I0671442

The Sullivan Secret

The Sullivan Secret

Jake Jacobson

ABSOLUTELY AMAZING eBOOKS

ABSOLUTELY AMAZING eBOOKS

Published by Whiz Bang LLC, 926 Truman Avenue, Key West, Florida 33040, USA.

The Sullivan secret copyright © 2018 by Jake Jacobson. Electronic compilation/ paperback edition copyright © 2018 by Whiz Bang LLC.

All rights reserved. No part of this book may be reproduced, scanned, or transmitted in any form or by any means, electronic or mechanical, including photocopying, recording, or any information storage and retrieval system, without permission in writing from the publisher. Please do not participate in or encourage piracy of copyrighted materials in violation of the author's rights. Purchase only authorized ebook editions.

This is a work of fiction. Names, characters, places, and incidents either are the product of the author's imagination or are used fictitiously, and any resemblance to actual persons, living or dead, businesses, companies, events, or locales is entirely coincidental. While the author has made every effort to provide accurate information at the time of publication, neither the publisher nor the author assumes any responsibility for errors, or for changes that occur after publication. Further, the publisher does not have any control over and does not assume any responsibility for author or third-party websites or their contents. How the ebook displays on a given reader is beyond the publisher's control.

For information contact:
Publisher@AbsolutelyAmazingEbooks.com

ISBN-13: 978-1949504002 (Absolutely Amazing Ebooks)

ISBN-10: 194950400X

This book is dedicated to my late mother, Sandra Jean Kiner Jacobson, for her unbelievable faith in me.

The Sullivan Secret

Chapter 1
The Heist

THE OLD BATTERED BAKERY VAN moved steadily along the country road. It was the perfect vehicle for the night's task. They were abundant in the Bordeaux region of France, fitting in perfectly in the French landscape.

The thirty something driver deemed the van good enough to last the night. It was stolen that morning from the neighboring town of Limoges. The tires were new, and the long bed could hold plenty of precious cargo.

Alongside the driver, in the front passenger seat, was another American who happened to be the driver's lifelong best friend. He had balls of steel along with an icy stare that served his lukewarm personality well. His skills as a major-league alarm expert would be tested very soon. This wasn't his first heist, but he never participated in anything of this magnitude before. If everything went per plan, he'd have more than enough assets to finally go legit.

Squatting on milk crates instead of a backseat were two local thugs from Limoges. They had good reputations in the Southern France underworld, but they had nowhere near the confidence of the two Americans. But for ten-thousand American dollars upfront with the promise of another forty grand, they were doing their best job of faking it.

The instructions for the double duos were very explicit. A soft but compelling voice on the phone instructed the players as to what each of their specific responsibilities would entail for an errorless crime. Bring your own equipment and destroy it afterward.

More important was rule number two. No speaking amongst themselves. Pure silence was required as someone always wants to be the alpha dog. Eliminate the verbal interaction and you eliminate most of the egos. Considering that nobody spoke anything other than their native tongue that task wouldn't be too daunting. Coincidence it was not.

The van crossed over a wooden bridge and Ambassador Jerome Patterson's country estate lay a quarter mile ahead. It was situated on the left bank of the Gironde Estuary which is world famous for its Cabernet Sauvignon wine. Patterson turned down an opportunity to buy a larger estate on the right bank which is equally famous for its Merlot, but he detested Merlot. His nickname in the States was the 'King of Cabs' as he also owned a massive vineyard in California's Napa Valley. Appearances are everything in the prestigious wine business.

By most accounts, Patterson was a mediocre United States Ambassador to France at best. He was more interested in living a celebrity lifestyle and promoting his wine business than serving his country. There's no better way to do this than raise a horde of cash for a presidential candidate and have your horse win. An appointment to France was the logical request when it came time to call in your marker.

This weekend would be another social event for the Ambassador. Along with his wife, he would attend the Monaco Grand Prix with their good friends the Browns. They were also American's who liked the good life and had re-located to France after Gerald Ford lost his re-election bid. The plan was for the Browns to leave their three children with the Ambassador's trio and return Monday. Hopefully, the Ferrari Team would do well as that's what the Ambassador drove on weekends.

The van pulled onto the winding road of the Patterson estate without slowing down. The guardhouse a quarter mile up was barely visible with a light mist and dark skies absent of moonlight. A thief couldn't handpick a better night than this for a sinister act. With the Ambassador in Monaco was most of his Diplomatic Security Force. The remainder stationed in Paris. Only a light security force was anticipated at the estate.

The driver pulled the van up to the guardhouse holding a road map while hand cranking the window down. The lone guard slid the security window halfway open with a look of annoyance. At least once a day some tourist mistook the estate driveway for a nearby forest preserve entrance. No hesitation, no mercy, the driver put two slugs into the guard's chest with a 9-millimeter pistol bearing a suppressor.

The van's front passenger jumped out and entered the guardhouse with a small tool kit. Within thirty seconds the fence alarm was disabled, and the gate opened. Almost as an afterthought, he dragged the guard's body behind some bushes and re-entered the van. A treasure of a lifetime was only another quarter mile away.

Headlights were turned off and dome lights disabled as the van rolled to a stop about a soccer field short of the target. It was go time as everyone left the van with adrenalin flowing and their hearts pumping blood like water flowing through a burst dam. Except for the front passenger as he was too close to the Promised Land and his demeanor was calm with his trademark icy stare focused on the end goal.

All four men sidled up to the north side of the estate next to the alarm box. The expert had the alarm schematic memorized and within sixty seconds any entrance was freely penetrable. But first, a slow walk around the building was in order.

No rooftop security was noted. The estate had thirty-two rooms with only five first floor rooms illuminating light. Inside the grand library, a butler and maid were entertaining six small children. The butler looked rather exhausted while sipping on a Louie Royer Cognac. Even though it appeared easy at this point, extreme caution would be exercised until all rooms were secured.

A side kitchen delivery door was picked open and all four men entered the premises and headed straight for the library. The butler and maid were petrified upon seeing the intruders but defensively huddled with the children next to the fireplace. The noise level dropped to silent mode within seconds. The alarm expert held them at gunpoint while the other three men left to search the remainder of the house.

After a dozen long minutes, the men returned to the library giving the all clear sign. The occupants were tied and bound with black electrical tape and locked in the library. The van was retrieved by the driver and backed up to the front door. The looting was about to begin, and it was like a pirate's dream.

They would start with the heavy work first as it was the most valuable at least from a time and economic standpoint. It was known that Patterson had an enormous standup black J. Baum safe which dated from the early 1900's. The safe itself was a collector's item but it would not be leaving the premises. The contents would though. It was a highly regarded safe and the alarm expert had been practicing daily on one of its mates.

The four men entered the upstairs office. There was no safe in sight and they already knew that it wasn't a wall safe. The alarm expert went to the wall sconces and pushed the one closest to the northeast corner upwards three times in succession. Nothing happened, and a slow sweat broke out on his brow. It was the correct wall sconce but perhaps the cadence was wrong. He was hoping a sledgehammer wouldn't be needed as he tried it again but speeding up the cadence. This time the bookcase slowly opened revealing a small passageway. The nerves of steel worked once again as the men stared into an old-fashioned panic room.

The men entered the panic room which appeared to be around one hundred square feet at most. The alarm expert was braced for his biggest challenge of the night as he had oversold himself a bit as an expert safecracker. Truth be told, the J. Baum safe had been giving him fits every day.

The apprehension was unnecessary. Patterson must have been lazy or figured nobody could find the panic room. The safe door was wide open.

Inside the safe were two thousand bearer bonds in five thousand-dollar denominations. There's nothing better in the entire world to steal than bearer bonds. They are unregistered, and no owners of records are ever kept. Whoever holds them physically owns them. Even if you get caught holding them proving theft is impossible. International airports every day comes across shady characters travelling with bearer bonds, but Interpol is helpless to do anything about it.

If the heist ended now the thieves were already up ten million bucks. But on a table next to the safe lay four gray Zero Haliburton briefcases full of bundled one hundred-dollar bills. A half million bucks of c-notes weighs about 114 pounds and all four of them combined seemed to total that. Even the rich are prepared to run from something bad at a moment's notice.

The heavy part of the theft rested in two burlap bags next to the safe. They were full of Kruggerands. Owning the South African gold coins was no longer fashionable due to the apartheid government of South Africa. Unfashionable as it was, they weren't leaving a million bucks of gold coins behind.

All the panic room contents were loaded into the bakery van. As expected, there wasn't a soul around nor was the cavalry on the way. The next phase would be orderly as the inventory list was etched into the two American's minds. Only take valuable paintings that could be sold with little effort. No need for breathtaking but unmovable museum pieces except for two notable exceptions.

Out of the one hundred plus original paintings on the walls of the estate only eighteen were taken and loaded into the van. One Goya, one Degas, three Renoir's, two Frida Kahlo's, three Salvador Dali's, five Claude Monet's and one ugly Jackson Pollock. It was an impressive lot, better suited for an auction. The art world value was close to thirty million for the collection. But, a pre-arranged sale price of six million dollars had already been brokered with a black-market aristocrat from Italy.

The paintings were gingerly loaded into the van and the four men made their way to the master bedroom suite for the final two paintings. Above the super king-sized, four post bed were two opulent paintings known as The Dutch Sisters. Technically, their existence was unknown as they were believed to be destroyed or stolen during the Nazi surge in World War II. Despite a lengthy search, the Monuments Men were unable to find the Dutch Sisters, but they did recover thousands of other art pieces in the final months of the war.

The Dutch Sisters were commissioned by a wealthy Dutch shipbuilder. As the legend goes, it was a gimmick to get his daughters married off and out of his home. No written history exists as to the sister's fate. It's believed they were painted sometime between 1605 and 1610 and the artist never signed them. Art historians theorize that they were painted by an up and coming Frans Hals before he started painting group portraits.

The paintings bounced around Europe from one private collector to another for about three hundred years before they disappeared in the 1940's. The Nazis burned and destroyed many paintings at the end of the war and it was believed that The Dutch Sisters had met this awful fate. There hadn't been a sighting or even a rumor of such for over forty years. Now, they were hanging side by side over the stately bed in the Bordeaux region of France.

The first painting was placed on the bed and wrapped up with the bedspread. The second painting was wrapped with a blanket in a likewise fashion then both were whisked away with kid gloves and placed in the van by the hired help.

It was time for the Americans to check on the library occupants. As they entered the library it was obvious that nobody could loosen their ties, nor had they made much of an effort. Much like the Titanic crew they seemed resigned to their fate.

As they waited for their cohorts to return from the van, a glass case on the wall above a table caught the attention of the driver. Behind the glass were a mounted sword and a bottle of wine. The sword was an authentic Japanese Katana sword used by the Samurai. The bottle of wine was a 1785 bottle of Lafite Rothschild Bordeaux once owned by Napoleon Bonaparte himself. Napoleon had a wine cellar of thirteen thousand bottles at its peak. Owning one of these bottles was a prized coup in the wine world.

Smashed glass trickled to the black and white marble floor as the driver whacked the case with a table lamp. The sound made the children shudder, but pure fear kept them from crying out. The driver carried the cased items to the van while the alarm expert stared up towards the ceiling in frustration. These items weren't on the inventory list but deep down he understood. Greed runs rampant in a thief's heart.

As the trio returned from the van with a mid-summer sweat the alarm expert checked his watch. They were a few minutes ahead of schedule due to the safe being an easy mark. They might as well grab something else of value to add to their profit margin. Besides, deep down he wasn't prepared for the final act.

He motioned to the basement door which housed the wine cellar and all four men rushed down the steps. The cellar only appeared half full, but three or four thousand marquee bottles lay in the wine racks. Some full cases rested next to the stairs so they each grabbed a case and made their way back to the van.

The allotted time for the operation was nearly up so it was time for the inevitable. The dirty work was for the hired help as it would make them unlikely to talk if something went wrong. At least that's what the voice on the phone had told them.

The six children were all very close in age with the oldest appearing to be about four years old. The instructions were to take the three Ambassador's children with them and dispose of the other witnesses. The children were being separated as the American's started to exit the library. The nanny sensing her final moments started to run towards the kitchen with her bound hands dangling in front of her.

As the alarm expert looked over his shoulder he saw a puff of smoke and the nanny dropped to the ground like a deer in hunting season. The butler charged the shooter gallantly but suffered the same fate. During the commotion, the two smallest girls inadvertently switched spots.

No one seemed to notice or care if they did. As soon as the larger thug herded three children out the front door, faint suppressor shots could be heard followed by an eerie silence. The ghastly final act was complete.

The three children were loaded into the van and made to sit cross legged in what little room was left. The adults grabbed their seats and the van retraced its steps off the estate grounds. Within thirty seconds it was just another set of taillights.

Chapter 2
Discarded Baggage

NOBODY MADE A SOUND for ten minutes. Finally, the van turned north onto a gravel service road. It travelled another half mile before stopping two hundred meters short of a white moving truck parked under an enormous oak tree on the opposite side of the road.

The heist crew blinked their headlights three times and the moving truck responded in likewise fashion. Everything was clear on the dark deserted road and the bakery van maneuvered so the backs of each vehicle were about five feet apart.

A medium height slender woman wearing tight European jeans, black mid-calf boots and a matching leather jacket jumped out of the box truck. She was alone, and her long brunette hair was tied back in a ponytail. Her outward demeanor was calm, but her stomach was churning as she walked to the bakery van to meet the four men as they exited the vehicle.

"Did everything go okay?" she asked looking squarely into the eyes of the alarm expert.

"It was even easier than I expected," he replied.

"See what great planning does." She smiled wryly. "Are the kids in there?"

"Yes, just as you requested."

"Good, let's get them into the truck then start unloading fast." She moved to the bakery van and opened the side sliding door.

The tiny children stared up at the woman with helpless eyes from their cramped positions. It was obvious they had no idea what was happening, and their bound hands didn't give them a secure feeling on this lonely stretch of road in the middle of nowhere.

"Why didn't you untie their hands already?" the woman demanded to know as she turned around.

"We forgot, we were a bit pressed for time at the end."

"I see you had some time to grab a few items not on the inventory list," she snapped. "Untie them now and get everything loaded. We have a schedule to keep."

The alarm expert hurriedly untied the children as he motioned for the other men to start the loading process. As soon as he finished the woman smiled big at the children in a whimsical attempt to comfort them as she escorted them into the back seat of the box truck.

All four men transferred the contents into the box truck. Except this time, they carefully wrapped the stolen cargo in thick gray blankets and secured them with various sizes of bungee cords. They didn't want the cargo to shift as the next ride would take a lot longer.

After the transfer was complete, the alarm expert produced two white envelopes from the glove box and placed them next to each other on the rear floor of the bakery van.

"Better count it." The alarm expert motioned with his finger towards the envelopes. "I don't want to hear we shortchanged you after the fact."

Despite not understanding English, the two thugs understood the criminal payoff code quite well with no translation needed. Always count your paycheck before you leave the table. Even on a dark road in the middle of the night one couldn't help but see the pure joy of a big payday in their body language.

It was a short-lived joy as both thugs simultaneously realized their envelopes were full of cut square shaped newspaper. Before either man could turn around or make a move for their guns they both took a shot to the back of the head. Their dreams permanently expired.

Both bodies were tossed into the rear of the van. The driver grabbed a large can of petrol from the moving truck and doused the van in its entirety. Within minutes the accelerants did their job turning the van into a blazing inferno. The physical evidence was destroyed, and the hired help might never be identified.

It was a crapshoot which would be discovered first, the burned-out van or the looted estate. Either way it didn't matter. The moving truck was heading south to Spain along the Bay of Biscay under the guise of a happy family relocating their household.

Chapter 3
Tension in Paris

IT WAS A STICKY HUMID DAY in Paris. The Parisians were still in a buzz as their countryman Alain Prost won the 1986 Monaco Grand Prix three days earlier for the McLaren-TAG Porsche team. Prost started from the pole position and ran an almost flawless race. His teammate Keke Rosberg finished second and Team Ferrari was never much of a factor much to the chagrin of Ambassador Patterson.

Stuart Rivers negotiated his way on foot through the Louvre District on his way to the local commissariat. It was a bad choice to wear a light blue dress shirt as sweat marks were already showing. Despite the heat outside, he felt it would be an even hotter meeting. Rivers was scheduled to give a communication update on the Ambassador incident, but he didn't have much to communicate.

Rivers had only been working for Diplomatic Security for eighteen months. It was his first job and considered a plum assignment. Due to recent retirements and reassignments, Rivers was the temporary agent in charge despite his youth and inexperience. In his mind, he was critiquing how a kid from Stony Point, New York could be strolling through an elegant park such as the Jardin des Tuileries. It was a lifestyle he'd grown accustomed to.

Upon graduating high school, Rivers was accepted at the United States Military Academy in West Point. It was during a military history class when he gave an oral presentation of the Battle of Stony Point which occurred in 1779. Rivers grew up only a mile from the Stony Point Battlefield, so he had no problem relaying all the facts about General 'Mad' Anthony Wayne and his glorious victory over the local British garrison. After class, his first name, Stuart, was replaced with Stony and that's how he acquired his nickname.

After a stint in the Army guarding high-ranking officers including some five-star elite Generals, he put in an application for Diplomatic Security. No action ever happened on his watch and he was disillusioned with the slow pace of Army promotions. Stony was almost stunned when he received his acceptance letter. Surprised would be an understatement when they assigned him to Paris. For a kid from Stony Point this plum job was his lottery prize.

Stony arrived at the local commissariat and gazed upwards at the magnificent four-story renaissance building. Everything is beautiful in Paris, even the police stations he thought to himself. As he walked up the marble steps to the second-floor meeting room he hoped the reception wouldn't be hostile. As an American in Paris, he seldom received a warm reception, so his expectations weren't high.

After a brief greeting from the receptionist he was ushered into the meeting room. Despite arriving early, he was still the last one there which is never a good sign in tense situations. Seated at the twelve-foot mahogany table that dated back to the French Revolution were four no nonsense men with a vast array of international policy experience. On the far left was CIA Station Chief Gene Tanner with Interpol Bureau Chief Lyle Hendricks on his right. Smoking a pipe with his legs crossed was French General Intelligence Directorate Chief Albert who had brought in famed Paris Inspector Andre Baudin as his right-hand man. Baudin showed a bit of mercy and eased the awkwardness by rising to shake Stony's hand. They had met once before at a charity dinner at the Louvre Museum. Baudin was not impressed by Stony whom he thought to be raw and inexperienced for a position of this magnitude but a personable fellow just the same.

Stony took a seat facing the four men and reached out for the pitcher of water pouring a large glass anticipating a case of cotton mouth. Tanner took the lead. "Tell us what you have so far Rivers?"

"Certainly," Stony said. "We were notified that something was amiss at the Ambassador's estate during the morning guard change. I was contacted about an hour later as I was in Monaco with the Ambassador. We immediately rushed back to the estate and arrived mid-morning. By that time all the bodies were found in the library besides the missing gate guard who was found on the grounds. Three children are still missing but no ransom demands yet. The alarms were all disabled. There is a ton of artwork missing in addition to the contents of a large safe. It looks like a professional job and they were most likely finished before midnight. There are not a lot of leads, but we are working around the clock gentleman, I assure you of that."

"How come you only had one guard at the estate?" Tanner asked accusatorily.

"Budget cuts," Stony replied. "The embassy in Paris was fully staffed and I had a crew with me for the Grand Prix. The country estate was deemed low risk without the Ambassador there."

"Any ideas on the missing children?" asked Interpol's Hendricks. "I have alerts all through Europe, but it seems rather odd that some are dead if this is a ransom job."

"That has me stumped as well. They could be dead also. If they are alive, I'm thinking it's for the black market but then why not take all the children and double your profit?"

Inspector Baudin calmly stood up and walked to a nearby window adjusting his blue bow tie. He was rather famous for solving high profile and celebrity cases. As much as he appeared in the local news he still retained a high degree of humbleness.

"Gentleman, I think perhaps we need to look at this from a different direction. Before Ambassador Patterson retained counsel, he admitted to me that he was in the possession of two paintings known as the Dutch Sisters. He was in a bit of a quandary as we couldn't very well look for these paintings if he didn't acknowledge his possession. So, my question to you is rather simple sir. What is an American Ambassador doing with two paintings that the Nazi's stole during World War II?"

"I have no answer for that," Stony replied defensively. "To me it's just paint on a canvas from some long dead artist. I know we met once at the Louvre, but I don't follow this crap and I think you know that."

"Let's keep it professional gentleman," said Henri Albert never flinching as he remained motionless puffing his pipe. "One last question Mr. Rivers anything solid that we can report to the press, so we don't look like a collective lot of fools?"

"Just one sir, we found a burned-out van about ten minutes away from the estate. It was empty except for two charbroiled bodies. I'm sure it's related. The van was reported stolen and the owner of record has an alibi that's solid. The bodies should be identified very soon. Hopefully their identification will lead us to something worthwhile."

"Let's hope so Rivers, let's hope so," said Tanner. "I know you're still fairly new, but you've been around long enough to know one thing. If you don't come up with something solid this temporary position could be a lot more temporary than you imagined. That will be all. Thank you."

As Stony retraced his path down the marble steps he wondered how much a two-bedroom condo in Stony Point was going for. He was on his last legs in Paris and everyone knew it.

Chapter 4
A Bad Exchange

THE METALLIC BLUE MASERATI Gran Turismo glided down Collins Avenue without enough room to open-up the V-8 engine and do it justice. Bradley Dunbar was heading for an evening meeting at a warehouse in Port Miami. The port boulevard wouldn't be any roomier, so Dunbar would have to wait another day to show off the horsepower. Open road seemed to be the only disadvantage to living in a penthouse condominium in the Art Deco section of Miami.

Dunbar was listening to ESPN radio as the cool ocean air filtered through the open windows. Miami Heat fans were still in an uproar from the LeBron James announcement that he was returning to his hometown Cleveland Cavaliers. Dunbar couldn't understand the move himself. Miami was so exotic for a United States city not to mention that Florida had no state income tax. At least David Beckham was in negotiations with Dade County to bring a major-league soccer team to Miami.

The non-stop radio chatter didn't remain a distraction for long. Dunbar couldn't help but be pissed at himself for getting into this mess. Some things had certainly been good. He had managed to remain a committed and wealthy bachelor with a stable of twelve fine dining restaurants and clubs. Throw in some commercial real estate and a fat brokerage account and his name was well known in Miami social circles. Best of all, he had just turned sixty and was still kicking it with models half his age.

Unfortunately, Miami real estate was hit extremely hard in the 2008 recession. When occupancy rates fell below forty percent in his buildings he let the banks have them. His stock broker was an incompetent fool as he had way too many margin calls. The jet setting lifestyle finally caught up with Dunbar and he was cash poor. The free and clear penthouse now had a mortgage and the restaurant business was like a roller coaster.

Dunbar still had an ace up his sleeve or rather an expensive painting to sell to be more precise. He hated to part with the painting, but it had to be worth at least twenty-five million dollars by now. It couldn't be sold at an auction, so he had to resort to private collectors. He made discreet inquiries in art circles to no avail then offered it to his best friend who replied with a firm no. Business advisors suggested he sell his restaurant empire, but he loved the fast-paced business so much that he couldn't bring himself to do it. Desperate, he sought the advice of his pal who happened to be a Unites States Senator. His pal read him a phone number and whispered the name Santora before hanging up.

Santora was a well-known American born Cuban who lived in Miami. He was in the import-export business. Some of it was legitimate. Most of it was shady as a three-dollar bill. But, desperate men can't be choosy and Santora was offering five million dollars in cold hard cash. Dunbar was expecting twice that price but Santora wouldn't negotiate. It was his business style and it worked. The transaction was set that evening at the Southern Global Imports warehouse.

He slowed the Maserati to a stop in front of the yellow warehouse that needed a new paint job. At first, he thought it was a starry night until he realized it was the nearby cruise ship lights. Port Miami was one of the few world ports that were used for both commercial and passenger ships.

As he approached the warehouse office door with the painting he studied the landscape. The lights were very dim inside. An Audi sports car and a Ford pickup truck were in the tiny parking lot. Dunbar had wondered about his personal safety as he was instructed to come alone. He trusted the Senator to not put him in a bad spot. Besides, he had a snub-nosed pistol in an ankle holster and he was known for doing some dirty work back in the day. True toughness never fades away.

Dunbar turned the doorknob and walked through the northern entrance as previously instructed. On the west wall were about twenty cargo containers that were labeled and ready for shipping. Or perhaps it was an excellent facade. A shipping dock on the south wall was littered with smaller empty wooden crates. Two rather unremarkable Central American men were standing on his left looking him over before he noticed a small wood table nestled between pale yellow forklifts. Sitting at the table was Santora who starred silently at Dunbar. He was large for a Cuban, six foot five and looking about two hundred and fifty pounds without an ounce of fat. His shoulder length hair was pulled back into a ponytail revealing a small scar above his left eyebrow.

"Good evening Mr. Dunbar," Santora said. "I trust that's the painting. Bring it over here by the light please."

"No small talk, I like that," Dunbar replied as he walked over to the table and placed the painting onto it.

Santora pulled the painting out of the carton and inspected it holding it up to the light.

"It really is one of the Dutch Sisters, one of the most mysterious paintings in the history of the world. I'm surprised you didn't bring an art expert with you for authentication purposes," Dunbar stated.

Santora smirked out loud. "Mr. Dunbar, if I found this to be a forgery later, I would hunt you down and kill you in a most painful way. We both know that." Santora paused and nodded towards the door. "That canvas bag weighs over a hundred pounds. Don't strain your back my friend."

As Dunbar started walking to claim his newly acquired canvas bag one of Santora's henchmen was fidgeting with his silver Harley-Davidson belt buckle. Just as Dunbar swung the bag over his shoulder the door exploded open followed by a small army of DEA agents in full body armor.

The Harley-Davidson man and Dunbar immediately hit the deck with their hands covering their heads. Dunbar kept the canvas bag close still thinking he had a chance at keeping its contents. The other henchman started running towards the back of the warehouse then wheeled around pistol in hand. He never fired a round as he was simultaneously felled by three different DEA agents. Santora had seemingly done his best Houdini imitation and was nowhere to be seen.

Dunbar was handcuffed and relieved of his bag and escorted outside along with the painting. The Harley-Davidson man stood up casually brushing himself off. It was obvious that Santora had a rat in his operation or even an undercover cop. Dunbar was pissed that the Senator had led him astray but now was no time to panic. He needed a brilliant cover story and he needed it fast.

Suddenly, a rumbling explosion from inside the warehouse shook the ground and Dunbar leaned against his Maserati to balance himself. One of the DEA agents found a tiny trap door behind some pallets in the southwest corner of the warehouse. Whether it was an adrenaline rush or a quest to be a quick hero, he opened the trap door with pistol drawn and the flash before his eyes would be his last vision in this world. Santora was no fool and booby traps were an acceptable form of protection in his world.

The Dade County Bomb Squad arrived as per protocol for any explosion along with two ambulances anticipating the worst. Sargeant Torrino had already ordered everyone out of the warehouse while the bomb squad did its due diligence. He hated paperwork as much as he hated Santora and tonight's fiasco would entail a lot of paperwork for the eighteen-year veteran.

Torrino was looking baffled as he watched the bomb squad from the perimeter safety line of miscellaneous emergency vehicles. As the ambulance bagged up his downed comrade he was holding an old painting and staring at a bag of cash lying on the hood of his vehicle. His mole had informed him that something was going on at the warehouse tonight and it was a last-minute event which wasn't Santora's style. He was a careful planner who always tried to minimize risk. Torrino was expecting a large cache of guns or a truckload of cocaine since Santora rarely deviated from his routine. Now he was in a quandary as this spectacle didn't fall into the spectrum of his jurisdiction.

It was getting late and Torrino just wanted the botched up bust to be over. Santora was gone and he would be hard to find. His men would do a search of the warehouse for illegal contraband and his report would be due first thing in the morning since he lost a man. This would be an all-nighter and he could feel his blood pressure rising. He marched over to Dunbar holding the painting with a pissed off look.

"What the hell is this Mr. Dunbar?"

"I'm not answering any questions without my attorney. I know my rights," Dunbar quietly responded.

"After I saw your Maserati, I figured that would be your response. You're under arrest for an unregistered firearm, possession of explosives and murder of a DEA agent."

"None of that's true and you know that," Dunbar exclaimed.

"At this point, I don't know what I know except that one of my guys is dead and I need to call his wife now. Let your attorney earn his fee as I don't give a crap."

Chapter 5
Duval Street

SINJIN JONES WAS SITTING at the middle of the stylish bar at the Little Jazz Room drinking a mojito. Wearing black Teva sandals, khaki shorts and a white linen shirt he looked like a typical Key West visitor enjoying the local music scene. He moved to the island seven months prior after his discharge from the army.

It was still rather hard to believe in his mind that this southernmost point was part of the United States. It was an island of only eight square miles in size with a population of twenty-seven thousand give or take a thousand. Laid back and casual were the norm, not the exception. Jones thoroughly enjoyed living in Key West and all that it had to offer.

Jones was chilling and killing some time listening to a couple locals play who had toured with some big-time bands including Jimmy Buffett. He was due at the Chart Room in two hours to meet up with a tourist girl named Susan who was staying at the Pier House. He had met her earlier in the day while wave running by Higgs Beach. She was a blonde-haired beauty who seemed like she could hold a decent conversation.

The band finished their song and went on a scheduled set break. Jones finished his mojito and decided to head down to Willie T's outdoor bar on the five hundred block of Duval Street. As he exited the club he ran smack into a drunken Ernest Hemingway look-alike. It was nothing to be surprised about. It was the Hemingway Celebration Days in Key West and they were having their annual look-alike contest. It wasn't his first Hemingway encounter this week nor would it be his last.

As Jones walked down the narrow historical street he couldn't help but wonder how different his life might be if his parents hadn't died. His father had been a casino executive for the MGM Grand in Las Vegas, Nevada. An innocent to the world, Jones was sitting on the couch at his parents' house watching the local news three months before his high school graduation when the local reporter broke in with news of a small plane crash outside Aspen, Colorado. His dad took his mother there that weekend for a surprise skiing trip that very morning to celebrate their anniversary. He was piloting his Beechcraft Musketeer which he had flown for years.

Jones could vividly recall jumping off the couch and making a beeline for the landline in his father's office. It was ringing before he could dial an outbound call. The achy feeling in the pit of his stomach was confirmed and that event changed the course of his life forever. With no siblings, he went from an only child to a very lonely kid.

With youthful innocence lost forever, his Aunt Gloria moved in with him. Two days after his high school graduation he was on his way to boot camp intent on becoming an Army Ranger. Las Vegas was like a long-forgotten taillight on the darkest of nights and he never returned.

At six foot one with a slim but muscular two-hundred-pound frame and shoulder length brown hair he was a familiar sight amongst the locals in Key West. Several people gestured hello as he entered and ordered a Red Stripe beer at Willie T's. He put his hair into a ponytail as he grabbed a stool at the bar when he noticed a man carrying a briefcase on Duval Street. About the only thing strange in Key West was to see anybody carrying a briefcase in this southern city of characters.

Jones always felt comfortable at this open-air gem of a bar. Signed dollar bills were tacked all over the walls of the joint. Every so often, they took them down and donated the cash to the Wounded Warriors Project. He respected that, being a veteran who considered himself lucky to escape Afghanistan fully intact both physically and mentally.

From his brief time in Key West he knew that some of the locals viewed him as a complicated man. Others viewed him quite the opposite as a very simple man. He could be very private or swing to the opposite end of the spectrum and be very outgoing especially at the Green Parrot after midnight. The truth be told, Sinjin Jones always decided what a person shall see about him. It was a conscious decision and he lived life on his terms, and his terms only.

The solo guitarist at Willie T's finished his set and went on break as Jones finished his beer. Apparently, his social timing was a bit off tonight and he was hoping that it would be improved by the time he arrived at the Chart Room. There was still time to kill and he was feeling a bit antsy without music. A longer walk to Captain Tony's Saloon was in order. He grabbed a ten-dollar bill from his money clip and signed it as Ernest Hemingway with a pen lying on the bar. Then he tacked it onto the wall and headed back up Duval Street.

As Jones continued westward he couldn't help but reflect upon his own military service. Special Forces found him as he completed basic training in the most fearless manner. Perhaps it was his youthful bitterness towards life, but he was always cool and calm in stressful situations. Combined with his natural athleticism he became one tough soldier.

Jones was assigned to a Special Forces Unit in the Paktika Province of Afghanistan. It was considered the most dangerous province and a soldier's lifespan was measured by days. Their mission was in the simplest terms. Kill terrorists and don't get killed yourself.

The rules of engagement were just as limited, but one couldn't find them in some military manual for this unit. High level terrorists were somebody else's problem and relied much more on expensive technical resources. The mid-level terrorists were part of the food chain and needed to be eradicated before they moved into the kitchen.

Sleep and good food were scarce at times. Goat was often on the menu. Most of their work was done at night and they slept in caves out of sight during the day. Taking no prisoners, they sent a strong message throughout the province.

Per the armed services rumor mills, about one thousand bodies were found in various places throughout the Paktika Province. All the bodies had the same signature wounds. A gunshot wound to each knee from varying distances. No other signs of trauma. Most bled out and died in a most painful way ten to thirty minutes after being shot. No other shoe or boot prints were left by the bodies. Was it eradication or a type of borderline torture? That wasn't for an enlisted man to decide. They called it mission accomplished if indeed it was them. After all, Afghanistan was full of rumors and ghosts going back to the beginning of time.

Captain Tony's Saloon on Greene Street was a piece of Americana. Besides being the home of the original Sloppy Joes, it had been a morgue, a bordello, an ice house and a wireless telegraph station. When the battleship Maine exploded in Havana Harbor in 1912, all the news provided to the world came from this peculiar yellow building which has a tree in the middle of it. In the pirate days, this same tree became the gallows for the guilty.

As Jones took a leak in the ultra-small bathroom he couldn't help but think of how many famous people had relieved themselves in this very same spot. Captain Tony himself was a Key West legend. He was good friends with Jimmy Buffett who helped get his favorite saloon keeper elected Mayor. Any place with a whisky slinger as Mayor has a certain degree of uniqueness to it.

Jones left the nostalgia trip with his excess beer and walked back to the bar. He noticed his half full beer had disappeared. As he ordered another Red Stripe he noticed the man with the briefcase again as he stood out in the crowd. He was talking to two wannabe Hemingway's and appeared slightly agitated.

After Jones killed his beer he still had thirty minutes until he was due at the Chart Room. He was always leery of being early to anything and waiting for people. For some reason, it made him self-conscious and uptight. He wasn't about to change this habit now, so he made the one-minute walk to Sloppy Joe's for one more beer.

When you walked through the open-air doors at Sloppy Joes it's like walking back in time to the 1930's. Not much had changed to the building since then and it was the first gin joint Jones walked into after his discharge from the service.

During his last month of service, he was approached by the CIA. They were informed he was not going to re-enlist so they offered him a contract position. It paid well, and it wasn't an office job. The only setback was the danger which Jones was already accustomed to. So, Jones became a CIA ghost, unofficially of course.

Sight unseen he headed to Key West. During his many days in the caves of Afghanistan he had read some books and articles on the island and decided that was where he would get his fresh start. His father's attorney finally finished liquidating the estate as he had died without a will. Jones was flush with cash and spent most of it on a decent sized house in the Old Town section of Key West. The rest of the cash was spent on a small Donzi powerboat and a Jeep Wrangler. There was enough left over for a few months of fresh fish and his nightly beer rounds.

As Jones ordered a beer at the longest bar in town he was reminded about his low cash flow as he put the beer order on a credit card. If he didn't get an assignment soon he'd have to take a deckhand job on a commercial fishing boat. The utility companies didn't care that he was hired to protect his country; they just wanted their cash for keeping the lights on.

The bartender gave him his receipt as Jones once again noticed the briefcase man standing outside the entranceway. He appeared to be around fifty years old with short brown hair, mustache and piercing blue eyes through horned rimmed glasses. Wearing khaki pants, boat shoes and a blue polo shirt he was giving Jones a hard look.

Jones didn't mean to give a sly smile towards the man, but he couldn't help himself. In addition to holding the briefcase with his left hand, he was holding an overpriced key lime pie on a stick with his right hand. It was dipped in chocolate and the heat had it melting down onto his palm.

The man then turned away walking back onto Duval Street in an eastbound direction. Jones gave the man a five-minute head start before slamming his empty bottle onto the bar top and heading towards Whitehead Street with a devilish grin on his face.

Chapter 6
Hemmingway's Shanty

SINJIN JONES BROKE A SLIGHT SWEAT as he briskly walked towards the Key West lighthouse. He had already left a message for Susan on her voicemail breaking their Chart Room date. Only a tinge of regret existed as he was finally getting what he wanted and needed. Besides, she would likely find his replacement at the Garden of Eden rooftop bar and everybody would be happy. She'd go back to Kansas or wherever she was from and he'd be long forgotten.

After one last deep breath, he rounded the corner and stopped right in front of 907 Whitehead Street which is better known as the Hemingway Museum. Hemingway spent most of the 1930's in Key West and lived in this spacious tropical house. There was a charity cocktail party on the eastside lawn as part of the celebration. All the guests seemed oblivious to the briefcase man sitting on the sidewalk leaning against the stone seawall.

Briefcase man took a pull from his sidewalk café Corona then looked at Jones. "Sit down Mr. Jones, if I didn't have a personnel shortage, your very first assignment would have ended before it ever began."

It was a rookie mistake and Jones knew it. All he had to do was briefly acknowledge the briefcase man and meet him at the museum within thirty minutes. True, it had been seven months since he'd last seen Graydon Bullock, but Jones was too focused on history to even gander a look at the man's face. He should have recognized Bullock earlier in the evening.

Graydon Bullock wasn't exactly the good humor man. He was a southern raised, Yale educated, eccentric fifty-year-old man. He was a twenty-four-year member of the CIA who had cut his teeth in the Bosnia conflict in the early nineties. Now he was a handler for messy issues that most political ass kissing hacks didn't want to oversee. Therefore, he received more discretion than most of his contemporaries and was well respected on Capitol Hill.

"Sorry Mr. Bullock, no excuses, it won't happen again."

"No apologies Jones. Let's make this brief as I need to get back to Langley to monitor another situation so listen carefully please. Last night a man in Miami was arrested in a warehouse sting. According to a DEA informant, he brought in a painting and sold it to a well-known drug dealer named Santora. Unfortunately, Mr. Santora made a miraculous escape."

"You want me to go to Miami and find this Santora guy?" Jones asked.

"No. Well, maybe at some point it will come down to that. I could really care less about him or the painting for that matter. It was stolen by the Nazis during World War II. Or so they thought until an Ambassador reported it as stolen years later."

"Doesn't the FBI have an Art Theft Division?" Jones asked.

"Yes, they do. And I tried my damnedest to pawn the complete matter over to them. Unfortunately for me, the NSA recorded an unofficial phone call from this Dunbar fellow to Senator Warren out of Miami. They're investigating the Senator for something which I'm not privy to."

Bullock paused for a second taking another swig of his beer.

"So, I had to find someone for a joint operation with the FBI. You're close to Miami, you're available, it's not too complicated and I have absolutely nobody else for this task force. I need you to poke around a bit very carefully with an FBI agent named Rivers. See what you can find out. Be discrete and give me a full report. Think you can handle that Mr. Jones?"

"No problem sir. Technically then, is the FBI in charge?"

"Absolutely not," Bullock snapped Bullock. "The CIA doesn't answer to anybody except to the President occasionally. That being said, it's your first assignment, start off cooperating with Agent Rivers. No need to ruffle feathers on a matter that is probably irrelevant. You'll need to pick him up at Opa-Locka Executive Airport tomorrow morning. He'll coordinate a plan with you."

"Thanks for the opportunity, I won't let you down."

"This briefcase is for you. Inside you'll find a burner phone; my number is programmed in there. You also have a mini iPad with appropriate apps already downloaded. An ordinary looking Zippo lighter, unscrew the bottom and it has some GPS chips and bugs. Coordinate those with the iPad if needed. Weapons are a Glock 19 and a Glock 26 with plenty of ammunition and a suppressor. Also, a Visa card for expenses and a white envelope with a grand for cash expenses. Last, but not least, a brown envelope with thirty grand for services rendered. Any questions Mr. Jones?"

"So, I actually get to keep the briefcase?" Jones asked with a grin.

Bullock stood up without cracking a smile. "Yes, keep it. Once I tell you the assignment is complete someone from Langley will reach out to you with procedures for destroying the rest of the equipment. But you may keep the briefcase as a token of my appreciation."

A few seconds later a black Mini Cooper pulled up next to Bullock. He looked back over his shoulder before getting in. "One piece of advice Mr. Jones. Don't kneecap anyone. If you must shoot anyone, just shoot them."

Chapter 7
Just a Call Away

BRADLEY DUNBAR, WEARING AN orange Dade County jumpsuit one size too small, was being escorted to a phone room by a jail guard. After his arrest, it was a total law enforcement quagmire as to where he would be taken for custody. After many phone calls between department heads, Dunbar was taken to the Metro West Detention Center on 41st street where he sat in custody for the last thirty-six hours.

Despite being a temporary bag holder of five million in cash and losing a valuable masterpiece, he was in an upbeat mood. His attorney had arranged a bail hearing for later that afternoon and he should be eating dinner at one of his restaurants later that evening. The most serious charges were still in limbo and not likely to move forward so in a profound way he thought he was sticking it to the man. Yet, this next phone call he was about to make pained him in a merciless way.

Derek Sullivan sat behind his aviator wing desk watching the Today Show and eyeing his Calloway golf bag when the phone rang. He should have left five minutes ago for his golf engagement, but he knew the call would be coming to his private line.

Speculation had been rampant the last thirty hours concerning the Dutch Sisters. Only one painting had been recovered. Where had it been for the last twenty-eight years? Where is the other one? Why was it in Miami? Reporters weren't going to let this go anytime soon and Derek Sullivan was uneasy. Few people knew any of the answers. Connections would come up and questions would be directed his way. He was in dire straits desperate for a quick solution. The longer this black cloud lay above Miami the larger this mess could become. It took a long time to get a stately mansion on Star Island. He sure as hell wasn't going to give it up easy.

Sullivan answered his phone on the first ring and accepted the charges. He understood it was being recorded. The call would be brief and vague, but he wanted to hear the atonement in his voice. He needed the atonement more than he needed the why.

"I'm sorry. I'm so fricking sorry. But I'll make this right. I'll be out sometime today, and I will make this right," Bradley Dunbar said trying to keep his emotions in check.

Sullivan replied in a very quiet and deliberate tone. "You better." Then he simply hung up the receiver. Atonement was felt.

Chapter 8

On the Links

DEREK SULLIVAN LOVED GOLFING at the Biltmore Course. It had been around since 1925 and famous celebrities like Bing Crosby had often graced its links. Sullivan himself had been a caddy at this championship course back in his youth for the rich and famous. Today, he arrived via a chauffeured Rolls Royce Silver Cloud and he wouldn't be carrying anyone's clubs.

The four-hour game at Biltmore had been absent of the good-natured banter that was customary. Sullivan finished five over par but Senator Warren being a scratch golfer was a shot under. Sullivan had paid for a foursome but made sure today's game would just feature the duo. They'd be forced to talk about the latest matter in moments and didn't need extra ears around.

Senator Warren bought two ice cold Coronas from a scantily clad girl at the concession stand and they both walked slowly and stopped under a palm tree. Only a talented lip reader could eavesdrop on this conversation.

"I don't even want to know why our mutual friend did what he did. But it's paramount that this story ends now," The Senator stated.

"I'd like to know how he hooked up with Santora," Sullivan replied.

"I said it doesn't matter. It just has to end."

"We've been friends since we were ten. I'd like to know. I need some answers."

"Would you find some solace in a jail cell? I'm sure you can get some answers there. He knows too much. It's too risky. I have no answers for you Derek. Bradley

39

was a resourceful guy. He got himself in a jam and he made a bad move. I like the guy, don't get me wrong. We've had some good times. But, he got himself into this mess. We cannot be brought into this matter."

Sullivan was looking down at his Corona wishing he had about twelve more. Deep down he knew the Senator was right, but this was his buddy. They grew up watching each other's back.

"He called me before I came here, and I spoke with his attorney last night. The real serious charges will be dropped, he's quite confident of that."

"Yes, at what price? State's evidence possibly?"

"He would never do that." Sullivan replied.

"You didn't think he would sell the painting neither but he did. You think the Washington Post, or the New York Times will drop this? It's not that simple Derek. We're not choir boys. We both look in the mirror in the morning. We didn't get where we are today by playing nice. Dunbar is like a roadmap to the penitentiary. People put people there. Skeletons don't, and you know I'm right about this."

Sullivan finished his beer and dropped the bottle to the grass. He walked five feet away putting his hands on his hips gazing at the horizon. July was a tough month to golf in South Florida and sweat was still dripping down his brow. Now he had to make a split decision that could have a profound impact on many people. Deep down he knew the Senator was right no matter how callous he could be. There was too much to lose and nothing to gain. Maintaining their childhood friendship had been tough at times but loyalty kept it together. Dunbar had always been the reliable muscle that meshed so perfectly with Sullivan's ideas. Loyalty was a hard thing to find in the world today. Now he was being asked to dismiss it like a poorly made martini.

He finally looked over his shoulder and stared into the Senator's eyes. He gave a slow nod and the price of loyalty had just been determined. As the Senator reached for his cellphone, Sullivan's own phone rang which he walked further away to answer.

"Ceci, so glad you called. It's been a rough day."

Chapter 9
The Airport

THE SUN WAS BEGINNING TO RISE over the Atlantic Ocean when Sinjin Jones pulled his sandstone colored Jeep Wrangler onto A1A. Miami was further away from Key West than Havana, Cuba was and this fact always amused Jones. In the near future, he was planning on visiting Cuba, unofficially of course.

It was a slow uneventful drive with narrow lanes and only one stop for some Cuban coffee. There's plenty of traffic stops but it's the only way to navigate the Florida Keys since the Flagler train route was wiped away in the Labor Day hurricane of 1935. Nevertheless, Jones arrived at Opa-Locka Executive Airport slightly north of Miami with about fifteen minutes to spare. He grabbed an orange juice from a vending machine and took a seat in the terminal waiting for his new best friend from the FBI.

The egg white FBI Gulfstream G150 landed and made its way to the tarmac. An aged yet determined looking Stony Rivers sat in a window seat staring out at something called redemption. Since the heist and murders in France twenty-eight years ago, there hadn't been one solid clue or promising lead that led anywhere.

The perpetrators seemed to vanish in thin air. Not a single piece of art was ever recovered. The bearer bonds were impossible to trace and likely long gone. Nobody in the European underworld seemed to sanction the heist as even they looked for the culprits for a shakedown opportunity.

Rivers was correct in his assumption that the heist would bring a swift end to his career with Diplomatic

Security. He was allowed two months to follow up hopeless dead ends throughout Europe before he was re-assigned to a low-level desk job in Washington D.C. Before he was officially terminated he found an entry level job with the FBI. He used a West Point connection for the position which he gratefully accepted.

His career at the FBI was solid but unspectacular as most careers are. At least he was never embarrassed again as he was in that hot France summer which most people seemed to have long forgotten. Rivers never forgot though. The FBI formed an Art Crime Team in 2004. Even with his firsthand knowledge of art crime, he was not among the fourteen original team members. It took another three years to kiss enough hierarchy asses to make the appointment.

Rivers solved quite a few art crimes but not a month went by when he didn't chase down a new rumor or make some calls regarding the Dutch Sisters. Nothing ever developed but he never gave up hope. Now, one of the paintings ends up in a Miami warehouse a few hundred miles from his home in Virginia. Second chances don't always become available in the game of life. Rivers was assigned this case from the Director personally and he was going to get some answers. Even if he had to bend a few rules or forget some regulations. Redemption time had arrived.

Rivers disembarked the plane with an aura of importance. Despite wearing a wrinkled lightweight beige suit, he had a strut in his step. He was immediately met in the terminal by a well-built Italian looking man about ten years younger than Rivers. The Italian man was carrying an oversized cardboard file box and appeared to be a local judging by the subtle Hawaiian shirt.

Jones approached the men cautiously as Stony checked email messages on his phone. Out of the corner of his eye Rivers caught a glimpse of Jones and pulled out his identification while turning his phone towards Jones who was instantly glaring at a photograph of himself.

"Hello amigo. Looks like you're my hired gun courtesy of Bullock. This is my local associate Terrence Oliver."

"Pleased to meet you," Jones replied shaking both men's hand. Oliver juggled the heavy box to free his right hand.

"Before we go any further Jones, let me make one thing perfectly clear. I don't need a babysitter, nor did I request any outside help. I know this isn't your idea. This case is very personal to me. I'm in charge. Is that understood?" Rivers asked.

"I'm just here to assist. Whatever you want me to do, you have my full cooperation." Jones replied keeping a stiff upper lip as to not smile thinking back at his conversation with Graydon Bullock.

"Great. We start right now. Let's go over to that table."

All three men walked over to a table by a small newsstand selling the latest gossip rags. Oliver placed the heavy box on top of it. Rivers pulled off the top and glanced around before pulling out a manila folder marked Santora in bold black magic marker.

"Phase one, I want to talk to the main conspirators immediately. Oliver and I will head over to Metro West Detention Center. We're going to have a long talk with Bradley Dunbar and he's going to tell us everything he knows."

"What if he doesn't talk? I'm sure he's lawyered up by now." Jones stated.

Rivers hesitated and wrinkled his nose. "He'll talk. That's what Mr. Oliver is here for. Everybody talks to

Mr. Oliver. That's probably all you want to know about that son."

Oliver slid the folder in front of Jones and opened it up showing several photographs of Santora.

"I want you to head over to Little Havana. Find out anything you can about this prick. Known associates, family members, business connections, anyone who can help us find him. This folder contains the most current up to date information that we have. Rome wasn't built in a day. Just beat the streets and see what develops. I have rooms for all three of us at the Fontainebleau. Let's coordinate our cell numbers and we'll meet at the pool bar about five."

"The Fontainebleau, I like your style Rivers. See you gentleman there." Jones said.

Chapter 10
The Angry Man

SANTORA ENDED HIS PHONE CALL from his makeshift office above a Cuban cigar store on Calle Ocho which is the heart of Little Havana. He had accustomed himself to the Miami high life and now he was back to where he had started. Above a crappy little store fighting for survival in the toughest part of Miami.

He sat down in a chair behind a desk if that's what anyone wanted to call it. It was a slab of doubled up plywood painted red balancing on four piles of cigar boxes. He placed his head in his hands and rested it on the desk. How did he get in this mess?

The anger was welling up inside his head. Deep down he knew it was his own fault for aligning himself with them. He never should have associated with the Miami elitist from day one. Stay with your amigos. At least you know who you are dealing with. Those Miami elitists pushed him over the edge. Their fancy cars, designer clothes and massive mansions all acquired on borrowed dimes made them think they were important. Legitimize yourself they said. It will open doors and you can be a big shot businessman and own half of Miami. Those fricking Miami elitists!

Taking a hike out of the country was still an option. He would be welcome in Cuba and he had friends in the Castro regime. They'd take all his cash though. Panama might work if they didn't pull a Noriega on him. Too risky he thought, plus most of the country was a shit hole. Columbia would wine him and dine him with open arms. It would be good for a while, but the clock would be ticking on his head. Eventually, he would be the recipient of a Columbian necktie.

No, his best option was to keep to the plan from his phone conversation. Eliminate Mr. Bradley Dunbar. Dead co-conspirators make terrible witnesses and he would plead ignorance. In fact, he would never have to testify and the case against him would falter and he could return to the good life. Blame everything on Dunbar through his attorney including the explosion. The informant didn't know anything about the booby trap and he could pay off a reporter or two for some favorable press.

Not only did he need to make this happen fast, but he needed it done before Dunbar was released and went into seclusion. It would be a costly endeavor and it was on his dime. These fricking elitists loved rubbing the salt in a wound. Even if he walked his five million wouldn't be coming back his way. This operation was putting a serious dent in his pocket book.

This would be an inside job and currently none of his crew was being detained. Sure, he knew plenty of people on the inside but there was no room for hacks. He needed a professional job and that would be expensive. No time to be thrifty even though he was bleeding chips. It was time to place an uncomfortable call to Simon.

Before Santora made the call, he made himself a promise. He would get some of his cash back from the Miami elitist's or he'd make them pay with a body count. No hired guns for that task. The pleasure would be all his he thought to himself as he punched in a phone number.

"This is Simon."

"I've got a special project that requires your attention," Santora stated.

"I've heard about your recent woes. How may I be of assistance my friend?"

"I need Bradley Dunbar eliminated. Today, before he sees daylight on the outside."

"That will cost you double," Simon replied without hesitation or emotion.

"You just said you were my friend."

"It's a figure of speech. Four hundred thousand and he won't see the sunset. It's guaranteed."

"Fine, it's on the way over within the hour," Santora said with exasperation.

"Done" Simon replied.

Chapter 11

For Momma

RUBEN CASTELLANOS WAS DOING THIS for his momma he kept telling himself as he was being led down the Detention Center's cell corridor. His pulse was pounding, and his tight orange jumpsuit made every muscle on his three hundred and twenty-pound frame bulge out. Sweat was streaming down his shaved head almost soaking his goatee.

Castellanos had killed a man last night in a bar fight. It was caught on a surveillance camera, so it didn't matter if witnesses came forward or not. His meth fueled rage was there for the entire world to see. This was his third felony offense after a childhood of misdemeanors. He would never see the light of day again and Florida had a death row. It was time to do something for his momma.

Ruben's momma migrated to Miami via the Mariel Boatlift pregnant with Ruben courtesy of a prison guard. She was a career petty criminal serving time in a Havana prison when Castro decided he could get rid of two for the price of one. Ruben grew up in the streets of Little Havana being unwanted by two countries. That it came down to this moment should never have been a surprise to society.

The prison guard would get fifty thousand and explain everything as a tragic timing mishap. It happened at times and the detention center was close to capacity. Ruben's momma would get one hundred thousand as a reward for bringing a scumbag into the world. Simon would keep the rest for one day's work. It wasn't quite that simple though. It took years of favors and bags of cash to cultivate the connections to make it work.

As they approached the upcoming crime scene, trusting Simon was Ruben's only worry now. After the deed was done, he wouldn't be available to oversee the transaction. Simon had a good reputation on the street, so he'd take his chances. Besides, he had nothing to lose and everything to gain for his momma. That cash could get her out of Little Havana where she could enjoy her golden years.

The guard unlocked the cell door with Dunbar gazing out from a seated position on the top bunk just before 2pm. Castellanos entered the cell and took a seat on the bottom bunk.

"Relax Dunbar," the guard growled, "you still got another hour of plush accommodations until your paperwork is processed."

"Anyway, you could speed it up? I'm not above showing some gratitude," Dunbar replied.

"This isn't Club Med and we're almost at capacity. Be patient."

The guard felt like throwing up as he locked the cell back up and retraced his steps. This wasn't the first time this type of incident would happen or be the last. The internal investigation would be a bitch, but he'd be fine. He couldn't very well say no as he felt like he was being watched. He had a family to consider. His tracks were covered well. There were no phone calls to be traced as a note was left on his car windshield which he already flushed down the toilet. He took the cash home at lunch time and buried it. He'd wait six months before touching it. By then this would be long forgotten. It would look like a simple overcrowding issue. Besides, these weren't good people. He would be doing Miami a favor was his justification.

Within five minutes Bradley Dunbar had a bed sheet wrapped around his neck. After nearly thirty years of glamour it left quicker than it ever came to fruition. Dunbar's world went permanently black.

Chapter 12
A Step Behind

RIVERS AND OLIVER WALKED BRISKLY through the front doors of the Metro West Detention Center. Rivers could feel his heart pounding in his chest. He was so close to finding some answers that he could taste it. As much as he wanted all the answers, part of him didn't want any answers. Everybody has an ego and learning how ignorant he was almost three decades ago could be painful.

Rivers thought back on that Monaco Grand Prix weekend. Working for the Ambassador was never a dull moment. He spent more time guarding the Ambassador from women than he did foreign enemies. The Ambassador entrusted Rivers with a stash of hush money to pass on. Naturally, he kept a large cut for himself and developed a fondness for the good life in Paris.

They were stopped by a security officer on the other side of a glass security counter. Credentials were provided, and signatures logged onto a clipboard. When the officer noticed that they were there for Bradley Dunbar the Shift Captain was notified and they were escorted to a conference room. Rivers was expecting this, and he was prepared to argue with the Captain over his demands to interview Dunbar in a camera less room.

There are bad days and then there are bad days Captain Hughes thought to himself. His slicked black hair and head were working up a sweat as he ambled down the hall toward the conference room carrying a prisoner intake folder. Normally, he'd chalk it off to the fifty pounds he'd been meaning to lose. But today, it was a public relations nightmare when a high-profile prisoner gets murdered in his jail. To make it worse, the FBI shows up like a late charging thoroughbred that finishes just out of the money.

Hughes decided to take an aggressive approach and not beat around the bush. He wasn't a fan of the FBI arrogance and he expected the worst possible treatment. Besides, Dunbar's body wasn't even cold yet and he didn't have any answers. He burst through the door to see the agents sitting in an agitated manner at a bare table.

"Gentleman, I'm Captain Hughes." Let me spare you the formalities and give you the bad news. You're here to see Bradley Dunbar and I'm here to tell you he's on his way to the morgue. He's dead."

"You're fricking kidding me?" Stony replied in astonishment. 'What the hell happened?"

"Another inmate attacked him. It happened less than an hour ago. A complete investigation will be conducted," Hughes stated defensively.

"We all know that won't get us any answers," Oliver chimed in.

"But maybe his residence can. I'll need his address and if you dare use the subpoena word I swear I'll come across this table," Rivers threatened.

"No need for that tone sir." Hughes replied as he opened the folder showing the booking information. "It's only about twenty minutes away."

"I can make it in fifteen, let's go," Oliver replied.

Within sixty seconds Oliver had the black Ford Explorer peeling down the freshly laid blacktop towards the Dunbar penthouse on Collins Avenue. Instinct told Oliver that time was of the essence. If Dunbar needed to be silenced behind bars, then his residence would be at risk. It would be an easy target.

The Explorer weaved in and out of traffic with tires squealing around every corner. Being familiar with the area, Oliver didn't need the GPS and made the jaunt in a scant twelve minutes. Stony looked up and saw a black Bell helicopter departing the building's roof.

"Tell me that's one of our birds," Stony stated in a hopeless tone.

"Nope," Oliver said glancing up "it's a ghost. Look at the tail. The numbers are covered up."

"Let's grab building security and get up there."

The helicopter was long gone by the time they made it to the penthouse with the aging rent a cop. It was a simple smash and grab job. The Bell hovered over the penthouse while someone climbed down on a rope ladder. They smashed the glass patio door with a heavy object and knew they had at least seven minutes before anyone would answer the alarm.

The inside was hardly disturbed. It was hard to tell what was missing unless one had been there before. Rivers wanted to review the surveillance tape but was informed that none existed at the penthouse level per Mr. Dunbar's request. Dunbar valued privacy at all costs. Rivers admired this trait. Unfortunately, it was hindering his investigation.

Rivers and Oliver perused the entire residence. It was the typical open-air Miami flair with plenty of leather furniture, a twenty-foot bar and a giant big screen television. The view was fit for a king. The only disturbance seemed to be in the office with a broken glass case and the contents missing. It was long and narrow and possibly a rifle was displayed inside. Rivers noticed a laptop resting on the floor next to the desk. It was in about a dozen pieces. He gently scooped it up. It would be going to the FBI lab for inspection.

They exited the building handing off the laptop to another agent. The midday humidity was making the back of his navy-blue shirt into a puddle. He didn't know what to make of the last hour's activities, but he would need to process it over a cold drink. He removed his tie and looked over towards Oliver.

"Let's get to the hotel."

Chapter 13
Little Havana

LITTLE HAVANA WAS WEST of downtown Miami. The Jeep was cruising down SW 8th street which was the main drag better known as Calle Ocho. Jones found a metered spot and eased the Jeep into a tight spot between a white Porsche and a canary yellow Honda Civic. After he turned off the engine he could hear the distinct echo of a clacking noise. Upon further review, he could see the old Cuban men playing dominos. It was called Domino Park for a reason.

Before 1960, very few Cubans lived in Miami. After Castro took over there was a steady influx of exiles into the Gateway to the Americas. Naturally, the Mariel Boatlift added to the population, but Little Havana was home to many Central and South Americans also. Jones was a Las Vegas gringo who would be looked over carefully if he drew too much attention to himself. He was well aware of that fact, so he planned to operate in a very low-key fashion.

Nothing spells tourist better than buying a Cuban affiliated cigar and walking around seeing the sights. Jones ducked into a quaint but authentic family owned cigar store. It had tobacco leaves in a bin surrounded by piles of old wooden cigar boxes. Some of the boxes were hand carved. He picked out a nice hand rolled cigar from the humidor for ten bucks. The shop clerk didn't speak much English but seemed to indicate that it was the real deal. For all Jones knew it was a nice Romeo y Julieta. It didn't matter. His intent was to look for the local information man. Every community has one and they usually deal in black market goods. Asking for Santora directly could bring him a heap of unwelcome trouble. Since his communication skills with the shop clerk seemed strained at best he decided to try elsewhere. He figured he only had a couple attempts before word spread about his real intent.

Jones walked back through Domino Park towards a small coffee shop with a bright blue sign. The park tables were completely full with weathered exiles playing their favorite game in straw hats to keep the afternoon sun out of their eyes. The exiles were a loyal group. They hated both Castro and Kennedy with equal passion. Their last dream of returning to the motherland before dying was fading with each passing sunset.

Jones entered the dark blue tiled shop and took a seat at the counter in a lighter blue stool. Coupled with the blue outdoor sign it was apparent that blue was somebody's favorite color. He was the only patron at the counter. A few locals were in the back room having a late lunch at a row of tables along a bamboo wall decorated with photos of the Havana Malecon. The smell of hot Cuban sandwiches permeated the air.

It appeared to be a mother with her college aged daughter working the counter. Jones couldn't take his eyes off the daughter who was simply stunning with long dark hair and eyes full of desire. The older woman caught him starring as she approached him with a menu and a stern look. She took his order before the Yankee gringo visually assaulted her daughter any further.

Jones ordered a cortadito. He loved Cuban expresso drinks. They were both sugary and strong unlike the American version. He decided to test his charm on the older waitress as she delivered his drink.

"Excuse me ma'am. I'm trying to find an acquaintance of mine in the neighborhood, but I've forgotten his name. Is there a local around here who knows everyone? I'm thinking if I could give a description someone might know him."

"No." The woman replied without even giving it a second thought. She picked up three drinks to deliver to the back-dining area.

Smooth Jones thought to himself. He knew he didn't have all afternoon and he wanted to show the FBI something at his Fontainebleau meeting. It was a matter of pride more than trying to impress his fellow task members.

The younger waitress walked over smiling towards Jones and she snuck a quick glance into the back room making sure nobody could hear. Then she leaned over across the counter giving him a good bosom shot in her tight Florida Marlins crop shirt. Her long hair partially hid an angelic smile and Jones didn't know what to think as she leaned in even closer.

"Sir, your cortadito is one hundred dollars. The man you need to speak with goes by Torres. He knows everything that happens in Little Havana. I don't know what you want, nor do I need to. But he will know."

Jones reached for his black leather money clip and asked one question. "Where is he now?"

"I saw him at Domino Park ten minutes ago. Red pants, white linen shirt, slicked back hair, no facial hair. He watches the old men play and collects information. He takes a lot of bets on sports also."

"Does he have a first name?"

"Only his mother knows," she replied taking the hundred off the counter and walking away.

Jones exited the coffee shop without ordering lunch even though he was famished. He thought it best not to loiter and grabbed a chicken croquetas from a street vendor. He was a kindly old gentleman who didn't speak a word of English. Ten feet away a little boy working a fruit stand looked disappointed. Fruit stands in Little Havana were almost as abundant as cigars. Jones gave the kid five bucks and grabbed three mangoes for later and took a seat on a nearby park bench.

As Jones finished his croquetas he spotted his target. A man in red pants had stood up and started to leave the park. Nonchalantly, Jones followed suit and slowly began trailing the man. With those ghastly pants, he was certain that it was the man known as Torres.

It was a painfully slow walk. Every few yards a new person stopped to greet Torres or slap his back and whisper into his ear. No wonder he knew everything. There was a decent chance that Torres knew where Santora was hiding. After about fifteen minutes of walking, Torres grabbed an empanada and a Coca Cola from a street vendor. Jones bided his time at a newspaper stand until Torres continued his way towards the Tower Theater.

The Tower Theater was a classic art deco style building. There was a small line of locals waiting to pay at the box office. Torres walked through the entrance without paying for a ticket. The no outside drink or food sign was just a suggestion for Torres as well.

Jones stayed down the block for a few minutes to make sure Torres wasn't picking something up. His best guess was that Torres had a meeting there. A movie theater is the perfect place and great cover. It's dark and loud, nearby ears would have a hard time eavesdropping.

In fact, Jones couldn't think of a better place to corner Torres. He would sit behind him and put a gun to his ear once the movie started. He'd be gone with his information before anyone else figured something was amiss.

Jones strolled up to the box office window and purchased a ticket to see 'Viaggio Sola.' It was billed as "one woman's quest for personal and professional fulfillment." Great, he was going to sit close to a strange man to see a chick flick, Jones thought to himself.

The popcorn laden concession stand smelled great but Jones bypassed it and headed straight to the ticket taker who gave him a strange look. He would have given himself a strange look also if the circumstances were reversed. He took a step inside the black door curtain and waited a moment for his eyes to adjust. Red pants would be easy to spot, and he was hoping the seat behind him was still empty.

The sound of wood hitting a hard rock echoed in his ear a split second before realizing it was his head taking a mighty blow. The bag of mangoes hit the floor before Jones dropped to his knees with his back arching backwards before instinctively rolling sideways while catching a glimpse of Torres running out the front door while dropping a small club.

Holding his head with his left hand he reached for the concealed Glock with his shooting hand. The site of the Glock scattered the arriving crowd and Jones struggled to his feet in hot pursuit of Torres. Luckily, Torres wasn't a big man as more velocity from the club would have knocked him out cold. He probably pegged Jones for an undercover cop and was looking for a quick getaway rather than deadly force.

As Jones burst through the door he could see Torres sprinting towards Jose Marti Park and he had a good one-hundred-yard lead already. Normally, even with a head start he'd be able to run a guy like Torres down. But, he was feeling a bit dizzy, so he held back a bit, so he wouldn't go into deep oxygen debt.

Even with his head throbbing he was staying about even with Torres until he ran out of real estate. Once

Torres crossed out of the park he embarked onto a
black and red Scarab Impulse powerboat parked on the
Miami River which abutted the park. The pursuit was
over, separated by four hundred horsepower. Jones
stood there catching his breath as the powerboat
became a tiny spectacle down the riverway. So much
for being low key he thought to himself.

Chapter 14
Cocktail Time

JONES GRABBED HIS NAVY-BLUE duffel bag from the backseat and tossed his Jeep keys to the valet. His head was still throbbing as he walked through the lobby of the ultra-luxurious Fontainebleau Hotel. In the sixties, stars like Frank Sinatra and Jerry Lewis graced the premises. Sean Connery and Al Pacino filmed movies at the hotel. After recent major renovations, it now boasted over fifteen hundred rooms on a large beachfront property which made it easier for the casual visitors like Jones to blend in on South Beach.

It wasn't a good start for Jones, but he decided to pocket his ego and tell his task force friends the truth. Hopefully, they wouldn't think that he wasn't up to the task. Maybe they found some good intelligence and his Little Havana fiasco would be of little consequence. Wishful thinking was all he had going for himself at this point.

Both men were seated at the end of the Glow Bar working on mojitos. Judging by their glum greeting, it wasn't their first drink nor were they celebrating good news. Oliver kicked out a barstool. Jones ordered a simple Red Stripe beer and took up the offered resting piece.

Rivers looked at the bartender with a slight nod. "Put it on my tab. How did it go Jones?"

"Well," Jones sighed and decided to summarize it as best he could. "I was hit on the head and lost a bag of mangoes. How about you gentleman?"

Stony gave a slight shrug of the shoulders without looking up from his mojito. "Well, Dunbar got whacked by another prisoner right before we got there. Then, we scrambled over to his penthouse in time to see a helicopter flying off. His place was gone over good. We did recover his smashed laptop though. The local office is looking at it as we speak."

"Anything on the helicopter?" Jones asked.

"A black Bell," Oliver chimed in. "Probably a 427, the numbers were taped over. There are a couple hundred of them in Southeast Florida alone."

"What about the prisoner?" Jones was starting to feel like a pesky freshman high school student, but the answers weren't being offered for the obvious.

"Aww. Forget about that. He's not going to talk. Even if they do, they just make crap up. He's already in jail for another murder. No leverage, therefore no truth," Rivers replied with no attempt to hide his disgust with the question.

"There's always leverage somewhere," Jones replied so matter of fact.

Rivers glared at Jones like a gauntlet had been thrown and decided he better exercise his due authority accordingly.

"I've been doing this a long-time son. Don't second guess me. That stops now. Besides, you've got zilch so far also."

"Not true," Jones replied cautiously trying to ease the tension. "The guy that hit me is named Torres. I believe he knows Santora and maybe even his whereabouts. I'll find one of them tonight."

"Nope, save that for tomorrow," Rivers replied. He was impressed with that information, but he wasn't going to let Jones know it. "Let's move on to Plan b. Somebody higher up orchestrated today's charade, that's for sure. This Senator Warren down here is connected to Dunbar. To what extent? I do not know. I know you're here because of the Senator connection but we aren't going to protect this clown. If he knows something, I want to know it."

"I'm not protecting anybody Rivers. If he's dirty, I'll help you all I can," Jones replied defensively.

"What do you have in mind?" Oliver chimed in.

"There's a fundraiser tonight at the Lowe Art Museum down on the University campus," Rivers explained tapping his finger repeatedly on the bar. "The Senator will be there along with most of the Florida art community. Someone there will know something. Forget Little Havana, forget helicopters, and work the case from the inside out. Work the people that are in the know. We need to get close to the Senator and get close to who he knows."

"Won't we need invitations? Jones asked.

"It's already been arranged by the Bureau. Tuxedos and invites are in your rooms. Call the concierge if you need an alteration. We all arrive there separately. We don't know each other. Pick your room keys up at the front desk. See you there in three hours. Remember, work the room. Beat the bushes." Rivers chugged down the rest of his mojito and walked away eager for a quick nap.

Chapter 15
Stuffed Shirts

THE LOWE ART MUSEUM wasn't hosting special events this year due to renovation plans. However, Senator Warren brought so much cash to the University coffers that exceptions were made and the sawdust swiftly cleaned up. Naturally, a percentage of the charity proceeds would make its way back quid pro quo to his campaign fund.

With over seventeen thousand pieces, it was a world class museum. Important people from all over Florida would be in attendance, not solely art lovers. Ten pieces from a recently deceased benefactor's private collection would be auctioned off tonight after a lengthy meet and greet session fueled by expensive champagne and cocktails.

Jones arrived at the museum doors courtesy of a Fontainebleau limousine. He wasn't foreign to these events. In fact, being the son of a casino hotshot, he lost count of how many he had attended. They were all pretty much the same modus operandi. Whether it be an event for politicians, sheiks, kings or oil barons the underlying theme was always the same. It was money plain and simple. Dress it up or rename the hype but money was always the underbelly of the beast.

A beautiful hostess in a tight silver sequin dress with long brunette hair took his invitation after giving it a once over. An Asian girl with a sexy smile in a matching dress gave Jones a glass of champagne. Although he wasn't a champagne drinker by any stretch of the imagination he recognized a good Moet brand by taste. Not bad for a guy who took a blow to the head like some bleeding amateur a few hours ago.

The museum was sparkling and the dull roar in the air was the echo effects from multiple conversations due to the high ceilings in the marble foyer. Out of the corner of his eye he spotted Senator Warren holding court with four splendidly dressed men. Judging by the smiles and back slaps they were no doubt reverent supporters. Rivers was already attached to that group like an out of place adolescent.

Jones wasn't sold on his taskforce colleague's tactics. In fact, he thought Rivers was downright sloppy which was the likely reason things went south in France during his security days. Not being thorough with the prisoner interrogation or looking for black helicopters was puzzling. Almost like these events didn't matter. The missing art seemed more important but the former usually leads to the later in his opinion.

As Jones was making small talk with a Ft. Lauderdale couple he noticed the arrival of Terrence Oliver who seemed a bit mysterious. Was he really a hardline mercenary type like Rivers alluded to? He seemed more like a career FBI agent putting in his time. If he really was a mercenary, then Rivers should have had him interrogate Dunbar's killer. It was only logical if it was true.

Another twenty minutes passed with Jones talking to a Coral Gables couple who brought a large group of friends with them. Nobody seemed to know Dunbar personally but they all heard about his untimely demise. The most anyone would fess up to was that they ate at several of his restaurants. Bradley Dunbar was either that inconsequential or he was that good. There is no in between. To be under the radar with nobody being suspicious when you're shady is an art form.

Jones mingled his way into the southeast corner. He heard some gregarious laughing right before he accidentally bumped into Oliver. Startled, Oliver made his way to the reception area bar to order another mixed cocktail. Not only did Oliver seem like a jittery character but he liked to get his drink on as evidenced by his ruddy face. The poor guy probably wasn't a hit with the ladies.

A Miami area woman who looked like a cast member from the movie Scarface admitted that she knew Dunbar well. After ten minutes of worthless conversation, he determined that she was a second-rate hooker with useless information for his purposes. At least he had found someone who knew Dunbar while Rivers was becoming a member of the Senator's entourage.

Lowell Watkins, a self-proclaimed loud and rich Texan and his trophy wife struck up a conversation with Jones. They only lived in Miami part of the year, but they knew of Dunbar from frequenting his steak joint. Mrs. Watkins seemed to have had a fondness for the good-looking Dunbar which was likely the reason Lowell Watkins seemed to dislike him. Either way, neither of them had anything of value regarding the situation.

In the middle of the painful conversation with the Texans, Jones noticed Rivers depart the Senator;s circle as another couple approached. They were a decadent and well-known couple judging by the reception they received. Even Senator Warren momentarily stepped off his high horse for a hardy handshake to the gentleman and a lovely cheek kiss to the lady. They seemed to know the Senator's younger female companion quite well.

Whoever she was, the young female looked stunning in a shimmering Gucci dress. Jones wondered if she might look better with her hair down. Either way, she was a looker beyond belief and appeared to be single. Hopefully, she wasn't the Senator's mistress. He made a promise to himself to try to find out later. Girl X, whoever she was seemed to know all the players. There was a decent chance she could connect some dots.

Unlike Rivers, Jones wasn't convinced that the Senator was the key to unravelling the Miami connection to the French art heist. Politicians are quite adept at insulating themselves from the dirty side of the business. This guy appeared dirty from a political perspective, but he hired people to carry out the grunt work. Sure, on the way up he was more involved. Even then, he would have worn gloves and have a fall guy kept close. At his level in the U.S. Senate, he was almost untouchable which was the real reason that an FBI agent with a checkered past was on this case. It was also the reason that an unknown and new CIA asset such as himself was on the case. If something went south, this taskforce was getting the blame. Rogue was the favorite word in play this century for the finger pointers.

The event looked to be a solid success. Jones estimated the crowd to be north of three hundred people. They brought their checkbooks and were more than willing to use them. Rivers had been completely out of sight from his new vantage point. Oliver was now near the Senator's circle talking to a couple of trust fund guys in their early thirties.

Jones finished his third glass of champagne and pretended to be mildly interested in what a filthy rich Manhattan couple were telling him. Out of the corner of his eye, he spotted Girl X walking back from the restroom area absent any glass at all. He excused himself mid-conversation and made a beeline for Girl X grabbing two fresh glasses of Moet from the waiter. In a matter of seconds, he caught up with the vibrant woman.

"You appear to be a little parched. Allow me," Jones said handing her a glass of Moet.

"Thank you. You've read my mind. I don't believe we've met."

"Sinjin Jones. Las Vegas, Nevada. Very pleased to meet you." He replied shaking her hand gently.

"That's an interesting name," she mused.

"It's the English version of St. John phonetically speaking. My mother was born over the pond and always had a fondness for the name."

"Nice. I'm Rachelle Sullivan. I don't recall seeing your name on the guest list."

"I must confess it was a last-minute venture. I flew into town for business at the last minute."

"I see." Rachelle smiled softly. "Easy on the eyes and a bit of a mysterious art lover."

"Not really. I like old things that interest me. Especially if there's a profit in it." Jones replied with a nervous chuckle.

"I pictured you more of a high stakes gambler once I heard Vegas."

"Hardly, losing bothers me too much and the house always wins in the end. I buy and sell things."

"And that's how you ended up here?" Rachelle smirked with a tint of disbelief.

"Exactly. What's your story? You seem way too young to be hanging around this crowd," Jones countered to put the focus on her.

"Well, I'm legal I assure you. No kids, I'm a career girl. I work for the Senator. I set events like this up, so he looks good," Rachelle answered laughingly.

"A job well done." Jones toasted, and they clanked glasses.

"Thank you. It was nice meeting you. I have to go check with the staff and make sure everything is okay." Rachelle started to walk away.

73

"I'll be in town for a few more days. How about lunch tomorrow?" Jones asked.

"Maybe," she replied without turning around.

"What does maybe mean?" Jones asked befuddled.

Over her shoulder, Rachelle smiled while making eye contact. "Tap Tap, it's by the beach. Make it noon Mr. Jones."

That smile made the whole night worth it Jones mused as he walked to the bar for a simple beer. Guzzling Moet with the aristocrats made his stomach sour. After the bartender placed an ice cold Pacifico in front of him he felt the presence of somebody on his left side.

"Nice Jones, real fricking nice. We're working the crowd and you're working a girl," Rivers whispered harshly trying to be unnoticeable.

Jones didn't make eye contact with Rivers and held in a tight smile. "Sorry boss. I thought you told us to beat the bush."

Chapter 16
A Quick Diversion

A GENTLE MORNING BREEZE woke up the coconut palm trees. Jones had a simple task on this bright sunny morning. He pulled his Jeep away from the Castellano's residence and headed for the Metro West Detention Center. He hadn't visited Mrs. Castellanos. He required a current photograph of her. Even though it was a simple task, he wished he was still lying in his hotel bed because his head was still throbbing. The combination of being hit and drinking Moet wasn't kind to the old noggin.

The trio had a late-night strategy meeting in Rivers' room after the museum gala. Oliver turned out to be the evening's hero, at least from an information standpoint pertaining to the case. Two of the brash men he encountered were in the helicopter business together and knew Bradley Dunbar. It was a solid lead and this aspect would be followed up this afternoon. Maybe he had misjudged Oliver.

Rivers decided that he wouldl around Cecilia Sullivan around for the day. She was better known as Ceci in social circles and certainly was an expert at spending her husband's money per the gossip circles. Jones thought this was another twist in the wind like the Senator Warren angle, but he wasn't going to argue with Rivers' strategy now. Rivers was technically in charge but if Jones needed to make a bold move, he felt confident that Graydon Bullock would have his back.

In fact, Rivers initially wanted him to cancel his lunch date with Rachelle and head back to Little Havana. After five minutes of bickering, Rivers finally relented and agreed that cancelling anything at this point might raise suspicions. Jones conveniently left out the fact that Sullivan was Rachelle's last name. He would nail down the connection at lunch and see if it was even relevant.

After retiring to his room for the evening, he placed a call to Bullock. Surprisingly, Bullock was quite agreeable, and arrangements were made for Jones to visit Ruben Castellanos at nine a.m. He would have preferred a bit later in the morning but kept his mouth shut. He was thrilled that Bullock showed some confidence in him.

Jones arrived at Metro West Detention Center exactly on time and was escorted hassle free to a tiny corner room where he sat down directly across from a beastly looking Ruben Castellano.

"Who are you supposed to be?" Castellanos asked.

"Call me Jones."

"That supposed to be your real name?"

"Maybe, maybe not but since we are never going to exchange Christmas cards, it's Jones,

"Well Jones. Whatever you're selling, I ain't buying."

"I want information. Who hired you to kill Bradley Dunbar?"

"No offense Jones, but I've got at least a hundred pounds on you. Even in these bracelets, your scrawny ass don't scare me."

"I'm your worst nightmare Ruben. Let's do this the easy way, shall we?"

"Even a killer has rights." Castellanos smirked. "Can I see your badge officer?" Castellanos jokingly added.

Jones anticipated this obstacle. Castellanos was predictable but even big guys are capable of crying. Bullock had made the necessary arrangements citing some legalese from the Patriot Act. Alleging the standard phony terrorism threat was made even easier with Castellanos being a Cuban.

After a conscious pause with a blank stare, Jones calmly stated. "I'm a ghost Ruben. I don't officially exist. I have no credentials and there's no record of this visit. Look around. There's no guard. There's not even a camera. It's just me and you. You are a terrorist suspect against the United States of America. Tell me everything you know and that all goes away."

"That's bullshit, and you know it man." Castellanos said getting visibly angry.

Jones pulled out his iPhone without getting up from his chair or taking his eyes off Castellanos.

"Yes, it is Ruben. Absolute crap but people get hurt none the less. Tell me what I want to know. Or," Jones paused putting the phone close to Castellanos face. "I will kill this woman exactly how you snuffed out Bradley Dunbar and not even break a sweat."

Castellanos went berserk trying to get out of his chair and rush Jones. A simple shove backwards kept him at bay letting him know who had the power.

"You've got five seconds to talk Ruben. Once I walk through that door, I'm going to strangle your mother. And I will send you a Kodak moment of it every single day. You can count on that!" Jones raised his voice for the first time during this encounter.

Castellanos started crying like a newborn baby. Jones broke him in a style of his own. Even though he let this woman down time after time, she never stopped loving her Ruben. Now she was in great peril due to no fault of her own.

"I'm not going to count out loud Ruben." Jones was getting tired of Ruben very quickly. His head still hurt and frankly he didn't think he was all that tough. Letting him out of the cuffs and kicking his ass might release a bit of pent up aggression.

"Okay, okay. I got a call from Simon. He said this Dunbar guy needed to be done before he posted bail. They put me in his cell and that's that."

"Why?" Jones asked.

"I'm the hired help man. They give some cash to my momma and that's all I know. In my position, I don't ask questions."

"Where do I find Simon?"

Castellanos laughed right at Jones. "Nobody finds Simon. Simon finds you. He's a much better ghost than you Jones."

Jones stood up and started towards the door. He knew when a broken man was telling the truth. Plenty of them littered shallow graves in Afghanistan. "Did your mother get her cash?"

"I'm not sure yet. His reputation is solid though," Castellanos answered albeit a bit puzzled.

"Thank you for your time Ruben. When I find Simon, I'll make sure Simon paid her."

Jones left the room as quietly as he entered.

Chapter 17

The Oliver Twist

THE MORNING SUN REFLECTED brightly off the windows of the art deco building on Collins Avenue. Terrence Oliver sat slumped behind the wheel of his SUV parked down the street. Rivers and Jones seemed genuinely pleased with his work last night at the museum gala. The Sullivan brothers were both helicopter pilots. They seemed to be well connected and wealthy the trust fund way. It wasn't confirmation of anything, but it warranted a good investigation. Besides, it was better than anything else the taskforce came up with. Rivers seemed to suspect Senator Warren was involved and wouldn't pull his head out of the sand to look at anyone else. As for Jones, the kid put in a half ass effort and came away with a date in his opinion.

Most people considered the twice divorced Oliver quiet or downright aloof. Nobody considered him a people person. It was the nature of the business to play your cards tight. Too many vodka tonics though could make Oliver a full-fledged dangerous man. He'd split a loudmouth's drunk skull open without regret or repercussion. He was a selfish bloke with his only real allegiance to himself.

Public records showed that the brother's old man, Derek Sullivan had bought up every unit of the twenty ninth floor at a foreclosure auction in the nineties. It was only two blocks south of the Dunbar residence. Rumor had it that the Sullivan boys spent three million bucks remodeling the entire floor. It included a gym, full size bar and a stripper pole with plenty of guests who knew how to use it.

The palm trees on the sidewalk barely moved on a near windless day when a white Porsche Targa flew out of the parking garage and sped down Collins Avenue. At first Oliver thought he had been spotted but quickly realized he was in the clear. The Sullivan boys were a couple of rich boys who fancied themselves as thrill seekers. Putting the pedal to the metal added to the illusion. The helicopter business isn't cheap, but Oliver surmised that daddy's money had bankrolled this venture. Oliver despised guys like this and wanted to go out of his way to add some misery to their enchanted lives.

Oliver kept a loose tail on them exercising great caution on the men he spoke to the night before. Sunglasses and a baseball cap pulled low would keep them from making a visual identification. It was overkill though as the Sullivans seemed oblivious to anyone else on the road and pulled into a Porsche dealership ten minutes later. Oliver parked across the street in a fast food parking lot and tucked himself into the passenger seat like he was waiting for someone. The Sullivans exited their vehicle and made a beeline for a black Porsche Targa.

The younger brother Rick seemed dumber than a box of rocks. Cocky also, but deep down he knew he couldn't back up anything without the family name. That didn't even help him at the University of Miami. His grades were so poor that he only made it through one semester before deciding to join a band that faded into garage band history.

James Sullivan was the complete opposite. A graduate of Boston College preparing himself to take over the family business ventures someday. Smart and quite capable of handling himself in pressure situations. Kind of like a helicopter pilot willing to cover up his FAA numbers and do a rooftop heist.

Oliver kept the engine running and looked through a small set of field glasses to watch the drama.

An extremely tanned fast-talking salesman in a gray lightweight suit greeted both Sullivans with a hardy handshake. "I called you Rick the moment it arrived."

"I was expecting it two days ago. Do I look happy?" Rick Sullivan snapped.

"No sir. No sir you don't. I'm very sorry." The salesman looked down shaking his head with some of the color draining from his face and his stomach starting to churn from nervousness. "These things happen sometimes on fine luxury automobiles such as this one. But rest assured, I fought hard to get this car delivered here for you Rick."

"Sounds like a sorry ass excuse to me. My father wouldn't put up with crap like this. He'd walk away."

"Except you aren't father and we are in an extreme hurry today," James Sullivan interjected as he handed the salesman an American Express Card. "Please put it on this and take off a grand for the delay. Have it ready in twenty minutes please."

The salesman took the card with a dejected but grateful look. "I can live with that for you fine gentleman."

Right on cue, Oliver was now following matching black and white Porsches through the streets of Miami. He was having a hard time keeping up with the racing fools without looking obvious and he was getting pissed. His anger was growing by the second as he remembered how hard it was to talk his father into co-signing a loan for his first car. Now he was following two trust fund kids with toys wondering where he went wrong.

After ten minutes of gut wrenching lane changes, both Porsche's pulled into the valet lane of the

Fontainebleau. Oliver couldn't believe they pulled into his hotel without wondering if his cover was blown. He passed the hotel and parked in a nearby lot down the street and started walking to the hotel entrance. The valets were parking both cars carefully and the brothers were nowhere in sight.

Oliver tussled in his mind if it was a trap. Basically, he had two options. Sit down the street and possibly wait for hours. Or, go in and find out the skinny. It was a public place and he was a guest of the hotel. If they confronted him or accused him of following them he would simply deny it. He decided to play tourist and walk in.

After wandering through the resort grounds, he spotted them sitting at a table near the poolside lounge. Cocktails were already flowing, and they had four lavish beauties in bikinis beside them. Oliver took a seat on the backside of the bar and ordered a mojito.

After three drinks he noticed that he was being outpaced by a two to one ratio. Perhaps they planned on getting a room and spending the night but only time would tell. He ordered a fourth drink and sat back to watch the ever-gregarious show as more woman had joined the impromptu frat party.

When the Sullivans finally asked for their tab, Oliver threw three twenty-dollar bills on the bar muttering under his breath about Miami prices or something of the sort. He walked back to his vehicle keeping a low profile. If they left the premises, he wanted to be prepared for the drunken speed racers. If they stayed, he would head back to the hotel as they wouldn't be hard to find.

Oliver guessed correctly as the Sullivans tipped the valet and squealed out of the parking lot. This time the ride was a bit more subdued as he followed them to a helicopter port north of Hialeah. He slowed down and saw the Sullivans disappear behind a moving steel gate closing behind them.

A sly smile flashed across Oliver's face as he parked a good block down the street. These guys seemed dirty for sure he thought. All the signs were there under the surface. If he could crack this open, he'd find a way to make it worth his while. The area wasn't conducive to surveillance, but he decided to hang around for a little while.

A few minutes later Oliver watched the pair take off in a black Bell helicopter. Even he wouldn't fly a helicopter loaded up with that much booze. These guys were fearless or too drunk to give a damn. This one had FAA numbers visible, but it sure resembled the one he saw yesterday at Dunbar's place. Of course, his identification wouldn't hold up in a criminal court. But it would for a search warrant.

The Bell flew out of Oliver's binocular vision when he noticed that tower security had a visual on him. It looked like he had pushed his luck too far. In these days of terrorist acts, security was heightened at every facility and he should have known better. Hopefully, the tower wouldn't alert the Bell. It was Miami though. Drug cartels were always searching for chopper talent and maybe they thought he was working in a human resources capacity. Either way, it was time to vamoose before a patrol car came his way.

Chapter 18

Key Biscayne

RIVERS WAS HUNKERED DOWN behind the steering wheel of a rented white Fiat 500 sport peering at the Sullivan compound from a vantage point down the street next to a canal. A highly-secured brick wall separated the grounds from the rest of the neighborhood. Sullivan took his chosen occupation as a security analyst quite seriously. For the last ninety minutes, there had been neither sign of life inside the compound nor much activity of any sort in this land of mansions. He was determined to stay with his surveillance through the day no matter how hot and uncomfortable the summer heat was becoming. Luckily, he brought some ice-cold Gatorade and parked beneath a massive palm tree to bring a little relief. His field binoculars were steadied on the dashboard with a direct view of the front door visible through a service gate.

After another hour, a white Rolls Royce Silver Cloud pulled up to that same door. An elegant woman dressed in white tennis gear jumped into the backseat carrying a black gear bag. The gate opened, and it headed north. Rivers could tell by the familiar strut alone that the passenger was Ceci Sullivan.

Rivers pulled the Fiat onto the roadway following the Rolls Royce leaving a quarter mile of real estate between them. Normally, he'd tail a target a bit closer, but traffic was extremely light this late morning. Plus, it wasn't that hard to keep a visual on a Rolls Royce even in Miami.

A brief ten minutes later he followed Ceci and the Rolls Royce onto Crandon Boulevard and then into the

Crandon Park Tennis Center. She exited her status symbol and disappeared beyond the doors of the center. Rivers kept his head down and parked the Fiat in the last row of the visitor's lot as the Rolls Royce parked in the member's lot. Mrs. Sullivan seemed to adapt to her lifestyle quite well Rivers thought to himself.

Rivers waited five minutes before he entered the tennis center. It was a top-notch facility that was home to the Sony Open. World champions like Roger Federer and Serena Williams had graced center court. He walked the perimeter unnoticed when he spotted Ceci stretching out near the third hardcourt. Even though she was north of fifty, she could pass for someone twenty years younger. It was obvious she was waiting for someone, so Rivers speed walked over to the reservations desk.

"Excuse me sir," Rivers said to the desk manager as he approached him. "I'm supposed to watch my friend Ceci Sullivan play today. I'm embarrassed to admit that I forgot her partner's name. Could you help me with that? I'd really appreciate it."

The desk manager flashed Rivers a pompous smile as he checked his computer. "Yes sir, she has a lesson today with Jimmy Jensen. He's one of our finest instructors."

"Oh yes. JJ, she called him the other day. Is he here yet?"

"He's most likely in the men's locker room facility sir."

"Thank you, my good man," Rivers replied as he flipped the man a twenty-dollar bill and made a beeline for the locker room. This couldn't have worked out any better he thought but time was of the essence.

Another tennis instructor pointed out Jensen to Rivers who then approached him with a hundred-dollar bill.

"Excuse me Mr. Jensen. Mrs. Sullivan asked me to give you this and please cancel her lesson. An old friend dropped in unexpectedly and she's going to play with him today."

"Okay," Jensen replied. "But I usually get one fifty and this is a late cancellation."

"You're kidding," Rivers replied in amazement.

"No sir, this is Key Biscayne."

"Okay fine." Rivers fumbled another hundred dollars out of his pocket and handed it to him. "Go have yourself an early lunch. Is she any good?"

"She can hold her own."

Great, Rivers thought to himself. He was a very good athlete back in the day. He was the starting tailback on his high school football team, but he hadn't played tennis in years. Luckily, the FBI made sure he stayed in decent shape all year long.

Rivers moved through the pro shop with the precision of a hibachi grill chef. He grabbed a water bottle and picked out matching shorts and shirt. A Wilson racquet with Nike shoes and socks completed the makeshift wardrobe. No time to try them on as he paid with a credit card and made a dash for the locker room. This receipt would need an added narrative on next month's expense report.

Rivers scooped up a loose ball with his racquet as he entered court three. Ceci starred at Rivers with a slight smile as he stood there bouncing a yellow tennis ball on his racquet with a slow and steady cadence.

"I thought I caught a glance of you last night. Let's play a set since I'm sure you cancelled my lesson. I'll serve first."

"You always do kiddo," Rivers replied with a wry grin and a sparkle in his eye.

The set lasted almost an hour without one spoken word besides an occasional score update. Rivers lost the first game badly because he kept hitting the ball too hard and out of bounds. He finally lowered his adrenalin and reminded himself that playing a precision sport with anger is a fool's game. He won the next two games before Ceci played a brilliant fourth game to tie it up. Jensen was right, she could hold her own. She always could in almost anything the world brought her up against.

Rivers gulped down half his water bottle and started to dump the rest on his head before he thought better of it. She once called him 'unsophisticated' and that still bothered him all these years later.

Ceci came on strong the next game to blank Rivers but sloppy unforced errors throughout the match gave Rivers the set win. Either she had an off day or let him win. Rivers didn't care as they walked off the court together.

Ceci smiled. "Congratulations Stony, you win."

"About twenty-eight years too late Ceci."

Chapter 19
Taso Kabrit

JONES ARRIVED EARLY for his lunch date with Rachelle Sullivan and grabbed a Cuban coffee down the block. He hated to be early for anything. As a child with his parents they were always the first to arrive at any event. Whether it was a family reunion or a simple movie they were always the first ones there. Since then punctuality wasn't his thing. Sure, the army changed that world for a while. But most covert operations in Afghanistan operated in the darkness of night. His unit was usually sleeping in caves during daylight hours and staying out of sight. But in the darkness, they operated by feel, not a damn watch. Now, he lived in a place where only one hour of the day carried any significance. Some places called it happy hour. Key West conchs called it five o'clock.

The aroma of his coffee whiffed through the Miami air as he grabbed a seat at the outdoor café wondering if his new friend held any enlightening information about Bradley Dunbar. Her family was well connected in the Miami social world not to mention a powerful United States Senator. Even if she didn't, this lunch wouldn't be a waste of time in his mind. She seemed special and this stunning lady was close to Key West.

A few minutes later a sleek black new Mercedes 550 roadster pulled up to the valet who took the keys from one Rachelle Sullivan. Dressed in a white jumpsuit with a sparkling diamond necklace around her neck, she entered Tap Tap with a long line of gawkers behind her. Stunning was an understatement.

Tap Tap was one of the busiest restaurants on South Beach specializing in Haitian cuisine. Jones waited five minutes before entering the restaurant and finding her already seated. He approached her table with a slight smile keeping an even bigger one subdued.

"Good to see you again Sinjin, have a seat."

"The pleasure is all mine," Jones replied taking the seat opposite and feeling a bit underdressed next to her wearing navy shorts with a cream-colored linen shirt.

"I took the liberty of ordering us Mojitos and Taso Kabrit as an appetizer,

"Well it's a good thing I showed up then. What is Taso Kabrit?" he asked.

"Oh, I knew you'd show up Mr. Vegas," she replied with a happy confident smile. "Taso Kabrit is goat tidbits with a creole dipping sauce."

Jones stared straight ahead trying not to show any emotion. Just fricking great he thought to himself. Almost every day during his tour in Afghanistan he ate goat in some form or another. They were everywhere in the mountains and countryside.

"Great, sounds interesting," Jones replied with a small forced smile.

"Excuse me, I need to use the restroom really quick."

"Certainly," Jones replied standing up and watching her walk away. She had a nicer walk than any contestant in a Miss America contest. It was natural, not forced. Being the son of a casino executive, he was afforded the opportunity to see a handful of them. It was one of the perks of the job and Jones imagined he would have followed in his father's footsteps if he was still alive. He thought about his father a lot and missed him very much lately. But, his life now suited his personality well. Especially on days with a lunch date like this.

The mojitos and appetizers arrived as Rachelle returned to the table. She took her seat and raised her glass towards Jones.

"Cheers," she toasted.

"Cheers," Jones replied with a beaming smile thinking maybe, just maybe he could eat some goat without gagging now.

"So, Rachelle, tell me about yourself?"

"Well, born and raised in Miami. I even went to the U. Great football program but I didn't make the team," she joked. "Although, I did venture out to D.C. to get a master's degree at Georgetown."

"Is that how you ended up working for the Senator?"

Jones immediately wanted to bite his tongue. Always let people talk and ask questions at the end. Information one seeks will usually come out if you let a person talk freely.

"As a matter of fact, it is. A phone call and donation from my father probably didn't hurt." She laughed. "Don't get me wrong though. I did very well in the grades department and I can hold my own on anybody's staff. I have lofty plans of my own someday."

"Nothing like an ambitious woman. Were those your parents I met at one-point last night?"

Jones lied. Her parents were some of the few people he didn't meet last night. In fact, he was unaware of them until Oliver spoke about her brothers and he put the family tree in place.

"Yes. My father owns an alarm system company. Self-made man and all that. And my mother," she smiled sarcastically, "just likes being a socialite. She even bought a painting last night that she hated just to keep up the charitable impression in front of her friends."

"Well, it was for charity. Maybe she can re-gift it?" Jones joked.

"I'm sure she will. Enough about me. Tell me about yourself? You seem to be a bit of a modern-day nomad."

The waiter appeared to take their order. Rachelle ordered the conch creole and Jones ordered the blackened grouper with lime sauce and another round of mojitos for them. The first mojito wasn't enough to erase the recent memory of the goat bits.

Most operatives tried to re-invent themselves with a bland lifestyle to fit in as normal. Since he was freelance and formal training was minimal, he stuck closely to the truth. Except he would leave out Afghanistan which is where he received his only formal training that was overly simplistic. Learning how to kill others and come home alive was considered successful. Leaving the desert in a body bag wasn't. No girl would want to hear that.

Growing up in Las Vegas was a wonderful back story or at least entertaining. It was better than anything he could ever dream up and he learned something from them all. Among the gamblers, mobsters and entertainers that he met, they all served up a certain culture of success and advice. Listen and don't talk too much was preached upon him by the gamblers. Make connections and gather favors was the mobster credence. Keep secrets to yourself offered the entertainers. Always know where the bodies are buried from them all. They were his mentors growing up. As much as the city changed its landscape, Las Vegas was still very much old school.

The truth was better than a lie which is easily impenetrable from a worthy opponent. A mistake could be costly. No, he would use his own story rather than reinvent himself. Besides, everyone in it was dead anyway.

"Not much to say really. Rather boring and sad," Jones implied.

"A man of few words I see. Let me be the judge? Whatcha got Vegas?"

"Born and raised in Vegas. My parents were wonderful. I was the only child my mother could have but my neighborhood was great. One big family that grew up together. Everybody worked at the casino, including my father,

"I bet you met a lot of famous people?"

"Oh sure," Jones replied. "I saw Elvis and Sinatra in concert many times. Sammy Davis Jr. even came to my fifth birthday party. He gave me a saxophone that was almost as big as me. I still have it to this day. He was nice man to everybody."

"That sounds like a glorious childhood."

"It was." Jones didn't like talking about his past, but he knew he didn't have much of a choice to stop now. He liked this girl. He hadn't liked anyone in such a long time.

"Unfortunately, my parents passed away in a plane crash. I inherited a decent amount of money. Although they had more debt than I realized. So now, I travel around making investments and occasionally turning up at charity events such as yours."

"Sorry to hear that. It's so sad. Sorry I forced goat tidbits on you now!"

They both laughed hard which eased the moment's tension. Jones motioned for another round of mojitos as he caught the waiter's eye.

"Are you trying to get me drunk, Mr. Jones? It's only lunch time you know."

"Hopefully, I'll never have to resort to that." Jones laughed.

"So, is there a special woman in your life?" Rachelle hesitantly asked not one hundred percent sure that it was an appropriate question at this moment.

"No. Too busy traveling to get some roots. The craziest I get is ordering some room service and watching old movies. I saw Key Largo for the tenth time the other night."

"Bogie and Bacall, absolutely the best. Bacall is so beautiful. The way she walks, the way she talks, total class. I've seen all four of their movies together countless times," Rachelle said.

"I love that time period myself. It's something that grabs me. Men were men. Women were women. The whole era was so grand. Simpler times I guess. John Huston did a great job directing that," Jones remarked.

"It was a good movie, but I liked their first one much better. To Have or Have Not."

"Why is that?' Jones asked.

"Two words, Slim Browning. Bacall was nineteen and she hits a grand slam in her very first role. She's tough, elegant and aggressive. Ahead of her time but she should be every woman's role model."

"Should I call you Marie?" Jones joked.

"Very nice Mr. Jones. You know her characters real first name."

"That's probably why I'm fairly good at trivial pursuit. Any other reasons to like the film?"

"Well, there is Martinique. It's not presented well in the movie because it was filmed on a studio lot. People say it's simply gorgeous."

"Have you traveled a lot?" Jones asked.

"Not really. When I was a child my parents rarely ventured outside Florida."

"That's rather odd. Considering they are well off one would think they'd hit all the usual hotspots."

"It seems like they are content trying to be Floridian royalty. I've been to places like Mexico, Italy and the Bahamas. I'm playing catch up compared to my friends I guess."

"No France or Spain or that area?

"No. Hopefully someday."

The waiter brought out the lunch plates and ran back to the bar area for the mojitos.

"So, any steady man in your life?"

"No, not yet." She smiled. "But, I have a good prospect."

Chapter 20
Warrant Time

TERRENCE OLIVER SAT in the passenger side of his SUV to make it look like he was waiting for the driver running an errand. He could see the front entrance of the Sullivan brothers building once again. The sunny weather hadn't varied more than three degrees either way since he started this case. No wonder people love South Florida he thought to himself.

Getting a warrant for this residence was as easy as he had anticipated. All any agency needed in this world climate was to cite a vague reason for suspected terrorism. Any federal judge would sign off on it. Anything happening on their watch would start the blame game with a finger pointing squarely at them because they refused a simple warrant. Hell, the municipal dog catcher could get a warrant if they really wanted one. Luckily, nobody connected or inquired about family connections or it would have been a tough sell.

Oliver wouldn't be going in for the search. He didn't want to blow his cover, so he'd let the local agents perform it. They were well trained and experienced, so he had full confidence in them finding something useful. He was more worried about Rivers. This was a bold move and he went around River's back intentionally on this one.

Rivers would be pissed off when he found out. He would immediately know who called for the warrant, but Oliver didn't care. Sure, Rivers had a reputation as a hot head at times. They had worked well together in the past, but Oliver was tired of playing second fiddle to Rivers and everyone else for that matter. This was his time to make a mark for himself in the bureau. If it didn't happen now, he was a realist. It would never happen.

Two black GMC Yukons pulled to a swift stop in front of the building and four FBI agents rolled through the front door. It was going down now. Oliver had seen the Sullivan boys return to their condo twenty minutes earlier. They would be surprised but he didn't expect any gun play. Then again, trainers at Quantico drill it into every agent to expect the unexpected or suffer a sudden end to their respective careers.

Rick Sullivan never heard security call up, but he answered the door anyway. Despite the sudden surprise, he called out for his brother James in a calm manner. Rick acted even more aloof as he studied the search warrant produced by the lead agent.

As the agents put on matching baby blue plastic gloves and began their search James noticed that the warrant pertained to a helicopter incident with a Bell helicopter flying with no numbers. The warrant also entailed a search off all computers including email transmittals.

"Am I allowed to call my father?" James asked the lead agent.

"You can call anyone you wish but you need to stay in this room," the agent replied in a polite and professional manner.

Derek Sullivan was sitting in his plush home library office checking his massive diversified stock portfolio. He didn't believe in stockbrokers, financial advisors or money managers. No one would ever watch over your money as good as one's own self was his firm belief. His track record was better than anyone on Wall Street and he had the portfolio to back it up. Buy and hold was outdated in this world of technology. He preferred to buy solid companies beat down by some bad news. He was fond of spreading the bad news himself if need be by some slyly planted confidants for a price. A month or two later he would sell on the rebound due to some fortunate good news that often appeared out of nowhere, then look for another opportunity. It was a manufactured rinse and repeat process that served him very well. He was in a jovial mood now as he was up six figures for the day.

"What's up number one son?" Derek asked as he answered the phone on the third ring.

"The feds are here. They have a search warrant," James replied.

"You're kidding? For what?" Derek asked in a stunned tone.

"Something about a helicopter incident. Looks like they're going to take the computer. We haven't said anything."

"Keep it that way," Derek demanded. "Anything we should be worried about?"

"Not a damn thing," the cocky number one son replied.

"Good," Derek replied slightly relieved. "If by chance they take you into custody I'll have counsel down there in a New York minute. In the meantime, I'm going to try something else. We'll touch base very soon. Stay tough."

"Will do."

The anticipation was starting to put butterflies in Oliver's stomach. Waiting and patience wasn't his two biggest strengths. After forty minutes, he finally received his call.

"So far, we have a whole lot of nothing," the lead agent tersely stated. "Take away alcohol and clothes and this place is actually sparse. They actually have a stripper pole here."

"Great, they need an interior decorator. What about their computers? Oliver asked defiantly.

"There's only one and it was actually on when we arrived. Nothing so far. But we'll take it back with us and check the hard drive since inception."

"What was their reaction when you showed up?"

"Surprised but calm. Both were cool considering the circumstances. The older one called their father. They aren't talking to us. If we take them in, we'll have a seven-figure suit in our office but that's your call."

"No, don't take them in. We can't connect them to that numberless bird yet. If anything shows up on that computer call me right away. Thanks." Oliver hung up his cell phone with a glint of despair concerning the warrant search.

Oliver knew these developments weren't good, but he wasn't about to go into panic mode. He could check for witnesses at the heliport. Luck was sometimes better than being good. Appeasing Rivers would be a priority even if it meant blatantly lying to him. Mistakes happen, and he could plead ignorance. His cover was still intact and perhaps the sons had nothing to do with this whole incident. In that case, the only thing wasted was a bit of time.

Senator Warren was on a conference call with the Florida Travel Bureau in his downtown Miami office when Rachelle Sullivan interrupted him holding her cellphone. Normally, she would stall the caller or take a message in a situation like this. However, when the caller is your irate father it never seems to work that way.

The Senator excused himself and placed the conference call on hold while taking the cellphone from Rachelle.

"This better be good," the Senator barked.

"Unfortunately, it's not. The feds just raided my son's home with a search warrant. They didn't find anything. I'm not sure why they were targeted. But I need you to get them off my family's back."

"Calm down Derek. This is starting to get a bit old. I'll make some calls. But you have to be willing to help yourself my friend."

"I helped you get elected Senator, when no one else out there gave you a chance. I'll also help you get re-elected," Sullivan stated while grating his teeth.

"I appreciate that Derek. I'll make those calls. But God helps those who help themselves. And Senator Warren rewards those people also."

"I understand," Derek replied as he hung up the phone.

Chapter 21
Soho House

SENATOR WARREN TOOK UP a small table at the jazzy styled Club Bar inside the prestigious Miami Soho House. He nursed a gin and tonic while shaking hands and making small talk with a few patrons who periodically stopped by his table. After his phone conversation with Derek Sullivan, he thought it imperative to cancel the rest of his afternoon and set up a meeting with the real rainmaker.

The Senator didn't mention this appointment to Rachelle Sullivan. Meetings with her mother were always off the grid. Even to observers in the Miami social circles, people thought the Senator and Ceci Sullivan were casual friends. The Sullivans had always been good to the Senator. Much better than standard donors by offering multiple levels of support with different variances of legalities.

Life wasn't always pleasant and good for the Senator. He grew up in Pensacola which was closer to Mobile, Alabama than Tallahassee. It was a world away from the Caribbean atmosphere of Miami. His family was considered redneck hicks and he had a juvenile record a mile long. Larceny was in his soul long before he joined the world's most elite club called the United States Senate.

Fortunately, a social worker with a strong and patient heart took an interest in the young Warren and he made the honor roll at a community college. That was a huge first step as he repeated the same repertoire two years later at the University of Miami. Then again, three years later at the University of Virginia Law School. After a return to Miami to ply his trade at a leading law firm the hick moniker disappeared from his life. As did his complete juvenile record forever.

The 1980's were quite a boom time for Miami. Real estate and drug smuggling went hand and hand. Dummy corporations, legitimate corporations and offshore accounts were created by the brightest attorneys to clean up the drug money. The pre-Senate days awarded Warren quite handsomely during this era. The Sullivans had become his best client. But power was more important than cold cash, so he took his relationship with them to the next level.

Warren was a huge underdog in the 2004 election. The United States Senate welcomed him anyway with a one-point victory. Six years later he turned it into a nine-point victory and he turned into a real player in the old boys' club. The Sullivan relationship was mutually beneficial with no end in sight and they remained ardent supporters.

The Senator was still confident he could simmer down the heat and extinguish the fire. This rainmaker had the uncanny ability to fix any fiasco while letting others do the grunt work. All parties had a great deal to lose if the situation blew up. The relationship bonded tighter with the hiring of their daughter Rachelle. She was intelligent and tough and proved to be more than competent as she was promoted as his Miami liaison. She knew all the movers and shakers in Miami.

The Rolls Royce Silver Cloud pulled up to the front door of the Soho House and Ceci Sullivan exited her car and ushered it away. This was a meeting to be heard and not seen. She rarely met one on one with the Senator. She would have preferred the Tiki Bar setting but resigned herself to the Club Bar location. Old white men always preferred the elegant old school bar with unique charm from a period never known to today's youth.

Derek Sullivan always did most of the talking between the Senator's camp. Ceci preferred it that way and went to great lengths to keep Rachelle in the dark unless she needed information. So far it was a perfect relationship. Ceci was happy being a prominent socialite with a powerbroker of a husband. Having a United States Senator in your hip pocket proved to be very beneficial. It was originally her idea, but Derek did most of the legwork to get their man elected.

The favors in return were even more prosperous than anybody could imagine. Favorable trade agreements, real estate tax breaks and insider information kept the faucets flowing green. She was elated with her status in life. The only remaining goal was to keep it lasting forever which seems simple on the surface. It went well for a nice stretch until Bradley Dunbar became careless.

In another moment, she'd be in the Club Bar and force a loving smile. She wasn't in the mood to be downplayed by the Senator. He'd still be a nobody if it wasn't for the Sullivans and deep down he knew that. Sure, his electoral victory was beneficial to the family fortune, but the little redneck could show a deeper gratitude with a little more genuine respect she figured.

"Hello Senator," she said walking directly to his table.

"Good afternoon Ceci," he replied giving her a big hug. "I took the liberty of ordering you a marvelous Cabernet."

"Thank you. Judging by your phone call, you're suffering a little unrest?"

"Oh Ceci. Always straight to the point. Unrest isn't quite the word I would use. Disturbed would be more accurate after speaking with Derek today."

"The Dunbar incident has us all upset. Let's remain calm. This too shall pass."

"Your sons received search warrants today Ceci. Derek didn't seem too calm."

The smug smile disappeared along with most of the South Florida color from her face. She stared straight at her wine glass with anger boiling her blood. Her husband's first call should have been to her.

"Judging by your reaction, you didn't know?"

"I'm sure he's too busy working on solutions to contact me. That's what we do Senator."

"Let's not trade jabs Ceci. When push comes to shove, you're the powerhouse. You wear the pants in the Sullivan family. You need to take control of the situation."

"I'll take care of it."

"Time is of the essence Ceci."

"I said I'll take care of it," she snapped.

Chapter 22
Unexpected Guests

IT WAS DUSK AS SINJIN JONES walked down South Beach towards the Delido Beach Club at the Ritz Carlton Hotel with the cool ocean breeze in his face. Rivers had set up another strategy meeting and sounded upset with Oliver who went off the reservation. An unauthorized search warrant had come up with nothing useful and now the Sullivans knew they were under investigation. The element of surprise existed no longer. For once, Jones agreed with Rivers as every possible suspect would be on high alert now.

After lunch, Jones spent some time in Little Havana looking for Torres his friend in the red pants without success. Nobody was talking to Jones as they went out of their way to avoid him. Word of the cinema incident traveled fast so Jones cut his visit short.

He still had to find this Simon character and make sure he paid his debt to Ruben's momma before turning him over to the District Attorney's office. Even if he rounded up these two clowns, he wasn't sure they could provide all the answers to the Ambassador Heist. Somehow the Sullivans seemed tied into these events. They had a lengthy history with Dunbar. People tell secrets over the long haul to people they get comfortable with.

Even though Jones didn't agree with Oliver's tactics he understood why he took an interest in the Sullivan brothers. Rivers spent most of his time taking a deep look at the Senator. Jones thought that would lead to a dead end and evidently Oliver felt the same way. Rivers wasn't much of a team guy and he wasn't going to change his stripes now. Hopefully cooler heads would prevail at dinner and a new game plan would emerge.

Rivers and Oliver were leaning on a terrace railing waiting for a table as Jones approached them. Each of them sipped on an ice-cold Corona with a third one balancing on the rail which Rivers silently handed to Jones. The atmosphere was colder than the beer, so Jones desperately felt the need to relieve the tension.

Jones took a sip of his beer and inhaled a deep breath of ocean air. It was bad enough that they all stood in silence wearing almost identical blue jeans and baggy shirts to cover their handguns. Dinner in silence with these two buffoons would ruin the memory of his fabulous lunch a few hours earlier.

"If you two don't kiss and makeup, I swear I'm finishing this beer and heading to a casino or strip club. Anywhere but here," Jones stated staring straight ahead.

"For the record, I've apologized three times!" Oliver exclaimed.

"Is a fourth going to make it better Stony?" Jones asked. "Look, it didn't work out. But I understand. He was trying to make something happen."

"Look guys, I'm over it," Rivers said. "Just listen to me from now on. The Associate Director was all in my grill about the Sullivans. That guy barely nods my way when I say hi. But one of my guys rattles the frat boys and I catch holy hell. Someone in Miami called him and my guess is that it's the country club Senator."

"Well that's something," Jones replied. "Maybe Oliver rattled the right cage after all."

"Just because we didn't find anything doesn't mean there's nothing to find," Oliver stated with a sudden hopeful tone.

The white umbrellas over the outdoor tables were swaying gently with the slight ocean breeze. All the tables were filled with two or three patrons each enjoying the Caribbean evening. One couple brought their small daughter who was sitting in a makeshift high chair made with piles of colorful lightweight Mexican blankets. Jones had his heart set on the yellowfin tuna, but it looked like they still had a thirty-minute wait at least. Another couple rounds of drinks would be in order.

"I know. I'm over it so let's move on. All I'm saying though is that we need to find something soon or we'll be tooling around on dirt bikes like those three clowns," Rivers said while motioning his half empty Corona towards the bikers.

Jones and Oliver were straining to hear Rivers over the pinging echoes of the dirt bike engines. Three men in identical green, black and white Kawasaki KX450F dirt bikes were trolling on the beach looking for someone in the crowded terrace area. Sand was spraying up from the knobby tires and people on the terrace were irritated with the bikers.

Jones was hoping hotel security would do something sooner rather than later. He was always uncomfortable in situations like this. He differed greatly from his father is that regard. In the glory days of Las Vegas his old man would grab a pit boss and they would rattle some heads of anybody who acted up in his casino. Of course, it was always in a back room away from gamblers, showgirls and witnesses. Then corporations and camera phones arrived, and old Las Vegas was never quite the same.

The three bikers were having a hard time locating their target. Between the sun setting in the west in front of them and the patio lights to their east they were having a hard time obtaining a visual. Finally, the biker in the middle stopped his bike and propped his sunglasses on top of his head.

Like two long lost lovers in the night, Jones recognized Torres sans the red pants at virtually the same moment that Torres locked eyes onto Jones. This wasn't the first assassination team in Miami as it had been prevalent during the 1980's Cocaine Wars. As Jones started to motion for his colleagues to move the three bikers swung small submachine guns out from oversized backpacks attached to the gas tanks.

"Get down. It's Torres!" Jones shouted.

Shots rang out as Jones and Oliver returned fire from behind a small palm tree. Rivers ran to his right and pushed the lone couple with a child down behind a table he pushed over. Amid the chaos, Rivers sat up for one quick shot through the heart of the far-left biker and he toppled over with the Kawasaki laying on top of him with the engine still running and kicking up some sand.

Torres and the other biker sped off at the sight of their downed comrade south towards the Versace Mansion. Oliver started administering first aid to a woman with a profusely bleeding right shoulder. Rivers fired off a few more rounds but couldn't hit a moving target especially after he tripped over a chair and stumbled to his knees while swearing up a storm.

Jones wanted a piece of Torres as the lump on his skull was still fresh from this piss ant. With his Glock positioned in his back waistband he sprinted to the downed Kawasaki and did a full one eighty with it kicking sand on the new corpse. Jones had logged hundreds of hours on dirt bikes in the Mojave Desert as a kid and this had the makings of a great race even with lead flying around.

Torres and his accomplice had a football field length of a head start on Jones, but he was closing the gap. Throwing off a shot or two crossed his mind but with the bumpy surface it wouldn't be a high percentage shot. If he could keep closing the gap they would have to turn or make a deadly mistake. His biggest disadvantage was the sand kicking up in his eyes as his Oakley's had been lost on the patio.

Jones was having a hard time closing the gap any further on an open beach as all three bikes were of equal power. Exceptional driver skill wasn't helping him fast enough. Suddenly, Torres motioned for his partner to go straight as he splintered off to the right. Another half mile ahead was Highway 112 better known as the Airport Express to locals. This was Plan B for Torres if they didn't take Jones out on the beach.

Split decisions are called that for a specific reason. No time is available to weigh the odds or do some stupid ass corporate decision tree. Jones grew up watching legendary poker player Brian Reid play at his father's casino. A local reporter once asked him about the secret of his success. Reid thoughtfully replied, "I bet my gut and I bet big. If the other guy looks like he's going to puke I usually win."

Jones listened to his gut and veered to his right in pursuit of Torres. Within seconds of leaving the beach and cutting through a parking lot he narrowly avoided a valet parking a midnight blue Mercedes. Even with added obstacles Jones was closing on Torres. Then he noticed sirens everywhere. He wasn't sure how many people were hit in the beach firefight but Miami's finest were swarming the vicinity. Rivers and Oliver carried FBI identification, so they could fend for themselves. Without them, he was in no man's land which could be trouble. Time was of the essence and he needed to bring Torres down now.

Every time Torres glanced over his shoulder he would inadvertently throttle down a bit until Jones pulled his front tire even with his adversary's rear tire. Pure fear took over Torre's brown eyes as sirens were shadowed by actual blinking blue lights. There was no Plan C, so this chase would be over one way or another in less than a minute.

Two squad cars were bearing down on them about four blocks away with another one approaching from the south. As they approached a hairpin turn Jones took it tight, so he could grab Torres and pull him off his bike. It seemed like a good idea until he swerved to avoid a homeless man and hit a grocery cart which knocked him off his bike. The slower speed cushioned the fall a bit as Jones slid up into a kneeled shooting position while grabbing his Glock. One deep breath, relax, aim and squeeze the trigger. This sequence took less than a single second for one of the highest trained professionals in the world. Lead hit Torres dead middle in his right knee and his arms exploded off the handle bars as he flew back off the bike.

Facial expressions say a lot. But the agonized scream of a gunshot wound to the knee echoes loudly to a still night. Torres was finished for the immediate future, so Jones needed to make a quick getaway. Tomorrow he would get a face to face meeting. Bullock would see to that.

Torres was moaning in guttural agony and Jones took off on foot towards his hotel. He didn't need to look over his shoulder. He knew when he hit a target and he knew when he missed a target. The hits far outweighed the misses in his career. What kindled his old memories was how the alleys of Miami weren't that different from any major city in Afghanistan. Discarded food, discarded animals and discarded souls. Sirens and squad cars filled the neighborhood, but he knew these souls wouldn't point him out. In their world, they would never help the 'man' out. The homeless people stared at him as he made his way back to the comforts of the Fontainebleau.

Ambulances arrived, and yellow tape cordoned off the block. Ten squad cars sealed off the area and many more were at the Ritz. News crews were en route, and Torres was receiving medical attention. The intensive pain made it too hard for him to speak but the two detectives dealing with him didn't expect much talking from the Little Havana veteran.

The angry Cuban had been monitoring the situation from a twelve-story rooftop off the 112. It was the planned escape route and anybody chasing Torres could be easily dealt with. Deep down in his heart he knew it wasn't a great plan. Even a Chief Executive Officer of a drug cartel has a budget. Torres was great as the pseudo King of Little Havana but turned out to be a crappy assassin.

Santora loved loyalty and that was Torres in a nutshell. Sometimes we ask too much of others he thought, and this was one of those times. He had already brought out his Russian made rifle. It was the very same rifle that his grandfather used at the Bay of Pigs except it was outfitted with a homemade silencer and a scope. Nobody crossed the beachhead without a farewell shot from his grandfather. Back then they thought they were on the right side. Time changed that perception.

A deep breath and even deeper thoughts as Santora squinted through the scope, the hell with Castro and the Yankee bastard who chased his friend through Miami. As Torres was being loaded into Dade County's newest red ambulance a simple squeeze of the trigger made sure the pseudo King of Little Havana spoke no more.

Chapter 23
Eggs Benedict

THE SUN ROSE OVER the Atlantic Ocean with a bright orangish glow as the phone rang next to Sinjin Jones sleeping head. He was totally spent. Running from the police after you shoot someone tends to do that to a person. A four mile walk as the crow flies took almost three hours with squad cars on almost every block and a police helicopter buzzing overhead. No official identification meant a night in the Dade County Detention Center and possibly longer if Graydon Bullock thought this to be a brilliant teaching moment. Once he made it to the Fontainebleau all tattered for the worse he went straight to bed without communication to anyone.

Jones answered his phone on the fourth ring. "Yes," he simply said.

"Do you like eggs benedict Mr. Jones?" A serious voice asked.

"Excuse me?" Jones asked in a befuddled voice that cried more sleep.

"I'm not accustomed to asking twice. Come on down for breakfast Mr. Jones."

Jones finally recognized the voice of Graydon Bullock with an 'oh crap' moment in his mind.

"Well good morning Mr. Bullock. I appreciate the offer, but it will take me a couple hours to get to Langley sir."

"Oh, don't worry Mr. Jones," Bullock replied with a tone of glee in his voice. "I came to you. I'm downstairs at Vida. Would you like juice or coffee with your eggs?"

"Actually, a macchiato would be fine. Be down in five," Jones replied in a wary tone.

Jones threw on some clothes wondering if his first assignment would be his last. Sure, his FBI friends and he took some shots on the beach but only after being attacked. Split decisions had to be made and he shot Torres. Sometime today he would question Torres and the justification would be made with everything good. But if the situation was good Bullock wouldn't be here. He certainly didn't come for eggs benedict no matter how tasty they were.

Jones strolled into Vida wearing worn jeans, a striped polo shirt and flip flops. He spotted Bullock at a table on the far right as the food was being served.

"Good morning Mr. Bullock. What brings you to beautiful Miami this early in the morning?"

Both men sat in silence as they started to eat their breakfast. Jones added three sugars to his macchiato wondering if Bullock was enjoying this ball breaking moment. After a few more moments of silence, Bullock took a large sip of orange juice and looked straight at Jones.

"Well Mr. Jones, I heard last night that someone was shot in the knee in Miami. You're in Miami so it doesn't take Einstein to figure out why I'm here. This is your first assignment and the leash is very short may I remind you,

"I completely understand your concern, but may I point out that he's been the only one."

Bullock gazed at Jones in utter amazement hoping that he was trying to be funny.

"Seriously," Jones replied to the empty gaze realizing that Bullock wasn't even slightly amused. "I didn't have a choice. This guy Torres tried to kill us on the beach by the Ritz and he was getting away. By all rights, I should have rendered him dead, but I believe he has information on Santora. Police were closing in, so I took him down, so I could interrogate him later like I did with Castellanos. Surely you can set this up for today?"

"Not the worst strategy, I'll give you that. Except Castellanos is still alive and Torres is dead. Other than that insignificant fact it's not really a big deal I suppose," Bullock said while eating his eggs benedict.

"Torres is dead? He couldn't have bled out that fast from a knee shot. I know how long it takes, believe me," Jones replied in muddled thought.

Bullock looked up from his plate to meet the gaze of a foggy Afghanistan admission. He decided to ignore the comment completely as it wasn't his job to judge a highly-decorated combat soldier.

"Someone shot him from a high rise as he was being loaded into an ambulance," Bullock stated.

"Sorry sir. I didn't see that coming."

"I know that Mr. Jones. That's why I'm here. No worries. Your career is still intact. This simply means that you are close to something. I'm not sure what yet but an assassin team trying to take you guys out means there is a higher power somewhere who is very nervous. Good job. Now we need to take it to the next level."

"I really thought Torres would have some answers."

"I'm sure he did. Dead men tell no tales. He knew something, or someone wouldn't have blown half his head off last night. Very few people could have made that shot so be careful. You were on the right track."

"Yes, but where do I go now?" Jones responded in a dejected manner.

"I prefer the glass half full approach to be honest. One, you're not dead. That's a lot of paperwork for me so I thank you for that. How are the eggs benedict? I came to this hotel with my family as a teenager. Sinatra performed a show out by the pool. What a night that was. Good memories," Bullock stated trying to alter the mood a bit.

"It's an excellent breakfast sir. Thank you. I didn't think this far ahead to be honest. What's your advice?"

"I appreciate the honesty Mr. Jones. I really do. Maybe, I underestimated you a bit. That's why I'm here, to formulate a broad game plan away from a paper trail. Actually, it's an email trail these days."

"What is your broad plan sir?" Jones asked.

"Santora is so far underground now it isn't even funny. It will be hard to flush him out again. This guy Simon, he's a ghost and it could take months to find him, so I wouldn't waste your time there. The Sullivans are off limits to our FBI friends. That messed up search warrant sealed their fate. But nobody said anything to me about the Sullivans." Bullock smiled with satisfaction, as so few chances availed themselves to mess with a Senator.

"You think someone in the Sullivan family can put the pieces together for us?"

"I do. Maybe not too many specifics but they can lead us there. The Senator seems to be protecting them and I learned a long time ago those that need protecting always seem a little bit dirty. Dunbar's funeral is today. Check it out from a distant vantage point. Let's see who shows up. Maybe a new player will surface? Funerals are funny that way for a somber event."

"Maybe the Senator is protecting their reputation because they all knew Dunbar?"

"The only reputation I care about Mr. Jones is ours." Bullock stated with a firm gaze at Jones.

Chapter 24
On the Cheap

THE SUN WAS BEGINNING to creep through the closed yellowed blinds of the dingy room. Santora was in his third different safe house all provided by loyal Cuban confidants. He was short on sleep since the foiled fence job with Dunbar and last night's events didn't help the deficiency.

It had been years since he did the dirty work himself. His reputation had always remained intact though because he had twenty notches on his belt and he lost sleep over none of those notches. But this was different. Torres was his good friend, a true friend who knew every detail about his operations. Nobody knew that he was his own trigger man last night and he would keep that to himself. Santora didn't know who he could trust, and his natural paranoia was at an all-time high. The drug trade eventually did that to everyone. But now, he had a dangerous man tracking him and sleeping with one eye open was making him weary.

Santora walked a few paces to the door of the small room wearing nothing but khaki shorts with a pistol in the waistband when his cell phone rang. He yanked open the door first and motioned for his armed guard to grab a Cuban coffee so he kind fight his constant weariness. The call was blocked but only one person had this particular number and he was expecting this call after last night's events.

"Good morning Simon," Santora stated with a forced smile even though nobody else was in the room.

"I wish I could believe everything is all good. But, it looks like someone went on the cheap last night. Did you forget us professionals?" the voice known as Simon sarcastically asked.

"I'm sorry Simon. But I'm bleeding cash and nothing is coming in. I can't afford you."

"You know, you and Dunbar have a lot in common with money issues. Be careful my friend or you might end up like Dunbar sooner rather than later."

"Is that a threat?" Santora asked with his neck muscles bulging out like a body builder.

"Don't be silly my friend," Simon replied calmly. "I'm actually here to protect both of our interests."

"How so?" Santora asked.

"Word from my people at the detention center is that some fella named Sinjin Jones is looking for me. He knows what really happened there."

"That's unfortunate. Any suggestions?" Santora asked while trying to figure out Simon's angle.

"It's time for us to join forces. Let's work together and take him out first. I wish I would have known about last night's debacle. I could have helped. In other words, it would have been done right," Simon stated with a tinge of anger in his voice for the first time.

"Hindsight is not a luxury we have my friend. Believe me, I wish I could go back in time. I was living the good life and keeping it real paying off politicians and cops. But no, I get myself mixed up with the jet set crowd. Now, I have some madman trying to get me."

"He's just a man," Simon replied.

"Do not underestimate this man. He rolled off a moving motorcycle and made a one in a million shot. I saw it with my own eyes. Someone trained him well. He's tough and he has skills," Santora spouted with the lack of sleep showing in his manic voice.

"That's why my way is better. Your plan was flawed from the start. We'll get up close and personal to this guy, I promise you that."

"That's going to be tough now I'm afraid. Torres had the best chance in Little Havana but didn't want to make a mess in his backyard."

"And look where that got him. From now on, let's do this my way with my people. If I need support your guys can provide that. Deal?" Simon asked.

Santora paused long and hard. The logic made sense and his options were few if any. Besides, Simon never offers his services for free.

"Deal," Santora replied with a sense of relief. "Just get it done."

Chapter 25
Funeral for a Friend

IT WAS TOO NICE OF A DAY for a memorial service Jones thought to himself as he drove over to St. Patrick's Church in Miami Beach. It was Dunbar's sister's church and she arranged the service for her bachelor brother. They weren't close siblings, but she always portrayed it to friends as if they were. She was hoping to inherit some property or cash as his lone survivor, but she also heard the rumors of a cascade of debt.

After breakfast with Bullock, Jones made a quick dash to the nearest Sears. He would need a dressed-up disguise, so he bought an off the rack old man's tan suit along with a plain white colored fedora, so he could tuck his long locks underneath it. Next was a stop at an optical store for black framed glasses with plain glass lenses. All show and no functionality.

Jones arrived early at the 1920's era Catholic Church. The bell tower was a magnificent site as Jones passed it and parked six blocks away as a precaution. He found an inconspicuous side door and found his way onto the small white balcony at the back of the church. He took a seat in the back row with a complete view of the altar.

Jones wasn't quite sure what he would find out from this funeral. Often, it's what one doesn't see that is more enlightening. He turned off his cellphone as the first people arrived. Judging by the way they knew each other, he gathered the first dozen people were distant family members.

After another ten minutes a group of young women walked in. They dressed like well-mannered club girls and Jones figured they were some of Dunbar's service industry employees. Four large young men walked in together. They acknowledged the girls, so they were bouncers or bartenders in the same circle.

No one from the Miami jet set crowd appeared to pay their last respects. Dunbar was radioactive even in death. He had committed the three ultimate sins in South Florida. Going broke, getting arrested and getting killed. The flowers were abundant though, so he wasn't a forgotten man.

The organist started playing "Greensleeves" as everyone took a seat. The Priest approached the altar to begin the brief service. Out of the corner of his eye he spotted a stealth beauty in a black St. John suit take a seat by herself in the middle of the church. Even with her hair up Jones recognized Rachelle Sullivan.

It was a good move by the jet set crowd. Senator Warren wouldn't set foot at this funeral for political reasons and Derek Sullivan along with his wife Ceci wouldn't want to tarnish their image neither. The media was unlikely to cover a funeral, but cautious and clever people always took precautions. Rachelle was the one person who could represent both parties for their devoted friend. She was the most beautiful sacrificial lamb as he had ever seen.

The service was over in twenty minutes. A sunny day is the secret to keeping a Catholic funeral short or perhaps it was spite for the deceased. Either way, nary a tear was shed except for the show tears from Dunbar's sister. The guests departed as quickly as they arrived with no graveside service scheduled.

Jones exited the side door after everyone else had left. He took a final glance at the coffin holding Bradley Dunbar. He looked at peace now, but Jones knew the last thirty seconds of his life were anything but peaceful. The funeral embalmer had done a remarkable job covering up the ligature marks underneath the jawbone. Obviously by a person who took pride in their work.

Rachelle Sullivan's phone rang as she was sitting at a red light in her black Mercedes roadster. She flashed a wide smile as she pushed the speaker button to answer it.

"Well hello Sinjin. I was beginning to think I was a boring lunch date."

"No chance of that. How's it going? What are you up to?" Jones asked with a big smile as he was leaning on the open door of his Jeep.

"I'm running errands for the Senator."

"That sounds depressing. Are you free for dinner tonight by chance?"

"As a matter of fact, I am," Rachelle replied.

"Great. Any suggestions?"

"Surprise me Sinjin. Pick me up at seven. I'll text you my address."

Chapter 26
New Promises

THE BEACH WAS FILLED with an assortment of well-tanned bodies a couple hundred yards away from the roped off crime scene on the beach. Stony stayed up half the night speaking to Miami detectives. Then, he spent the other half talking to FBI brass. Two fiascos on the same case was never a good move for one's career path.

Rivers was trudging along through the sand sweating from the midday heat. He needed to move the timeline up for his hidden agenda. At first, he wanted sweet revenge and money. Now, it was strictly about the cash as being shot at never entered the equation. He was starting to wonder if she would show up. The last time they planned to meet she disappeared off the face of the earth.

He learned the hard way that Ceci couldn't be trusted. A bad double cross cost him a job and a life planned for luxury which she enjoyed without him. Instead, he started over from scratch and did a decent job of putting himself back in play. For years, he wanted to crack the case and recover the Dutch Sisters and restore his reputation. Then Miami happened and put conflict in his heart. Did he need to crack the case anymore? Hardly anyone even remembered it anymore except for some pompous art historians and collectors.

Now his heart and his soul leaned towards the money. He could retire in fashion with a Swiss bank account and nobody in the U.S. Government would ever know. Maybe he could finally land one of those high fashion Paris runway models that he always fancied. Most of his happiest times were in France but also his saddest. For a brief moment, he even thought of getting Ceci back. Then again, did he ever have her?

Rivers saw a bright orange Frisbee soar to his left when he caught a glimpse of her silhouette against a small crashing ocean wave. This wouldn't be an easy conversation with her. Then again, most conversations with her never were even in the good old days. She was a master manipulator through and through. She always had a way of getting into his head, but he hung around anyway. The good times were good, and the great times were great. Unfortunately, he never dwelled on the bad times with the thinking head.

Ceci turned around with a sixth sense when Stony was ten feet away. At least she would let him think that as she had spotted him ten minutes earlier.

"Sorry I'm late, traffic was bad, and I'm not used to driving myself anywhere." Ceci said with a tone of defiance.

"I'm just glad you showed up this time," Rivers replied sarcastically. "I thought we had an understanding?"

"Understanding? It was more like blackmail. I said I would see what I could do. It was a little outrageous," Ceci replied.

"I didn't think ten million was unreasonable. It's a far cry from my original fifty percent. You start adding interest over twenty-eight years and I think it's pretty damn reasonable. It's a small price to pay for an FBI agent to sweep this mess under the rug for you. If you didn't like the terms, then negotiate but don't send some third world hacks out to kill me!"

"I didn't try to kill you. I didn't say no and I sure as hell didn't say yes. But either way, I didn't try to have you killed."

"Then who did?"

"I don't know, but it wasn't me. Seriously, it wasn't me," Ceci repeated staring into his eyes for assurance.

"Do you know who did it? Give me some names. I know, tell me who did this and we'll renegotiate," Rivers prodded as he negotiated against himself like she knew he would as predictability was still rampant in his nature all these years later.

Ceci started laughing. "Really? Renegotiate? This is the reason I didn't show up last time. I couldn't count on you. What are you really going to do Stony? Go to the police? And tell them what? That you planned a robbery but someone else beat you to it. You are incorrigible, you know that?"

Rivers starred at her with total disdain. "Did your husband try to take me out?"

"Don't be silly. If he knew anything about this or even knew who you were, you'd be taking a dirt nap right now. That's why it's so hard to get that much money together in secret. He watches over every single dime."

"So, you leave me at the altar once again so to speak and now you're going to stand by and let me get shot because you're that damn greedy?"

"I have nothing to do with this!" Ceci exclaimed in sheer exasperation. "I'm never in the loop on anything. I'm a philanthropic socialite with no limit on my credit cards. But if I had to guess it's probably the Cuban guy that Bradley became mixed up with."

"Why?"

"Simple. You're chasing him so he's bringing it to you. No offense, but he's a real tough guy from what I hear. Go away soon Stony, or he very well could win. It's not worth dying for luv."

"Everything does get complicated with you Ceci. Tell you what. Get me five million within forty-eight hours and I can stall this thing out for another week.

Then, I can officially label it an ongoing investigation which leaves it twisting in the wind for another twenty years. Everyone wins, and I do mean everyone."

"I can get half of that without raising red flags. That's the best I can do."

"Make it three million. Sell your damn Rolls Royce if you have to Ceci."

"Fine. I'll be in touch," Ceci replied as she turned and stormed away with sand kicking up in the air from her quick cadence.

Rivers turned and started walking back to the Fontainebleau. The wind in his face felt good against his unshaven face. He felt confident she would come through this time. She had the same look as she had the night before he left for the Monaco Grand Prix. Far away and distant like she just wished him gone.

This time though he grinned like the Cheshire Cat while patting a high-tech microphone concealed under his buttoned shirt. One way or another, the Sullivans would pay up with this new trump card. Incorrigible he was not.

Chapter 27
Common Ground

TERRENCE OLIVER TOOK UP a position outside the Sullivan boy's condominium complex in a rented white Ford Mustang. It was brand new with less than one hundred miles on it and the glare from the mid-afternoon sun was bothering his eyes even with dark Ray Bans on. Strict orders had been issued to leave the Sullivans alone, so he thought it better to approach them sans an official FBI vehicle.

Between Senator Warren crushing the investigation then getting shot at on South Beach, Oliver's career wasn't on an upswing. This was the true reason he worked so well with Rivers. They both knew deep down that they weren't destined for higher accolades, so they never competed against each other in the past. Both were considered solid agents but not politically connected. Ordinary gold watch types with a firm handshake from the top brass on their final day. Then some low-level security job until they found an affordable retirement condo on the beach.

No way, Oliver told himself. Today, he was going to escalate his retirement pension. Within a month, he would serve his notice and move somewhere exotic courtesy of the Sullivans. He wouldn't feel bad about it, neither. It was obvious the Senator was on the Sullivan payroll, so he might as well sign himself up and quit fighting the system.

It wasn't long before the Sullivan boys pulled out of the parking garage in their latest Porsche purchase. The sun in his face made it impossible to see which one was driving but he imagined it was the youngest son Rick probably running out to buy a new computer.

There's were returned by the local bureau office but paranoia of them being bugged usually drove suspects to purchase new ones.

Oliver hung back in heavy traffic as he followed the black Porsche. Neither brother seemed to have a care in the world. Having a United States Senator forcing the pesky FBI agents off your trail sure helps the carefree lifestyle. He couldn't wait to see their faces when he approached them.

Both vehicles turned on Lincoln Road and Oliver grinned as he followed them into the parking lot of an Apple store. He wouldn't gloat any further though as he considered these two brash hotshots nothing but a couple clowns living in the shadow of their father. Neither one would amount to much in his opinion, but a nice trust fund tends to get a lot of clowns through the game of life.

Oliver guided the Mustang behind the Porsche blocking it in and hopped out to confront a surprised James Sullivan coming out of the passenger side. He looked a little rough with a bad hangover and a wrinkled white t-shirt, plaid shorts and beige sandals.

"Didn't you get the memo?" James asked.

Rick Sullivan wasn't as subdued as he bolted out of the driver's side.

"Go away right now Fed or I'm calling my father," Rick warned.

"Please do Rick. Call him. This isn't official business. I'm playing let's make a deal. Tell him I'll make it worth his while. He wins," Oliver replied.

A silver Land Rover with heavy tinted windows showed up forty minutes later and Derek Sullivan exited the driver's side door. Oliver was a bit surprised at first that Derek was by himself. Then he processed it through and it made sense. The Sullivan clan was woefully paranoid due to recent events. The less eyes and ears for this conversation would be wise considering the deal about to be offered.

Derek stood halfway between the vehicle triage and motioned Oliver over. Without saying a word, he patted him down finding no recording devices. Customer cars coming in and out of the lot seemed oblivious to three flashy vehicles parked oddly in the corner with one man getting patted down. But it was South Florida and anybody that noticed would assume a drug deal discussion and not want to be involved.

Derek seemed satisfied with the impromptu pat down then took a long look around for accomplices. It appeared safe enough.

"What do you want Agent Oliver?"

"I'm here to talk retirement. Mine, not yours. Frankly, I don't care about this Dunbar deal anymore. Santora isn't my problem and I certainly don't care about art."

"That was obvious the other night. Specifically, what do you want? I'm very busy," Derek replied with a hint of annoyance.

"I'm here to deal information. I can be your inside man for the rest of the investigation. I'll keep you informed of everything I find out and everything the Bureau and the locals know. Most importantly, I can give you all the players keeping and unofficial eye on you and your family."

"Who's to say I don't know this information already?"

"How can you be sure that you know everything?" Oliver shot back.

"I got you off my back, didn't I?"

"Have you seen the congressional approval rating lately? I wouldn't bet on your friend knowing everything," Oliver replied as if he was making the ultimate sale which he was from a personal standpoint.

He had run several scenarios through his mind over and over and felt well prepared for this moment.

It was a point well taken. Senator Warren wasn't the most popular figure on the Hill like he made himself out to be. This wasn't the time to play hardball with Santora on the run. Oliver could be useful now or in the future. Derek decided to make a deal as it had the makings of a mutually beneficial partnership.

Both of his sons watched the discussion in total silence as they had been instructed when they called their father. Unbeknownst to Oliver, Derek's security guard was laying low in the dark tinted cargo section of the Land Rover filming the conversation with a high-tech camera. If it was a double cross Oliver would pay the price later. Derek had been choosing his words very carefully but struggled to parse the rest of the conversation in a satisfactory manner.

"How much will this cost me Mr. Oliver?"

"I'm not a greedy man Mr. Sullivan. Just a half million and you're on the information super highway."

Derek smiled ever so slightly then leaned in closely to Oliver's right ear, so the camera couldn't pick up the audio.

I'm going to make this simple and I want an immediate yes or no. I'm going to give you one million dollars as a matter of good faith. But if I need someone eliminated, no questions asked, there's an additional million in it for you. Yes or no?"

Oliver stepped back trying his best not to look surprised. This scenario never crossed his radar. This must be how it feels to deal with the devil. He pulled out a small piece of paper with a bank account number jotted down and handed it to Derek.

"Yes," Oliver simply replied.

The devil is in the details.

Chapter 28
Date Night

IT WASN'T UNTIL JONES stepped out of the shower before he realized he was close to blowing his cover. He couldn't show up in his Jeep with Florida plates. It obviously wasn't a rental vehicle as it was covered with too much Key West sand and stale suntan lotion on the inside. A quick call to the concierge and an almost new midnight blue Jeep Cherokee was awaiting him in the parking lot of the Fontainebleau. Jones stepped out into the ocean air wearing khaki pants and a solid blue collared shirt looking forward to his date with Rachelle Sullivan.

Jones drove to the Indian Creek address that Rachelle texted him. She lived on the top floor of the Eden House condominium and it was easily a million-dollar property. Clearly, she wasn't paying for it on her legislature assistant salary. Jones knew many girls with the same pedigree in his Las Vegas days. Except Rachelle seemed like a genuine and real person. A girl he wanted to get to know.

She answered her door looking wonderful in a simple tight white dress showing off a deep year-round tan. Jones felt a bit underdressed and nervous like a college kid dating an older woman out of his league. He was glad he decided to take her out to dinner and a bit of gambling at the Hard Rock Casino. He'd be more comfortable in his own element even if it was an element of a former life.

Thirty minutes later they pulled up to the Hard Rock Casino in Hollywood. It was the most elegant Indian Casino in the region, but it still wasn't the Vegas strip. He'd never been to Monaco or Macau, but the

Strip was a legendary place where fortunes were won, and fortunes were lost. Everything in Vegas was the home of the best. The best entertainers, the best high rollers, the best gangsters and they all rubbed elbows together at the same casinos.

Jones grabbed the ticket from the valet and made a mental note not to lose it as he had no idea what the plate number was for the rental vehicle.

"What's your favorite game?" Jones asked.

"Well, besides men I do favor some high stakes blackjack," Rachelle replied with a mischievous smile.

Jones burst out laughing as he stepped through the front entrance of the casino. He found a hundred-dollar minimum table hoping that it met her definition of high stakes. His father was used to oil sheiks playing a hundred grand a hand, but those types were playing with monopoly money. The real players would be at these tables and more than willing to push chips out there if a hot streak was recognized.

Jones pulled out a wad of c-notes and pushed half in front of Rachelle who pushed them back at him.

"Thank you anyway," she replied. "But I can cover my own losses. Besides, I seldom lose." She flashed another smile at Jones who was smitten with her overall style and grace.

After about an hour Jones was pushing about even but Lady Luck Sullivan was up about thirty- grand. It only takes a small hot streak when a person bets five grand a hand like she was. He was grateful to be hanging on so he ordered two whisky sours from the cocktail waitress and kept playing.

The cards finally started turning his way with two face cards being dealt his way consistently. Great players can recognize a momentum change almost instantly and start pushing piles of chips into play which is exactly what Jones did as he had his competitive juices flowing. Great players also know when the momentum swings back to the casinos favor. Billion-dollar casinos aren't built on hard sweat alone. It's a mathematical science combined with psychology that makes it very hard to ever win some serious cash.

The sound of your chips clacking in front of you is a wonderful feeling. When they quit clacking, it means you're doing poorly and losing your ass. Pigs get slaughtered and greed will make a gambler follow into the swine's footsteps if they overstay their welcome. The cocktail waitress brought them a second round of drinks and he noticed that Rachelle was giving back a lot of her chips. He estimated that she was still up seven or eight-grand but couldn't pull any small cards to save a hand.

Jones was up twelve-grand and everything was going his way. If he was dealt a thirteen he'd pull a seven or eight every time. If he doubled down on a ten combination he'd inevitably pull an ace. He still had some time on his streak, but he wasn't here to make money. He wanted to get to know this girl. Personally and professionally as he hadn't forgot the underlying reason for this rendezvous.

He leaned into her left shoulder and spoke softly into her sweet-smelling neck.

"Do you like Italian?"

"You don't look Italian," she replied with a smirk.

"I meant food smart ass."

"Only if it has great veal parmigiana."

"Let's hit Martorano's then. Nothing but great reviews."

Martorano's was a typical Italian eatery only it happened to be in a casino. Celebrity artwork photographs of famous Italians adorned the walls throughout. If an Italian joint didn't have a photograph of Frank Sinatra, then you knew it wasn't authentic.

The Sullivan Secret

The cheerful duo already primed with whisky sours were led to a step booth table past the Italian marble top bar. Jones grabbed the wine list and scanned over the Bordeaux selection. He wasn't one to check with an over-educated sommelier about specific pairings with certain foods as he knew what he liked.

After making sure that Rachelle liked Bordeaux, he ordered a 2006 Chateau Margaux which was a four-figure bottle. Even when gamblers make decent cash at a casino they offer temptation with extravagant means. That's why you always find high-end jewelry stores inside casinos or other exquisite luxuries. Jones wasn't any different than any other gambler tonight.

The server promptly returned with the expensive wine and poured it into some Riedel glasses. Jones turned down the opportunity to taste the wine and instead gave the honor to Rachelle who nodded with an approval. Ironically, it was from the Medoc region of France on the left bank of the Grande Estuary, not far from where the long-ago Ambassador tragedy started.

Thievery and mayhem were the farthest things from his mind right now. Sure, he'd been shot at the night before, but it wasn't like he was a banker walking back from work. Occupational hazards happen but he was blocking all that out tonight. These next few hours were reserved for personal time.

After forty minutes of small chit chat and a classic Italian salad, Jones finally asked a serious question.

"So, what's the long-term future for Miss Rachelle Sullivan? A membership in the One-Hundred Club someday following Senator Warren?"

She smiled for a minute then thought carefully trying to pick the exact words. Mr. Jones was a nice catch and she didn't want to sound cavalier.

"Well, elected office it will not be. Working for the Senator, I've realized that true power is in the people behind the scenes. People like my precious boss are mouthpieces with an ego for the most part."

Jones picked up that she was characterizing people like her very own father. Whether it was subconscious speak or not, he decided to remain silent and listen.

"Don't get me wrong. I like the Senator even though he's a bit full of himself. I went into this job all gung ho and from that vantage point it's been a bit disappointing. I've made a lot of connections though with this job."

"Maybe you could land yourself a gig on one of the cable networks?" he interjected after a few moments of silence.

"I'd rather die than be a chronic complainer," she laughed. "No, I'm thinking of being a big shot financier, buying half an island and making deals from distant places."

"What about you Sinjin?" You already have an exciting life. Maybe you need a change of scenery? Maybe you could be persuaded to hangout in Miami more often?" she suggested.

Jones stared back adoringly not knowing exactly how to reply. Luckily, the server appeared bringing their dishes, so he flashed a small smile as his answer. The server's unknown save would gladly be factored into the tip.

The meal was divine. In lieu of a traditional dessert they decided on a twenty-year Tawny Port from Portugal. Dessert wines were usually too sweet for Jones, but Rachelle made a nice call on the Fonseca. As he was paying the bill, she made another nice call in suggesting they drive back to her place while they could still drive.

Jones remained nonchalant as he walked to the valet but deep down he wanted to be sprinting for the rental vehicle. As they waited for the valet, he remarked to himself how every evening in Dade County had perfect weather with tonight being no exception. Then again, a tropical storm couldn't ruin this evening.

Traffic was on the lighter side as Jones pointed the Jeep rental towards Eden House. He was anxious to see the inside of her place and not just for the obvious reasons. Rachelle had tossed her purse in the backseat when the valet at the Hard Rock opened the door. Working for a politician never gave one a night off so she decided to check her cell phone for messages. Some of her purse contents spilled onto the floor under the driver's side seat so she leaned over awkwardly to retrieve them then sprang upright.

"Umm, Sinjin, are you storing a funny looking package under your seat for some reason?"

"Quit goofing around." Jones replied then caught the seriousness in her face.

"It sounds like it's ticking."

"Grab your purse." Jones shouted as he stopped the Jeep on the shoulder half leaning on a drainage ditch.

Jones exited the Jeep and sprinted to her side. Rachelle already had kicked off her high heels and grabbed her purse. Together they ran about a hundred yards up the shoulder of the road before stopping and turning around.

"Are you sure you heard ticking? Maybe it was a toolbox or something that was vibrating."

The explosion happened right as Jones quit speculating. Instinctively they covered their faces and turned away.

"Yes, I'm sure," she replied dryly with her near perfect hair falling across her face as she looked back at the burning Cherokee.

It was a small explosion as far as car bombs went. It was still big enough that it could have killed the driver. Flying debris were minimal and no damage was noted to other vehicles although the burning Cherokee grinded traffic to a halt. Within two minutes emergency vehicle sirens could be heard in the distance.

"Sinjin, is there something you need to tell me?"

"Yes, be very, very careful who you rent from these days."

Chapter 29
Dirty Money

JONES WOKE UP AT 5AM the next morning with very little real sleep to show for it. A hack car bomb ruined a spectacular night. It wasn't a good professional job. Nobody did it any better than the mob. It was a low impact explosion with a lot of fire and smoke. The front end of the Jeep rental remained intact.

His first instinct was to hightail it out of the area but that would have been even harder to explain to Rachelle. She was having obvious doubts as to his background, but he explained it off as some sort of mistaken identity. She managed to go with his cover story as he explained to the Dade County Sheriff that he heard a large backfire sound right before the explosion.

Nobody was injured so the Sheriff cleared up traffic and had the carnage towed away. He even arranged for a taxi, so they could make their way back to the Eden House. The bomb was a mood killer as Rachelle walked up to her unit alone while Jones continued to the Fontainebleau.

Jones was ticked off at himself. He let his guard down and felt like a fool. Obviously, his cover was blown at some level. Someone had followed him to the casino and he was in a rental none the less. He could try leaning on the valets but that would consume time and unlikely to produce anything valuable.

No, he would pursue this from a different angle and hit it hard this morning. His request for information from Graydon Bullock's office was expedited judging by the manila envelope that was pushed under his room door. The agency never sleeps.

The enclosed photograph was of one Thomas Maddox. Jones recognized the face from his brief visit to the Dade County Detention Center to visit Ruben Castellano. Maddox was a muscular guard weighing about 230 pounds with an ex-military look.

The Maddox dossier listed him living about thirty minutes away with a wife and two kids. Bank accounts and mutual fund balances higher than expected but nothing filthy rich as it showed he could be a decent investor. Bullock's number's jockey had Maddox statistically favored to be Simon's guy pulling the strings at the Detention Center. No data showing absolute guilt but statistically probable was good enough for now. Maddox would be starting his shift in a few hours, so he jumped into the shower thinking about a quick breakfast before paying an unannounced visit to Mr. Maddox.

Thirty minutes later Jones jumped into his Jeep and put the key in the ignition. Before turning the key, he jumped out and did a thorough inspection of his own Wrangler. Satisfied, he started it up and pulled out of the parking lot headed for North Miami.

It was barely 6am as Jones drove down a quiet residential street in a normal looking middle-class neighborhood. The neighborhood would be waking up soon, so he needed to set up a position with urgency. The Maddox house was a two-story stucco with an attached garage but no pool. A nice house but it wasn't extravagant. If Maddox was dirty he was playing it correctly being low key and under the radar.

Jones found a secluded spot a block away to leave his Jeep. He wore jeans, a black collar shirt along with a sturdy pair of black boots which was the difference maker in case he needed to kick down a door. Jones prided himself in being prepared and one step ahead of the competition.

As he walked by the Maddox house he noted lights and some faint silhouettes moving inside. He doubled back and sat next to the garage hidden from view by a cluster of still palm trees. Jones wouldn't make a move on Maddox in front of his family. It wasn't his style. He would give it ninety minutes to see how the situation played out.

The grinding sound of an electric garage door opening finally put a jolt into a quiet morning about forty minutes later. Car doors slammed, and a Honda Accord came to life backing out of the driveway with Mrs. Maddox and two children to boot. Jones waited until they were out of sight and walked into the open garage courtesy of Mrs. Maddox.

It was likely the inner house door would be unlocked. Nobody ever locked those doors figuring a garage door was like a moat protecting the inner sanctuary. Jones had to be careful as it was possible that Maddox was a law abiding citizen. A corruption profile based on statistical analysis wasn't an absolute science.

Jones looked behind him onto the street. Seeing nothing he silently pulled the door open after deciding to keep his Glock concealed in his back waistband. As the door closed, Maddox turned around from pouring a cup of coffee on his kitchen island holding it firmly in his massive right hand. Jones raised his hands in a peaceful gesture after realizing this man was built like a linebacker who could still play the game.

"I'm just here to talk. A few questions are all I have?" Jones asked in the most soothing calm manner he could muster knowing deep down that this would end up in a slugfest.

Maddox eyed Jones from head to toe but it was obvious that he recognized the man standing a mere ten feet away. He wasn't sure what outfit this stranger entering his home uninvited belonged to, but he knew he had some pull from a higher level. He also had a good idea why the stranger was there. Taking him out right now was his only chance to avoid trouble.

The punch was telegraphed and Jones ducked left so the punch connected to his right shoulder. Maddox was fast and agile, and his experience showed. Jones offered a hard kidney shot with his left hand and shoved him back on top of the kitchen island.

"I don't want to fight. I need information!" Jones shouted while trying to maintain control of his opponent.

In defiance of words, Maddox kicked Jones backwards then grabbed a sharp six-inch black handled knife from the Chicago cutlery butcher block and moved hard towards his target. Jones grabbed the larger man's right wrist while simultaneously kicking Maddox in the right knee. To gain total control he brought an elbow flush to the nose while turning sideways and doing a back-step move. Blood gushed out of his nose a split second after a popping noise echoed off the ceramic kitchen tile.

Maddox was trained better to break up fights than be any type of winning gladiator. Jones was no longer in the mood to talk. Maddox was scared now and overwhelmed with pain, so he wrestled the knife away from his beefy paw and drove it halfway through the man's thigh.

A garbled scream were the first vocals that Maddox had exercised. Jones covered his mouth and slammed him backside onto the kitchen island again, so he could look him directly in the eyes.

"Shut up now and deal with the pain. I'm looking for Simon."

"I don't know a Simon," Maddox moaned with a mixture of tears and sweat pouring off his chin.

Jones reached down and gave the knife a quarter turn. Over half the blade was in the thigh muscle now and the turning motion made it hurt like hell again. This wasn't the first knife fight for Sinjin Jones.

"Don't deny the obvious. I want his location and I want it now."

"I don't have a location," Maddox cried out.

Jones pushed the man back against the kitchen island and gave it another twist. Maddox grimaced in agony and was close to passing out.

"Go ahead and kill me mister. I don't have a location." Maddox was crying now as only a completely broken man can.

"How does Simon make it work?"

"If Simon wants something he finds you. Everything delivered by a note to my car along with a paper sack full of money."

Jones could tell that Maddox was telling the truth. He'd have to find a different way. But a promise was a promise.

"Where's the money?"

At first Maddox was going to bluff and say he already spent it. Then, Jones slowly put his hand on the knife handle again and he decided he liked being able to walk.

"It's buried in the backyard."

Jones pulled out his Glock and pointed it at Maddox.

"Tie that kitchen towel around your leg, grab a shovel and get me the money now."

Maddox grabbed a spade from the garage and limped his way to a large potted palm next to a backyard patio. Jones kept his distance but had to lend a hand to tip the potted palm over on its side. Maddox dug a small hole where the potted palm stood and within minutes handed over a plastic wrapped bag of cash.

"Simon's going to kill me. You know that, right?"

"No, he won't. I'll get to him first. Go to a hospital and keep your mouth shut."

Jones walked back to his Jeep and retraced his steps to the Castellanos residence in Little Havana. Only this time he introduced himself as a friend of Ruben's and Mrs. Castellanos let him into her small bungalow.

"Ruben made a deal the other day. I'm here to see if someone paid you yet?" Jones asked coming straight to the point.

The white haired portly Cuban woman eyed Jones up and down cautiously. She knew he wasn't a friend of Ruben's, but she was anxious to speak with anyone who had seen him lately.

"How is my son?" she asked.

"I don't have time to lie to you. He's in prison and this time he won't be coming home. We both know that. But we made a deal and I'm keeping my end of it. Did anyone named Simon stop by and give you fifty thousand dollars?"

"I've been compensated sir. But if you're here for your slice forget it. I've already stashed it somewhere safe," she replied in a defiant manner.

Jones was somewhat taken back. It only made sense though if Simon followed through on his promises otherwise nothing could be done on the inside. Word would spread on the streets if he didn't honor commitments.

"I'm not here to shake you down. I'm actually looking for the man who brought you the money."

"He was a young man, early twenties. He drove up in a fancy black BMW. There was another man in the car I noticed when he drove off. Silver hair is about all I could see. He didn't get out."

The silver haired man could have been Simon. A bit sloppy if it was but this information didn't lead him to a location.

"I don't suppose you caught the license plate by chance?" Jones asked with a hopeful smile.

"As a matter of fact, I did. We have carjacking's and shootings every day in this neighborhood. I write them all down on this street. Every day I write plate numbers down and file them away.

"Could I get those from you please?"

"I don't think so sir. I hate to be ungrateful to someone who was so generous to me."

"I can understand that," Jones replied holding open the bag of cash, so she could see it. "I'll gladly give you a bonus for that plate number. On one condition, though."

"What condition?" she asked sighing.

"You take this money and move to a safer neighborhood."

"Okay." The old Cuban lady smiled happily knowing she won a big lottery with the only cost being a simple son.

Chapter 30
Wake up Call

DEREK AND CECI SULLIVAN were both fast asleep in their Ethan Allan four post super king size bed when the unexpected wakeup call came in. It had been one week since the Dunbar debacle had started. Derek was bone tired as he looked at the caller id which showed an unknown caller. He ignored it and rolled over in a foggy daze as only continual stress could wear a body down that fast. Thirty seconds later he received a text to answer the damn call. It was obvious who the caller was now, so he answered the next call on the third ring to make a point to the Senator.

"Good to see that you're sleeping well this morning. Is Ceci in the room?" The Senator asked perturbed about something.

"Yes," Derek replied not knowing if this call was meant for his ears only.

"Good, put the phone on speaker."

Derek hit the speaker button and placed the phone in the middle of the bed. Ceci propped herself up while lifting her eye mask and folding down the red velvet bedspread.

"I'm guessing neither of you have read the papers or seen the morning news?"

"You're batting a thousand. What can we do for you this morning?" Derek asked.

"Oh, I don't know. Our mutual friend gets caught with a stolen masterpiece last week. There's a major shootout on South Beach days later. And last night my legislative assistant who happens to be your daughter almost died in a car bombing and you're both sleeping late. You tell me?"

Derek and Ceci looked at each other in astonishment with no immediate reaction as they processed the last statement. It was obvious in their faces that neither of them knew about the very latest event. Why didn't Rachelle call somebody they both wondered? "Are you sure it was our Rachelle?" Ceci asked.

"According to the news report it is. Why she hasn't contacted anyone?"

Ceci checked her cellphone which had been on mute. Indeed, she did have a text message from Rachelle indicating that she was fine and going to bed.

"I have a missed text. She's fine. You know Rachelle, she's Miss Independent," Ceci stated.

"Well that is good news. We have another problem though."

"What's that?" Derek asked.

"Some of the media is starting to ask questions. There's no linkage yet but it's only a matter of time. I don't want to be either on or off the record for any questions. I'm heading back to D.C. immediately. Anything you two could do to make the situation tame down a bit would be greatly appreciated. Understand?"

"I understand. I'll make it better," Derek replied.

"It's in all our best interests you know," the Senator muttered looking for a better understanding of the dire situation.

Derek paused a second, so he wouldn't sound exasperated. The Senator had a bad habit of over emphasizing every phone call like he was giving a sixteen-year old kid the car keys for the very first time.

"Fly to D.C. my friend. I'm on it," Derek replied.

The Senator hung up the phone without a signoff or a simple goodbye. It was his unofficial silent power statement when he was irritated with someone. Derek grabbed his cellphone and walked into the adjoining bathroom without even a glance towards his wife. Any look of disappointment in her eyes always sent him over the edge. He turned on the shower water, so she couldn't hear him and planted himself on top of the toilet seat.

His first instinct was to eliminate anyone in his way the old fashion way. It was the same strategy favored by his late friend Bradley Dunbar. Ceci wouldn't approve of what he was about to do. Quite frankly, he wasn't that fond of the idea himself. But the situation needed to be rectified today and this opportunity almost fell from the sky.

He thought long and hard before he hit the call button. Once it was out there it couldn't be taken back. Then, his second instinct kicked in which was don't ever second guess yourself. It had worked well for him so far, so he hit the call button with a quiet confidence.

As soon as Ceci heard the shower turn on she grabbed her cellphone and checked her email. She had been liquidating small positions from a vast array of investment accounts scattered internationally to avoid raising red flags with the federal banking regulators or her husband.

Stony's first demand was ten million dollars which wasn't even remotely possible without consequences. She made some concessions with her lowball offer although five million dollars wouldn't be possible unless she told Derek the truth.

A long time ago in another life she made Rivers her dupe. She made a gutsy plan together with him but found another partner when she doubted his performance for the grand finale. Derek was better looking and more intelligent, capable of near perfect execution. Of course, Stony was more charming but she knew she could live without wit but not wealth.

Stony was played until the bitter end. Ceci made sure he wasn't physically harmed by telling Derek it would arouse too much suspicion and lead back to her. It was true but she and Stony had been an item for almost a year and there was a negligible layer of love there.

She imagined that Stony immediately realized he had been played the moment he heard about the heist. It was originally set for the Bastille Day celebration. She knew he would come looking for her, but she covered her tracks well. After the first couple years, Ceci never looked over her shoulder again expecting to see Stony. Until the day Bradley Dunbar made a huge miscalculation. Once the Dutch Sisters made the international news she knew Stony would be Miami bound.

Derek never mentioned Stony once after that fateful night. They never actually met but came close to bumping into each other once on a Paris sidewalk. Nobody wanted a jilted lover or a criminal collaborator hanging over their shoulders. Derek never gave it a second thought as he was convinced he created a wonderful meaningful life with Ceci. At least he paid a small fortune to create that mirage.

Ceci wasn't sure what to make of the sudden appearance by Rivers. Twenty-eight years of angst wouldn't leave room for forgiveness. A broken heart alone never serves up forgiveness. Add in the missed-out fortune and luxury lifestyle and being bought off didn't seem plausible. She figured he wanted some level of revenge. Perhaps accept a quick payoff then an anonymous letter to the Attorney General. Whatever his plan, she still didn't want to hurt him.

She was in a quandary. Smart money would eliminate the problem which was Stony. But, a dead federal agent would bring an even more in-depth investigation. Besides, she wasn't that ruthless anymore or at least she fooled herself into thinking that. She was a Miami socialite and they didn't go around arranging hits on FBI agents. No, she would pay him off and hope for the best. It would have to be done today as the body count needed to stop. Besides, if events went south, old ruthless feelings could always resurface. She'd been poor once. She wasn't going to be poor again.

Chapter 31
Protected Foe

SINJIN JONES RECEIVED a text from Oliver to meet the FBI duo poolside for coffee and a chat. Their vaudeville act was getting old, but he had no choice, so he headed for the pool. He thought it odd that Oliver was texting the invite. When he arrived both men looked relaxed and chatted away at a small table with the cool morning breeze parting their hair.

Jones measured his words carefully. Rivers was still in charge, but his side of the investigation was handcuffed. He didn't want to give Rivers the impression that he had carte blanche. He took a seat at the table and ordered a Cuban coffee with sugar.

"Well, I have a lead on Simon. Not sure how solid it is but I'm still working the Santora angle. Hopefully, it starts coming together this afternoon," Jones stated.

"Get anything from the daughter?" Oliver asked smiling.

"Nothing but some grief. How about you guys? Anything besides a tan?" Jones replied eager to change the subject.

"Just working background stuff. We're hampered by the higher ups. The Senator has a lot of pull in the bureau," Rivers stated.

"We're probably done in a couple days Jones. Office politics don't give us much hope and we accept that fate. You've done a good job under the circumstances. Let us know if something turns up on your end ok?" Oliver interjected trying to hide his pleasure with the status quo.

"No problem, you guys are my first call."

Jones received a text to check his email. This must be the information he requested from Bullock's office. He made small talk for another ten minutes, finished his coffee and excused himself for a late morning shower.

The elevator ride to his room was long and slow, with a full car of hotel guests all disembarking on different floors. Jones couldn't wait to open the email and start on his quest to find Simon.

He didn't expect Simon to crack easily so he'd have to make a good plan. This man would be a key witness in exchange for a lenient sentence, so he needed to be taken alive. Some background work would be needed. Find something important to any man and threaten to take it away or harm it was the standard protocol.

Jones finally stepped off the elevator onto his floor and entered his room after struggling to find the key card. The mini iPad powered on and Jones went to the email application. His mood went from anxious to despair in a matter of seconds. He didn't see this coming.

Langley was telling Jones to back off and not apprehend the owner of the car. Do not pursue it any further and that was a direct order from Graydon Bullock. No further questions would be entertained.

His emotions went from disbelief to anger. This wasn't exactly a new situation to him coming from Special-Ops. Highly classified targets went mysteriously off the radar from one night to the next. Jones thought long and hard about the situation and he knew he had only two options.

Option one, he could try and track the vehicle by himself. It would likely be flagged by Langley no matter what avenue it was requested from. Whoever Simon was, he was obviously important to the agency. Jones put option one on the backburner and decided on option two. It was either that or go tanning for a couple days with his FBI buddies.

All roads seemed to go through Derek Sullivan. He was off limits to the FBI but not officially to himself. Sullivan wasn't going to volunteer information that was for sure. He had friends in high places and he used them well. No, the way to go was with involuntary information. He could bug Sullivan's office and listen to the inner circle himself and learn of all the co-conspirators. It was a tough job and he was capable of doing it himself. Bullock had already given him the big wink anyway. He should have hatched this plot a few days ago. Tonight, would have to be the night and preparations needed to be made.

This would be a tough feat to accomplish. Sullivan made a fortune in the alarm business. He would have the newest and best state of the art technology for his private residence. Even a professional burglary crew would need more than six or seven hours to make a winning plan. Jones needed another angle and he needed it fast.

Star Island was almost as secure as Alcatraz Island in its glory days with only a single road in and out. It was a man-made island in Biscayne Bay that turned into a secluded paradise for mega stars. A couple million bucks couldn't even get a prospective buyer an invitation to look.

Driving up to the gate was a non-starter. It would have to be a physical operation which meant taking out the armed guards. Not permanently though or Bullock would have his hide even if it was accidental. He would stage a robbery, plant the bugging devices and steal something of value. It was a three-person job, two minimum but no time to find someone reliable that he could trust. He would go it alone and not get caught at any cost.

Time was of the essence and he needed to make a shopping list. A quick trip to the nearest Goodwill store for old beat up clothes would be easy. Google would be his source for a quick lesson on proper robbery terms in Spanish. Ace Hardware would carry the basic burglary tools that he wouldn't need except to make the scene look real. A dark colored Ocean Kayak was available at a marina down the road. He'd wear a baseball cap and sunglasses for all the purchases which would be made in cash. After tonight the real hard work would start. He would have to sit around a hotel room listening to phone conversations or blank air.

Chapter 32
Deceit from Different Angles

THE CRANDON PARK TENNIS center was empty with the mid-day heat as Ceci and Stony played next to center court. Rivers wasn't surprised at the phone call but was a bit baffled at being asked to play tennis again. She wanted to meet in a public place he surmised, and this was a great place to avoid eavesdropping.

Rachelle Sullivan woke up to a voicemail from Senator Warren that he was going back to D.C. immediately. She found it rather unexpected and couldn't find anything in the news or business reports that required his attention back in the nation's capital. She felt completely out of the loop and regretted sleeping a bit late due to the casino fiasco.

Several calls to her mother went unanswered. Ceci always seemed completely informed of the Senator's schedule. This perturbed Rachelle to no end, but it was useful at times when nobody else on the senate staff knew where he was. Finally, a call to the Sullivan's housekeeper revealed a tennis game at the Crandon Park Tennis Center.

Rachelle parked her Mercedes roadster in the tennis center parking lot and brought along her gear bag hoping that she wouldn't need to play. Beach volleyball was more her sport although tennis offered the best after set cocktail. The front desk informed her that her mother was already playing next to center court.

As she strolled along the top aisle she could see her mother exchanging backhands with a man roughly her age. He looked vaguely familiar, but no name came to the tip of her tongue. Hoping they would be done soon so she took a seat up high listening to the echoes of the batted tennis ball.

A quick survey of the facility revealed only two other games being played and they appeared to be staff. Considering it was 96 degrees she could understand the low occupancy rate. The busy hours were early morning or late evening, so it seemed odd that her mother would be playing in the afternoon heat.

There was a man wearing black Ray-Ban sunglasses and a low brimmed green Gilligan hat watching the game on the opposite aisle in the stands. He was keeping in the shadows behind a support beam almost invisible. Terrence Oliver found it odd that Rivers would be getting some exercise in this heat, so he had followed him with a very loose tail. It only took a minute for Oliver to recognize his opponent as Ceci Sullivan.

After observing the game for a couple minutes, Oliver could tell by the conversation and body language that they were more than accidental acquaintances. Maybe Rivers was still working the Sullivan angle despite orders to cease operations or perhaps he was playing for both teams as well. The garbled conversation was hard to decipher exactly from this distance, but he heard both players mention money.

Rachelle picked up on the money conversation also and decided to dodge behind a support beam herself. Maybe that man across the aisle was doing the same thing as her. Her mother never handled money issues besides handling a store clerk a Visa card. In the early Miami days, she advised her husband well, but she was more than content being a well-known socialite these days. Something odd was going on down there but she had no idea what it was. The answer relied on learning the partner's identity.

A phone rang from across the stands. Oliver grimaced as he realized he forgot to turn off his ringer. He answered the phone while leaving the stands unnoticed by either player. Both players kept grunting away on their backhands while Rachelle observed the odd behavior from the man with the green hat.

It took Oliver a second to recognize the voice of Derek Sullivan. His cash was almost ready for pickup and this interesting tidbit regarding his wife's afternoon tennis rendezvous would be reported once he had cash in hand. Derek needed a couple more hours and wanted to reassure Oliver that he was soon to be a wealthy man. He would text him soon. A quick shower and early room service dinner was in order.

The hard part would be hiding his newfound wealth tomorrow. Quantico never taught him anything about money laundering his own cash. The timing of his retirement notice would need further thought. He'd have to lay low for a few months with cash burning in his pocket. That would be a nice feeling for once.

The tennis match came to an end with Ceci hitting a backhand well out of bounds. Her agitation didn't seem limited to tennis as her voice rose to an audible level.

"I have what I have Stony. I don't keep it around in sock drawers," Ceci said.

"I don't get it," Stony replied in a steady quiet tone. "How can you have so much money yet no available cash? That figure will simply not work."

A group of grade school players were coming towards Rachelle causing quite a racket. Rates were much cheaper in summer afternoons so the middle-class parents with dreams of Wimbledon for their children didn't care as much about heat strokes. They bought more Gatorade with their savings. Rachelle didn't want to get busted eavesdropping, so she left without greeting her mother. She would piece it together later, but she had some phone calls to make. The Senator would return her call tonight if he needed anything.

Ceci was sitting in a chair drying off her face and arms with a pink terry cloth towel. She shook her head in utter disbelief.

"It's mostly on paper. Trust funds, real estate, stock, a lot of complicated business arrangements. This is part of the reason you were cut out. You didn't have the business acumen to pull it off."

Rivers stared at her with total disgust. She played him until the very end always telling him how smart he was. She never meant it for a damn second and now it became perfectly clear to him. He swallowed hard and took a deep breath to maintain his composure.

"I understand it's not in a sock drawer. Most of it is probably in Switzerland or the Cayman Islands. I don't give a damn because that is not my problem. Listen carefully as 2.4 million is not enough. You must do better. You owe me Ceci."

"Owe you? Owe you? You didn't do anything. A tiny bit of planning was your contribution. The dirty work no. And now you want your cut?" Ceci exclaimed.

"No, I wanted my cut then. Nothing changed except people getting hurt, which was never in my plan Princess. My plan was classy. You sold your soul to the devil that day baby and now it's time to pay up. Get more money now." Stony leaned over so she could see his angered icy stare. "I deserve it."

Ceci never went down silently in an argument and for a moment, Rivers thought he finally may have won one.

"Or what?" she asked with a smug little smile unable to mask here surgically enhanced lips. "You can't very well call the cops and tell them a better set of thieves beat you to the heist."

Rivers sat silent for a moment. He had anticipated this last statement of hers but was praying that he wouldn't hear it from her lips. In a strange way, he still admired Ceci despite the double cross. It was her moxie. She still pulled the strings to his heart in some strange way like no other woman ever had before.

Maybe she was being honest about the available cash situation. But time was of the essence. She was doing him a favor anyway as he was likely to blow all the cash at once in Monaco or some other exotic place. In the long run, this proposal could be more prosperous, and he wanted to show her that he was smart enough to pull off something big.

"Ok Ceci, relax, I believe you." Rivers pulled out his phone and hit the audio play button.

It was only a conversation of mere minutes, but it was painfully long judging by Ceci's jaw dropped look. With age comes wisdom especially in the case of one Stuart Rivers who was very proud of himself on this sunny Florida day.

It was a fatal blow to Ceci being duped by Rivers. The beach conversation was damning and for all she knew this very incriminating conversation had also been recorded. Vengeance had reared its ugly head.

"I have a copy being released if something strange happens to me."

"I'll talk to Derek tonight and get the rest."

"Don't bother."

"What? You've just badgered me for the last ninety minutes for more money."

"Don't bring Derek into it. I'll take the 2.4 million."

"Really?"

"Plus, a monthly payment of 100k wired to an account in the Caymans."

"Until we hit the five million mark. Very well, that's doable," she replied with a feeling of relief that Derek wouldn't know she ended up being played by this meathead.

"Nope. Until one of us dies sweetheart," Rivers replied coldly. "Looks like I developed a little business acumen."

Chapter 33
The Cuban Fire Sale

SANTORA ENDED THE PHONE CALL knowing he didn't have a choice. He would be losing his local base of power which was always important to a Cuban's pride. But power was overrated behind prison bars. Besides, his temporary financial setback would be made up many times over if everything went right.

Deep down he prayed it wouldn't be a permanent move as he loved the United States and everything it had to offer both legally and illegally. He was still a young man full of ambition. But a lifetime in this industry had a shorter expiration date than most occupations. The jet set lifestyle without any power or real action to keep him feeling invigorated wasn't for Santora. Hopefully he could start over on some quiet Caribbean island and be a player again. It was in his blood.

Whatever the future might bring, plans were escalated and Santora would have to be ready to go with the next phone call. That meant finalizing his affairs, packed and ready to vamoose. He figured he had three days at the most. It was liquidation time.

Santora glanced down both sides of the street before stepping out of his safe house. It was a humid day and he would be doing a lot of sweating physically and mentally. He gave his crew members the afternoon off. No need for his amigos to see the fire sale. He still had his pride.

Luckily, Santora never invested in real estate. It took too long to sell, and it was too easy for the government to attach liens to it. The warehouses were all rented in various corporation names. All legal, but unfortunately his merchandise was seized or destroyed that night by the feds. Except for one warehouse which nobody knew about, even his amigos.

He called this one his toy warehouse. It's where he kept his three Ferrari's. Though he rarely drove these days due to security precautions, he couldn't part with these babies. After his first big score, he went out and purchased a brand new white one. On subsequent scores, he went out and bought the black model then the red vintage classic. They were always paid for with a briefcase full of cash. He drove them in rotation for a couple years until one day someone took a shot at him. They'd been in this Ft. Lauderdale warehouse ever since.

Through his attorney, the sports cars were sold for cash to a collector from Atlanta. He had no choice. Any large transactions into a Florida bank would be flagged and authorities alerted. His Cayman Island's cash was safe but doing him no good in this country and who knew if he would make it back for sure.

Santora started the ten-block walk through Little Havana. The more things changed in Miami the more they stayed the same in Little Havana. He migrated to this neighborhood years ago. The locals took care of him when he was young and watched his back. He was a success story in this neighborhood and they continually watched his back to this very day. In turn, he took care of them. When somebody was sick they didn't worry about medical bills. He was the insurance company. This was his home. It would be missed.

Santora ducked through an alley and entered through the back door of a tiny Cuban bar. It didn't have a name or a sign out front. It was a local's joint that didn't have a liquor license. Anybody entering had to know somebody so Santora knew he would be safe there for his meeting.

Robert Johnson, his overweight attorney was already sitting at a table working on his second mojito. Johnson had more sweat than normal pouring off his jowls as the past week had been especially tense. Local authorities had been all over his ass looking for Santora.

Mick the accountant was standing at the tiny bamboo bar ordering a Bacardi and Coke and it wasn't his first drink of the day. Nobody seemed to know Mick's last name not even Santora. Mick was an overly slim paranoid man who knew too much about other people's money, especially the non-taxed type.

Santora ordered a Red Stripe and motioned Mick over to the table where they were all seated. Johnson fumbled his oversized meat hooks into a briefcase and shoved three envelopes in front of Santora.

"I got you 180k for the cars," Jonson stated with a grim expression.

"That's all?" Santora asked.

"Needing cash today narrowed the market down quite a bit. There's another 30k for the motorcycles. Most of them needed work. There's another 50k for your Cigarette boat. I could have got a bit more if it wasn't for the bullet hole in the stern."

"Swell," Santora replied. "Any better news for me Mick?"

Mick slid a large duffel bag towards Santora.

"I've spent the last week closing out all your accounts in every name you had. Even that dog shit coal stock that never bounced back. There's about 300k there. Sorry, the market really sucks right now."

Santora took a pull from his sweating bottle of Red Stripe and ordered another round for the table. A week ago, he was on easy street. Now he was fleeing Miami like a thief in the night. Mick advised him against buying the painting. He should have listened to the wise old man as he was a Miami native who'd seen it all. History always has a way of repeating. Good or bad.

Now he had over 500k before him that he needed to make last for a while. The Feds had his painting and the cash he gave to Dunbar. His merchandise was confiscated in the warehouse and nothing was coming in as he was too hot for his clientele. The Cayman accounts couldn't be tapped until he was settled in a safe place.

Santora peeled off thirty thousand each for Mick and Attorney Johnson and thanked them for services rendered. He hoped to return someday but deep down he was a realist. There would be new power players in Miami taking his place soon and getting back to the top is nearly impossible. Oh well he thought to himself. Five hundred thousand to make his way in a new country was more than he had the last time he started. His new business partners better honor their promises. If not, there would be pain. More pain than they could ever imagine.

Chapter 34
The Allegiance

RICK AND JAMES SULLIVAN pulled up to Miami's Area 31 on their Chris Craft Barrel Back. It was a boat of beauty with the sun glistening over its restored finish. It was the most inexpensive boat they ever purchased but the restoration costs were ten times the sales price.

They docked at the Epic Hotel and waited a few minutes to make sure nobody was following them. It was Rick's idea once James suggested they have a private chat away from bugging devices or a smart tail job. Rick seldom had good ideas and James needed to know where his brother's mindset was and set it right if he didn't like what he heard. This wasn't a game anymore. It was jail time for them if something went south.

They made their way up to the gorgeous hotel pool and grabbed a couple chaise lounge chairs in the shade where they could see everyone else. Now wasn't the time to get loaded but they ordered a couple of mojitos anyway. A couple of known bikini clad working girls tried to start small talk, but James waved them off before Rick lost his concentration.

"So far we've covered our tracks up really well," James started off.

"I agree. If they haven't found anything yet they probably won't. The Feds are looking rather stupid in my opinion," Rick replied pleased with their work to date.

"Father's phone call shutoff the spigot. At least that's what he indicated."

"You have a reason to doubt him?" Rick asked.

"No, not at all. He certainly seemed satisfied the way we handled the search warrant."

"Almost as proud as the last-minute chopper caper," Rick countered.

"I'm pretty sure that's the first and last time we'll fly without numbers. They'll be checking that hard from now on. I just wanna make sure that if something goes wrong we keep our mouths shut until our lawyers get there."

"I know, I know. I'm not stupid," Rick replied agitated with the suggestion.

"If they actually take us downtown they will turn up the heat. Father pays a lot of retainers for these lawyers. Let them earn their check is all I'm saying."

"I know. But don't think for a minute it will go that far. Too many political hacks rub elbows with our old man. Plus, he has the Senator," Rick stated proudly.

"True. It's hard to imagine any more heat is coming our way. Be prepared if it does and be prepared if he needs to lean on us for bigger things. Much bigger things," James replied with a slow emphasis on his last three words.

"Like what?" Rick asked.

"I'm not sure. But I'm not going to give up this lifestyle easy, that's for sure. So, I'll do anything Father needs. He wasn't a choir boy coming up you know?"

"Yes, I've heard some stories. You think Mother knows about any of those things?" Rick asked.

"Hell no," James laughed. "She's too busy spending his money to care about where it came from."

Both brothers paused staring at the pool while sipping their mojitos. After several minutes, James finally looked at his Rick.

"It could get messy. The helicopter stunt was one thing but if he needs us to get our hands dirty we need to be mentally ready also. Father has been too good to us."

"I'll be right there with you brother," Rick replied tapping his brother's glass with his own.

Chapter 35

Midnight Waltz

AT MIDNIGHT JONES SLIPPED out of his room and headed to the parking lot carrying his new wardrobe courtesy of Goodwill. He thought it would be better to change in his Jeep rather than trudge through the lobby of the Fontainebleau lobby looking like a Cuban refugee seeking freedom on Smathers Beach. It was a bold plan, but he needed to make things happen. The FBI game plan wasn't yielding any results and the game plan itself was puzzling. The agency blockade on the plate number was baffling as well.

There was a surf blue Malibu ocean kayak sticking out of the back of the open Jeep. He would ditch it on the beach after the job which would make for a nice gift for someone tomorrow. It would be wiped clean of prints and blend in with the other multi-thousands of ocean toys lining the Miami beaches.

Jones changed into some beat up brown pants with a long sleeve brown shirt. He would pull on an oversized floppy brimmed hat low over his eyes and hope to look as much of a Cuban as the half-moon sky would allow. As he threw his good clothes into the back seat he caught a glimpse of a figure walking through the lot.

"Going rogue on me Jones? Rivers inquired with a sly smile.

Jones stared right into his eyes and shrugged his shoulders.

"That's a nice look on you Jones. I figured you had something up your sleeve. I noticed the kayak a couple hours ago."

"Listen Rivers, I'm just trying to get some answers."

"It's ok amigo. I'm not mad. In fact, I don't blame you. We've been handcuffed pretty good. I'm going with you though, but if things get too hot I might have to ditch. What's the plan?"

Jones was surprised at how Rivers relented. He could probably see his determination to get some answers and didn't want the fight. Or, maybe Rivers wanted to see Jones fail up close and personal. Either way another person would make the job much easier. He could cover Rivers up in the kayak with the tarp and use his help to overpower the dock security.

He filled Rivers in on the grand plan and Rivers seemed genuinely impressed. Deep down Rivers had ulterior motives. It was a three-pronged information super highway for the agent. He would obtain more information on the Sullivan family and know exactly what Jones knew. Best of all, he would know if Jones found out about his dealings with Ceci. It was a win-win situation and Jones was doing most of the dirty work.

They pulled out of the parking lot and headed south towards Ocean Drive. They parked close to a lifeguard stand and walked the kayak into the ocean. Normally it would be a ten-minute paddle trip. But a Cuban refugee would be approaching from the southeast, so they would paddle around Star Island and come in that way. Most refugees come in via the Keys on beat up makeshift vessels, so he didn't expect the ruse to last long. A few seconds to get up close was all that they needed.

The slight head wind and extra passenger made the trip longer than expected. Rivers was tucked down flat covered by the tarp. Jones couldn't tell another person was there and he was only three feet away. With the low hanging clouds coming in a person would have a hard time seeing the kayak. Don't rain he prayed.

As they approached the Sullivans dock it was eerily quiet. No motion coming from the dock house, but lights pointed brightly right on the upper portion of the dock. They would need the guard to walk down there to them or the whole operation would be over before it barely began.

The kayak nudged into the dock and not a stir from the dock house. For a moment, it appeared unmanned but suddenly a flashlight from the top of the dock ramp glared down upon them.

"This is private property. No trespassing," a security guard said in a stern but calm voice.

"Es este el EE.UU?" Jones asked in a halfway decent Spanish accent. Translated it basically was a question regarding if he was in the states.

The guard started walking down so Jones pulled down his hat and repeated the same question again knowing his moment was close.

"Look buddy, this is private property. You have to leave now."

The guard put his foot out towards the kayak to give it a swift push off the dock and Jones catapulted off the kayak and tackled the guard onto the dock. It was obvious to the guard now that Jones wasn't lost as they wrestled for a moment until Rivers relieved the guard of his pistol.

"Stop and be quiet," Rivers offered in a hushed voice while pointing the revolver at the guard.

"Do what we say and you won't get hurt," Jones promised.

They all marched up to the dock house after Jones tied up the kayak. The front gate guard was called for assistance by the first guard and was also jumped and tied up by Jones. They marched the first guard up to the front door entrance careful to remain in the shadows. He was quick to give up the floor plan and the number of people inside. The only occupants were Derek and Ceci Sullivan who appeared to have retired for the evening.

The guard was less than forthcoming when it came time to give up the alarm code. Jones gave the guard a half-hearted whack to the left knee with his crowbar before the guard spit it out. Jones went to enter the alarm code when Rivers stopped him.

"Wait," Rivers said while pushing the end of his cold revolver into the guard's mouth.

"There's only one thing certain tonight Mister. If he enters that code and a panic alarm goes off, that white stucco wall behind you is going to look like splattered tomatoes. Would you like to re-think that code?" Rivers asked.

The guard nodded yes and recited the correct code after Rivers removed the revolver from his mouth. Once the door clicked open Rivers retraced his steps with the guards in tow while Jones entered the luxury mansion. They would meet back at the kayak once Jones finished the mission.

Jones almost gasped in awe once his eyes adjusted to the interior foyer. On the opposite wall, a small light shone on top of a large painting of a mystical horse. This room alone was about half the size of his entire house. The imported Italian marble floor cost more than his humble abode.

If the guard was truthful, Sullivan's office would be at the top of the steps to the right. Jones was prepared to walk gingerly up the stairs, so they wouldn't creak. It took him two full steps before it dawned on him that marble doesn't creak. Tripping on the carpet runner would be more likely.

Being a cat burglar was an occupation that he never sought. He had done it once before in his youthful Vegas days but that was a prank. This was a pseudo agency operation and he would be alone on the reservation if it went south.

The French office door had a flimsy lock on it. Sullivan was an alarm system industrialist, so this wasn't impressive by anybody's imagination. It could be a trap if anybody dared to get this far. Or, maybe he felt secure enough and became lazy at the crème de la crème. Star Island had private security at the entranceway in addition to his newfound friends tied up in the dock house. Jones took a deep breath and slowly pulled up the door handle. After a few moments of silence, he walked in confident that he was undetected.

The office was more to his taste than the foyer. Almost the entire east wall was adorned with built in elaborate oak bookshelves. The only break was a half circle bar nestled into the corner with a four-bar stool accompaniment. A Captain's desk was laid out splendidly in front of the south wall with a magnificent view of Biscayne Bay through the window behind it.

The west wall was littered with various size paintings complete with attached dim viewing lights which enhanced the visibility of the office. The southwest corner was strangely void of anything. A perfect place for a dartboard Jones murmured to himself.

Enough of the envy society as Jones thought, ass he pulled the listening devices from his pocket. All four of them were pre-programmed to his device so he needed four strategic places for them. Obviously under the bar top was a prime location. Many men throughout history have poured out secrets and liquor together.

There was a curved red velvet sofa in front of the bookshelves, so he placed one underneath it. He could almost picture the smug bastard laying back and working some deal on his phone with his Senator buddy. Despite only seeing Derek Sullivan at the gala, his disdain for the man ran deep.

Outside the library doors a shapely silhouette of a woman stood motionless. The curse of being a very light sleeper sometimes had its advantages. At first, she assumed it was a Sullivan family member, but this person had a different vibe. She decided to remain silent and observe from behind a statue down the hall.

Jones thought of planting another bug in the landline phone but that was so cliché. No one used landlines anymore and if they did it was to order a pizza. He decided to put one on the top of the window frame behind the desk. People always liked to talk while standing and gazing out a window. More so when they had a million-dollar view.

The bugs were highly sensitive so four of them were overkill. Then again it was a spacious office so better safe than sorry. He crawled under the desk and planted one on the body of the desk. As he was crawling back out he spotted somebody else's bug attached to the underneath side of the drawer. Unbelievable, Sullivan was already bugged by someone else. The agency or the bureau could have beaten him to the punch and that's why he was put on the sidelines. Rivers might know something, but he could be out of the loop. Besides, if he did know, he wouldn't have put up with this last-minute Watergate imitation.

Jones took a photo of the bug with his cellphone and would work on the identification later. He wiped clean his crowbar and placed it on the day sofa. It was a perfectly good burglary tool gone to naught. Now he had to steal something to make it look good.

He had his choice of a couple dozen paintings. Three would be enough to carry as he sneaked out of the mansion. He removed a Claude Monet from the middle of the west wall. At least he had heard of Monet and since it was showcased in the middle of the wall it would have some value.

Keeping to the same theory Jones took the paintings on either side of the vacant Monet spot. They were an Edgar Degas and something resembling a high rise with flying objects by Salvador Dali. He liked the later one a lot.

At this point the shapely silhouette had a decision to make. Either wake someone or call the authorities. Instead, she went with a third option to protect her own best interests and slipped down the hall and out of sight without confrontation.

Almost done, Jones opened the office door holding his haul. This close to the finish line, he didn't want to do something stupid. He retraced his steps thankful they had no dogs and vanished out the front door. After a quick surveil of the compound to let his eyes adjust he walked by the dock house and saw the guards tightly fused together. They would be back at the Fontainebleau before anybody rescued the guards.

Rivers was lying low in the kayak with the revolver by his side. He laughed to himself as he helped load the paintings in the kayak and covered them with the tarp to protect them from the ocean mist. This time they paddled the direct route and were upon the beach in about ten minutes with help from the incoming tide.

Jones was exhausted, and he needed some sleep. Daylight would bring a long day with eavesdropping his only task unless something went unhinged. He took a long look at the paintings which were placed in the backseat of his Jeep. He had no idea what to do with them.

Once they arrived back at the hotel lot he let Rivers go in first. He needed to change out of his refugee garb and put the paintings in an empty suitcase which he bought earlier that day. Once Rivers entered the lobby, Jones stopped by his vehicle and planted a GPS chip under River's SUV bumper. What was good for the faithful Lieutenant was also good for the General.

Chapter 36

The Quarry Blues

TERRENCE OLIVER WAS still sleeping off the previous night's booze when his cellphone rang around 4:30am. From prior experience Oliver knew early morning calls weren't habitually filled with joyous news. Groggily, he answered it in the middle of the fourth ring.

"Are you alone Mr. Oliver?" the man on the other end asked.

"Depends on who the hell this is?" Oliver replied.

"It's James Sullivan. We're ready to receive the information you mentioned yesterday."

"And you're ready to procure payment for services rendered?" Oliver asked knowing that too much of this type of conversation on the phone wasn't wise, but time was of the essence.

"Yes, we have your money. Meet us at the White Rock Quarry in Hialeah in one hour. We'll drop down in our Bell at precisely 5:30am."

"That's not necessary son," Oliver replied.

"We want to make sure we aren't followed. Our money, our rules and I'm not your son," James Sullivan replied uncompromisingly while ending the call before Oliver could say anything else. Father would be rather pleased at his improvisation he thought to himself. He was confident Oliver would show up. No federal worker would ever miss a payday like this one.

Oliver rushed out of bed wishing his bourbon headache would go away fast. He googled the location for the White Rock Quarry, it was a thirty-minute drive tops. The place would be empty this early and it was an easy place to land a helicopter without waking up the neighborhood. It was a smart plan on their part. The sons weren't as stupid as he thought. Nevertheless, there would likely be some type of guard at the entrance. He didn't want a record of his appearance, so he needed to arrive even earlier and find another way in.

Oliver threw on blue jeans and a dirty booze stained brown long sleeve shirt from the night before. Then he grabbed his agency issued binoculars and his non-issued personal .38 pistol. No need ballistic wise to have anything traced back to himself if something went wrong. As he went out the door, he pulled a Marlins baseball cap low over his eyes.

Traffic was very light as he merged his SUV onto the A1A. Twenty-five minutes later and he was in Hialeah with the quarry in front of him. It was a massive place with huge mounds of limestone which would be trucked to Jacksonville.

Oliver was far from the front gate when he saw a decent sized oak tree next to the fence line. He parked the SUV next to the tree and climbed onto the roof. In no time, he climbed onto the tree and saddled out on a heavy branch which hung over the fence. He took off his belt and fastened it into a loop and lowered himself to the ground. The belt would make it easier to get back over as his vertical jump wasn't much these days.

He took up a position on top of the nearest limestone pile. It felt gritty on his stomach as he lay there scanning the quarry with his binoculars. He still had twenty minutes before his counterparts arrived and he hoped his information would be looked at favorably.

There didn't seem to be a lot of information that Derek Sullivan didn't know. His connections kept him in the loop and he was sure Sullivan knew more about the Bradley Dunbar murder than the FBI did. The search warrant turned up nothing which Sullivan already knew and seemed delighted to throw that in his face. Future information would be the catalyst for this business arrangement, but the tennis game yesterday was gold. Oliver was confident that Derek didn't know that his wife was playing tennis yesterday with Stony Rivers. Nor, that they seemed to be more than casual acquaintances.

Derek Sullivan would want more information about this rendezvous. With a little more time, he could fill in the gaps for him. If not, giving up some relatively new information would still prove his worth and a need for his services.

Oliver worked his binoculars back and forth over the quarry. Limestone piles were scattered about and the landscape littered with blue dump trucks and yellow Caterpillar loaders. An organized mess he assumed then he spotted a shiny object reflecting off the rising sun. It wasn't there a few minutes ago or the darkness hid it well. It was sticking out of a bucket of a front loader. This warranted further inspection from a different angle.

He took up another position on a similar limestone pile two-hundred yards to the south. Lying cheating bastards, he thought to himself. Rick Sullivan was sprawled out in the bucket with a scope rifle. He was being double crossed. It was a good plan when he thought about it. Walk up to the helicopter when it landed and take a head shot from behind.

Oliver's first instinct was to sneak behind Rick Sullivan and put two slugs in his head despite only needing one to get the job done. Anger however, wasn't going to obtain his early retirement funds. Otherwise, the young Sullivan would have taken his last breath already. No, he'd take him hostage for now and make a solid plan later. The black Bell would be here in ten minutes, so he needed to act fast.

He retraced his steps back to the first limestone pile then walked fifty yards to the north and started walking straight towards the front loader. He was directly behind the tractor and there was no way Rick Sullivan could see him while laying down in the bucket. As soon as he was ten feet away he veered to the right taking slow soft steps. Rick Sullivan saw a shadow over his right shoulder and turned his head which was promptly greeted with the butt end of a .38 pistol.

Oliver looked down at the unconscious Sullivan realizing they were closer to pulling off their plan than he liked. He thought they had a deal because he was a useful asset. Now he had to figure out what to do with the amateur assassin as the helicopter would be here in minutes.

He grabbed the rifle with his shirt sleeve and tucked it behind the seat of the front loader then walked over to the nearest dump truck. Sure enough, the keys were in the ignition. These trucks were moved quite often by a handful of employees and the joint was fenced in. Theft was an improbable occurrence.

The sound of the Bell chopper was in the horizon as Oliver threw the unconscious Sullivan brother onto the front floor. Oliver sat down on the seat next to him prepared to bash his head again if he woke up. The chopper landed about fifty yards away and Oliver scrunched down hard, so he couldn't see the bird. If he couldn't see it then they couldn't see him.

Oliver wasn't sure how long James Sullivan would wait it out. He turned off both his cellphone and his captives. He was tempted to look over the dashboard but decided against it. If one of the doors to the dump truck opened he was prepared to blast away.

A professional would have departed after a minute or two tops once the meet time was greeted by silence. Oliver understood a few extra minutes because it was his brother after all. But James Sullivan waited a full twenty minutes before taking off wondering what the hell happened.

Oliver stayed put until he could no longer hear the Bell in the distance. Without a visual he couldn't be sure if a passenger departed the chopper, so he cautiously peered over the dashboard until he was satisfied it was safe. Rick Sullivan started coming out of his unintended nap, so Oliver bashed his head once again sending him back to sleep.

The younger Sullivan was steadily bleeding now, and Oliver had splatter all over his shirt. He couldn't wait any longer, so he started the dump truck and throttled it towards the fence by his SUV. Holding a gun and driving a stick shift was a nearly impossible task. So he tucked it in his waistline and kept his head down in case he was wrong about another shooter.

Not a shot was heard as the dump truck barreled through the chain link fence at thirty miles an hour. He stopped the truck next to his SUV and tied Sullivan up with his belt that he left behind.

Oliver placed him in the backseat and figured even if he woke soon it was doubtful that he could put up a fight.

With an eye towards the sky Oliver retraced his route hoping to avoid any helicopters. It was doubtful that James Sullivan spotted the SUV, but he still couldn't let his guard down as he had underestimated their grit already. He needed a new plan and more importantly a place to stash the younger Sullivan.

There was an FBI safe house outside of Miami in Hollywood. It hadn't been used for a while and it should be good for the next forty-eight hours. At this point he didn't care if the kid lived or not, but it would be easier trading a live body for his cash. The terms just changed. Two million dollars for the half dead kid in his backseat and no further information would be provided. It would be a quick exchange then he would disappear somewhere in this vast great world.

Chapter 37
The New Deal

RICK SULLIVAN SAT GAGGED and bound in the corner of the safe house with a mixture of dried blood and sweat dripping down his brow. His headache was beyond migraine level. Terrence Oliver sat across the room staring out the window. Standard operating procedure required that he inform the local office when putting the safe house into use. But this was far from standard, so protocol would be ignored. Oliver had been gazing outside for a solid hour and no one seemed to notice their presence.

A phone call would be coming that much he was sure of. Why the double cross he wondered to himself? He offered his services in good faith at a fair price. Or at least he thought it was fair. After all, he was betraying everything he believed in and everything he had ever been taught by the bureau. Maybe the two sons had gone rogue? He doubted it though. Their old man always called the shots, so he never even bothered to ask his bloodied hostage.

This unplanned escapade changed everything. Keeping the same terms would be unacceptable. Besides, he would never feel safe now and always be looking over his shoulder. Even with a peaceful exchange there would be a mark on his back because he's a loose end now. No, he would have to up the ante, not only for his pride but for practical reasons. He would move up his retirement date, but it would cost them double the previous arrangement. It was small change for a guy like Derek Sullivan with imbeciles for sons.

His phone finally rang in the late morning. He missed breakfast and his stomach was growling like a third world refugee.

"Oliver," he stated into his phone showing no emotion of strength or weakness.

"Apologies would be in order Mr. Oliver but I'm assuming you're not in the mood," replied an unfamiliar Cuban accented voice on the other end.

"You assume right."

"I've been asked to rectify this mistake. I have your money sir."

"Who is this?" Oliver asked.

"I'm a grunt soldier like you doing the real work without the glory. I'm able to make the exchange right now."

"The terms have changed. The amount is doubled, even exchange, nothing else and you'll never hear from me again."

"That's a bit steep, don't you think?"

"I didn't try to ambush myself now, did I?" Oliver asked as he was getting agitated but trying hard to keep an even keel. "I could always put a bullet in his head and keep my day job. I'd be doing his old man a favor that way."

"That won't be necessary. You make a good point and you shall be compensated appropriately. I'll be ready within the hour. Meet me at North Beach at one o'clock. I'll come in a chopper, make the exchange and take off."

Oliver remained silent for a few moments. Meeting at a beach was going to be his proposal. It's a perfect place. Only one way in unless someone comes by boat which you'll see before they arrive. The only problem might be getting shot from the sky. He would have to keep the young Sullivan very close and not show himself until the bird landed.

"See you at one o'clock," Oliver replied as he ended the call.

Oliver pulled into the North Beach parking lot with twenty minutes to spare. Rick Sullivan was in the backseat in obvious discomfort. Oliver didn't care and didn't even try to pretend. The punk was going to put a bullet in his head a few hours ago and if he lost a finger or two from tight restraints he wasn't going to lose a minute of sleep. The parking lot was empty except for a handful of cars at the far end. He looked hard for a sniper's nest but didn't see anything suspicious. He would wait until he saw the helicopter land then take his hostage out into the open.

Oliver sat in the early afternoon heat with the windows down scanning the beach. Besides a couple of small leisure crafts the ocean was clear. It was a quiet afternoon with no foot traffic. For the second time today, Oliver was planning on being rich. If he was double crossed this time he was prepared to leave a dead body or two on the beach.

Repercussions would be severe if a Sullivan died. Oliver leaned back and closed his eyes behind his Ray Bans. Positive thoughts he told himself. Maybe he would start off in Switzerland, open a numbered account and make it a home base.

The sound of the Bell helicopter was heard several minutes before the allotted time. He grabbed the binoculars and made a visual. It was the right bird. As soon as it touched down about a football field away he grabbed the young Sullivan and trudged through the deep sand until he was twenty yards away.

The helicopter door opened outward and a well-built man wearing a flight jacket, Yankees cap and mirrored sunglasses jumped out of the back with a large blue Adidas backpack. As he approached Oliver and the hostage, he put up a hand then slowly opened and lifted his jacket while turning around to show he had no weapon.

Oliver seemed satisfied and pushed his hostage ahead of him as a precaution while keeping his gun aimed in the general direction of both men. The mystery man started to walk up to Rick Sullivan which set Oliver off.

"Put down the bag first," Oliver barked.

"Take it easy mister. I'm just the errand boy."

"Back up slow, next to the kid, with your arms up," Oliver ordered.

The man replied with his arms shoulder high. Oliver walked up to the Adidas bag and sized it up. It looked about the right size if it was full of hundreds. Either way nobody was leaving until he opened it up and had a good look through it. As soon as Oliver bent over to unzip the bag the errand boy flipped off his cap and grabbed a small .22 pistol nestled into his hair. The bullet plowed into Oliver's right shoulder sending his weapon into the sand. Oliver wasn't going down without a fight. He lunged for his revolver with his left hand, but the shooter was too quick and stepped onto Oliver's good hand pointing his .22 at Oliver's head. This was no ordinary errand boy and Oliver had severely underestimated the man.

"Relax Mr. Oliver. Derek Sullivan wishes to have a word with you about your new terms. Please get into the helicopter. You can still have the backpack."

Oliver looked up at the pistol pointed at his face then at the glare off the man's sunglasses. Considering he was lying on his chest with a slug in his shoulder it didn't seem like a bad proposition. He staggered to his feet and walked to the chopper like a beaten mule. Rick Sullivan jumped into the back of the chopper next to him. The errand boy followed them both and placed the backpack under the seat and made Oliver toss over his car keys.

"Fly straight back to your port. Your father will meet you there. I'll use his car." The errand boy instructed the pilot, James Sullivan.

James nodded, and Oliver looked down knowing this wasn't going to end well. He swung for the fences twice and missed badly both times.

The errand boy handed the gun to Rick.

"Do not shoot him unless you have to."

"I'll try not to," Rick sneered.

The errand boy shut the door and started walking to Oliver's SUV. It was a good spot as no one seemed to witness what transpired. It was even more deserted at night which is why he ran a monthly shipment there.

The Bell helicopter turned hard right after it's takeoff over the ocean. The errand boy better known as Santora looked over his shoulder and smiled as he took out his phone. He entered four numbers into the phone and pressed send. Santora felt a mixture of joy and relief that he was back to controlling his own destiny once again.

The explosion was small and deadly. At a height of around a thousand feet it doesn't need to be a giant explosion to reach your desired result. The Sullivan clan was now short two heirs and Terrence Oliver was put into permanent retirement.

Chapter 38
Unexpected Company

THE WIND CONTINUED picking up from the east scattering some clouds over the high noon sun. Jones decided to take his eavesdropping endeavor poolside, so he grabbed his ear buds and headed out for lunch Florida style. So far it was nothing but pure silence from the Sullivan office. Doubts creeped into his mind about the quality of the equipment, but Bullock struck him as perfectionist, so he was sure it was in working order.

Either way it was starting to feel like a waste of an afternoon. Maybe they left for the day and he was worried for no reason. The Cubanito sandwich was magnificent and briefly took his mind off his dull task. The bronze beauties lounging poolside were gradually leaving as the clouds started gathering above. Suddenly a shadowy figure appeared from the minimal sun.

"What kind of date are you Sinjin Jones? You almost get a girl blown up and you don't call her anymore."

"Actually, I was just thinking about you. Could I order you some lunch?" Jones replied instantly recognizing the beautiful Rachelle Sullivan.

"You're a terrible liar Mr. Jones."

"No, seriously, I'd be glad to order you some lunch." Jones replied with a wide school boy sized grin.

"In that case make it two mojitos plus something for yourself," she replied laughing.

"The Miami lunch, I love it," Jones countered as he proceeded to place an order with the poolside waitress. "What brings you into my neck of the woods?"

"I'm not sure," Rachelle replied then pausing for a couple seconds. "I guess that's why I'm here. I don't like unanswered questions. I find you very intriguing Mr. Jones."

"Well I'm glad you dropped by. I wanted to call, really I did but I've never been in an explosion with a girl before."

Rachelle snickered. "That's understandable. I'm sorry that someone is trying to hurt you though."

"Well the police are still investigating. I'm sure it was a case of mistaken identity. It was a rental after all."

The waitress walked up and passed out the mojitos. Rachelle raised her glass towards Jones.

"Here's to being alive. May all your dreams come true."

Jones saluted her back. "As well as yours."

A few minutes later the waitress dropped off a second round of drinks as raindrops started falling from the sky.

"Would you mind if we took these to your room? My dress is linen."

"Certainly. We can't have wet linen."

As they walked up to his room he was hoping room service had attended his room. It was starting to resemble a college dorm room late in a semester. Luckily, he did keep his weapons and issued equipment locked in a case.

They entered his hotel room and to his relief the bed was made. The housekeeper also straightened up his organized mess and made the room presentable. Jones realized that tipping generously had its perks as he set down his audio equipment and the remnants of his last mojito.

As he turned around Rachelle was standing ten feet away with a seductive look on her face. The green linen dress lay crumpled next to her ankles but the white strappy heel remained on showing the contrast to her tanned toned body. There's something about a rainy afternoon Jones thought to himself as they fell together twisted as one onto the king-sized bed.

Chapter 39
By Invitation Only

RIVERS EXITED HIS HOTEL room with a huff of exasperation followed by a half-hearted door slam. Both Jones and Oliver were avoiding his numerous calls. He left voicemails for both. It's so nice to be head of a taskforce where one can't reach the rest of the task force.

He'd been lying on his bed half asleep in a happy place with the television on. Local programming broke in with breaking news of a helicopter explosion a few miles north of the hotel. Television cameras scanning the accident scene showed that it was a black Bell helicopter.

Sure, there were plenty of black Bell helicopters out there, but coincidence didn't happen often in this case. This needed to be checked out immediately. Even though the Sullivan boys were off limits, Rivers didn't want to look stupid and be the last to know something. He'd drive up there and find out himself. His FBI badge would get all his questions answered but a little company would have been nice to bounce some ideas around.

Rivers had made an inquiry phone call to local headquarters but they didn't know any more than he did. He also thought about seeing if he could get Oliver re-assigned but thought better of it. It was bad enough that they were barely on speaking terms but better to keep the dirty laundry in-house. Besides, problems like this should never be dwelled on when a tidy sum of cash was heading his way.

The sexy voice at local headquarters informed Rivers that she would text him any information they received about the crash. Rivers hurried off the lobby floor elevator while glancing at his phone. The day was getting stranger every moment that his calls weren't being returned. Something wasn't right but first things first.

As Rivers walked through the parking lot amid a lazy Southern Florida day he noticed a young Cuban man eyeballing him from his distant right. His phone beeped, and Rivers looked down for a moment to read the text. It was the Sullivan boy's helicopter that exploded and crashed off North Beach. The cause was unknown as well as identification of the occupants. Further information would be forwarded as it became available.

A momentary disruption was all it took for the young Cuban to approach Rivers. Sunlight glared off the man's gun barrel and Rivers looked up knowing it was too late to reach for his service revolver.

"Relax Mr. Rivers. We have a mutual friend that would like to discuss a certain matter with you."

"I knew having an unlisted number would cause me a problem someday," Rivers retorted.

The young Cuban chuckled at that remark while his mirror image emerged from the shadows and relieved Rivers of his vehicle keys and his revolver. Rivers was motioned into the backseat. He sat there motionless with a gun being prodded into his ribcage. As they departed the lot they were followed by a Ford Mustang.

Rivers wasn't sure who was beckoning for him on a day where everybody should be holed up in a Tiki bar trying to stay dry. Maybe it was about the helicopter crash and he was being setup. If that was the case it was happening fast. Or, Derek Sullivan got wind of his off the grid demands. Either way, this wasn't a good situation.

Chapter 40
The Crash Site

JONES EXITED THE SHOWER almost as steamy as when he entered. He still couldn't wrap his head around Rachelle Sullivan. She was a dream girl with a mysterious side. She didn't shy away from his drama of which there was plenty of lately. Whatever it was, he was counting on seeing her again. The complexities of her family dynamics couldn't be ignored though and deep down he knew a long-term situation was highly unlikely. A man was entitled to his dreams though.

He turned the television on as he grabbed a bottle of Fuji water wearing only a towel around his waist. The cool ocean air coming through the open patio door felt refreshing. He knew he should get back to his mundane eavesdropping task but looked for a fresh distraction anyway.

The local news was covering a helicopter crash on North Beach. Jones didn't think much of it until he checked his voicemail. He had five missed calls from Stony and one pissed off voicemail. Now that the possible connection was made he threw on some jeans and a black hoodie. He could be at North Beach in twenty minutes and find Rivers. It seemed the tired old man had a lot of fight left in him after all. Jones was surprised twice by Rivers in the last day which brought a small smile to his face. There's nothing like fighting the good fight.

Jones took off for North Beach in his Jeep with the top on to keep out the steady drizzle. He hated having the top on because it reminded him of the Middle East where they were never allowed the freedom of riding in the desert sans the top. Jones tried hard to forget the war all the time. It didn't always come easy, but he did it better than most.

Both calls to Rivers and Oliver went straight to voicemail. They were probably both at the scene by now cursing his very existence. Oh well, his pleasant distraction was well worth it. They could curse him all they wanted, and he would take it with a concealed smile on his face. He pulled up to the scene and the beachhead was now full of people and emergency vehicles with lights twirling. The Coast Guard had four small vessels in the water recovering large pieces of the Bell. Jones put another call into Rivers with the same result. He looked up and down the beach once again but saw neither of his contemporaries.

He felt helpless as he stood behind the yellow crime scene tape. Without his FBI friends, he was just another bystander. Albeit a bystander with a gun but he wasn't going to force the issue with the authorities. He could see three black body bags up the beach about a hundred yards, so they must have recovered the bodies first. He surmised that the chopper came straight down from low altitude which would make the debris field compact.

There was still no sign of Rivers or Oliver anywhere on the beach. They surely wouldn't have left already. Jones was starting to get a bad feeling deep down in his gut. It was seldom wrong, yet he tried to push it aside. He had no choice but to throw a call into Graydon Bullock now. The Bell debris did look like it could be the Sullivan's bird. He needed some answers and they weren't jumping over the yellow tape coming to him. He wasn't sure if he should bring up his missing colleagues, but he was sure Bullock would ask about them.

Bullock's secretary was a sweetheart to him. Bullock was out golfing, but she would reach out to him and advised him to standby. Jones hung up and considered the sky where the drizzle was starting to let up. Bullock didn't strike him as a country club type, so he assumed he was out with some high-profile D.C. powerhouse types. He found it strange how department heads always had to beg Congress for money to help keep the country safe. It was no different in the Army where he experienced seeing half-assed equipment being blown to bits because some contractor took the cheap way out. It was always about somebody's profit margins.

Whatever Bullock may or may not be, he was certainly efficient. Within ten minutes a Coast Guard official approached him and asked his name. Receiving the correct reply, he was escorted up the beach next to the body bags.

Jones stared down at the body bags. He'd seen enough of them in the Middle East to last one-hundred lifetimes. Over there, staying out of a body bag was always the number one goal. Everything else was secondary.

"What do you have on the Bell?" Jones asked without looking up from the body bags.

"The tail was pretty much intact. We were on the scene within minutes and we've recovered most of it already. Very few witnesses but they all relayed that it was a low altitude explosion and it dropped straight down. NATB is due here any minute. It falls to them for the investigation. We're just recovery," The Coast Guard official replied.

"Who does the Bell belong to?"

"It came back to a Sullivan Cargo. They operate airfreight service."

"Yes, I'm familiar with them. Are these all the bodies?"

"As far as we know, yes," the official answered.

"Any identification on the bodies?" Jones asked.

"Yes sir, two of them. Rick and James Sullivan. Judging by the ages, I'm assuming they are brothers."

"You assume right. What about the third body?" Jones asked.

"It's in pretty bad shape mister. No identification on him. Then again, half of his ass is missing. He looks to be older than the other two by at least twenty years." The official was starting to get an uneasy feeling about this conversation. This guy was supposed to be some CIA operative, yet this seemed personal. Jones finally looked over at the man speaking. His mind was still hanging on the ass comment. It sounded like a small bomb or an undercarriage shot. Since there was no apparent small artillery on the beach he was betting on a small bomb in the cabin.

"Unzip it please?" Jones asked.

The Coast Guard official hesitated for a second. Viewing it once that afternoon was gruesome enough. He thought about referring the man to the Dade County Medical Examiner. Then, with another brief hesitation, he bent down and unzipped the bag exposing a half-scorched corpse with one leg barely attached to the torso.

Jones took a long look at the corpse. Shit, it could be Oliver he thought to himself. It could also be Rivers. Then again, it could be a hundred people that he had seen today. The body was in that bad of shape. It was an explosion that thrust directly upwards. It's why soldiers sit on their helmets when riding in a war zone chopper. There are no headshots a few hundred feet up but a villager with a high caliber rifle and decent aim can take your nuts off by shooting through the chopper floor.

"Unzip it more please?" Jones asked. "I need to see the feet."

The official grimaced and unzipped the body bag exposing a pair of black lightweight military boots. There was no doubt about the identity now. The boots belonged to the late Terrence Oliver.

Chapter 41

Intervention for Two

THE SILENT RIDE ENDED for Stony Rivers at the Crandon Marina. It was a true local's marina with plenty of diving boats and fishing charters along with a slew of middle class boats that wouldn't be confused with the international playboy jetsetters. The cloudy skies with the intermittent showers left the marina deserted.

Rivers was ushered into a nearby boat warehouse. It held a few boats in dry dock but most of the boats were in various boat slips outside. The smell of damp motor oil permeated the air near a Criss Craft Corsair in for repairs. Rivers was shoved into an empty beat up folding chair and instructed to sit which he reluctantly complied with. Facing him was another empty folding chair about five feet away.

If Rivers didn't know any better, he was a party to an intervention. Except his two new friends didn't seem the type to care about his welfare and his counterpart for the other chair probably wouldn't care neither. On the outside Rivers appeared calm but on the inside his stomach was churning like he drank a gallon of soda. Hopefully, he was being run out of town with a little bit of cash for his silence. After all, killing an FBI agent wasn't looked upon favorably even if he wasn't liked by the bureau hierarchy.

Rivers sat in silence with his eyes helplessly glancing around for any kind of weapon. There was nothing close but some tool chests on the other side of the building. The two goons behind him would have plugged him with a handful of well-placed shots before he made it anywhere close to them. Besides, a heavy

Craftsman wrench wasn't going to do the job against these guys. No, he sat there and tried to figure a way to talk his way out of this mess. He needed to think fast as he heard an automobile pull up outside of the front warehouse office door.

The Sullivan's Bentley idled outside with the wipers slowly going back and forth. One of Santora's men was behind the steering wheel where he stayed while Derek and Ceci Sullivan exited the backseat escorted by Santora.

The Sullivan's kept protesting about this unplanned stop and Santora kept getting angrier by the moment standing in the rain. He didn't like getting drenched. It brought back bad memories of a cartel member that once tried to drown him in a filthy bar toilet in Columbia when he was half drunk. Luckily, a long arm and a boot pistol helped eradicate him from that situation.

Both Sullivan's stopped their protests upon entering the warehouse and seeing Stony Rivers sitting alone in a darkened warehouse. Derek had no idea what was going on and Ceci wished that she didn't have one. Rivers wasn't thrilled to see the couple himself feeling like his shakedown didn't work. He was starting to feel like a carnival barker about to get tarred and feathered and ran out of town. Worse yet, his dream of riches seemed doomed.

The Sullivan's were sitting comfortably in their mansion less than an hour ago, when Santora and his cohort burst into their home. The daytime security detail consisted of two young men who reacted rather meekly when they recognized Santora at the front gate of the island. Nobody likes dying especially if it's for someone else's money.

Overall, Santora was rather polite with an urgent tone when he relayed to the Sullivan's that they had an emergency on their hands. Ceci protested loudly but Derek became more cooperative when he was informed that a large amount of money was at risk.

All three of them approached Rivers and stopped in front of the morose figure. Ceci couldn't bring herself to meet his eyes nor did Rivers try to meet hers.

"It's come to my attention that the three of you have some kind of prior relationship. Being that this man is an FBI agent does not bode well for my working relationship with you," Santora said as he gazed at the Sullivan's for a reaction.

Neither Sullivan uttered a word. They had always kept Santora in check before because they made him a lot of cash. They seemed to legitimize Santora which was his most basic need rather than be viewed as another crazy Cuban mobster. This time though he seemed different. He was borderline psychotic with a touch of frenzy. Better off not saying anything they reasoned rather than deny it to a dangerous man with a loaded gun who obviously knew something of their past.

Another car pulled up and two more Cubans entered the warehouse and approached Santora. The Sullivan's felt a sense of momentary relief but Rivers cringed when he saw his recording device that he used on Ceci for his shakedown. The Cubans were thorough and gutsy for tossing his room after he was forced into this meeting. Smart also as Santora now had physical evidence of his plot which could mean some serious jail time in a federal penitentiary. It was time to play let's make a deal.

The accomplice handed Santora the device and whispered into his ear for a few moments.

"Good work. Go take care of the other one now," Santora said.

Rivers didn't know what to make of that comment. Was he talking about Jones or Oliver? It didn't make sense if they were running him out of town. It could only mean they were turning him into the feds complete with evidence on a platter for a twenty-year sentence. That churning feeling was turning to full out panic now.

As the accomplice left going for his next hunt, Santora played River's trump card. It was the secret recording. All the parties stared straight ahead in silence except Ceci who looked down trying to think of something brilliant to say. Santora never offered her a chance as he turned off the recording.

"It all comes together my friends," Santora laughed. "One man scorned, one man does the dirty work and a woman who thinks of herself as a genius. You three deserve each other, you really do. Misery loves company and you're all miserable to the core."

"It was a long time ago!" Ceci shouted lifting her head up. "It doesn't matter anymore. Let's make a deal and go our separate ways."

"I'll make the damn deals!" Santora yelled his face red with rage. "You played me. I will make the damn deals. And tonight, we will make a very, very big deal."

"Leave her out of it Santora. Derek and I can work this out. We're all sorry you got involved," Stony pleaded solemnly.

"Oh, that's beautiful. Simply beautiful. She double crosses you with another man and you're still acting like a white knight trying to get in her pants. Do you have any pride Rivers?" Santora asked.

"Give me a gun. I'll finish this right now!" Derek yelled standing up.

"This isn't your call Derek. Sit down in that chair," Santora replied.

"No, I write the checks. I still call the shots."

A quick punch to the jaw from Santora laid Derek out flat on the oily warehouse floor. The two Cuban's behind Rivers ran over and placed Derek back on the other chair. They steadied him for a few seconds as he grabbed his jaw.

Santora took out his pistol and offered it to Ceci after he emptied it except for one lonely round in the chamber.

"This is about Ceci, the so-called brains of the operation. I do give you your kudos. It worked. You get away with a brilliant heist and you're worth billions now. What I don't like though is that everyone else always does the dirty work for you. That ends tonight dear. Tonight, you get a little dirty and then we all go home."

Santora pressed the gun into her hands with an icy stare. She returned the favor except it was even icier. He smiled slightly with a bit of admiration.

"Now, you have a choice to make. One of them dies and you get to make that decision. A decision which you should have made a long time ago but now you have an opportunity to make it right. Go ahead, shoot one of them. You have ten seconds to decide or my men will shoot you."

Both Cubans pulled out their side arms in case anyone doubted their seriousness. Ceci stood there holding the gun and looking at her feet in deep thought. She knew Santora was serious and she wasn't the one who was going to die tonight. No yelling, no crying and no protesting. Don't stare into anybody's eyes. Just choose, turn around and pull the trigger she told herself.

Derek's jaw pain didn't seem so important now. He worried for a second but knew deep down his co-conspirator wouldn't shoot him. For the first time in a long time he felt secure by true confidence rather than a false bravado.

Stony stunned, sat there feeling like the odd man out. All he wanted was some real cash and ride off into the sunset. Sure, he had a bond with this woman many years ago. It wasn't important to her though or she wouldn't have teamed up with Derek in the first place. He was still lost in thought and he hadn't noticed the shadow of Ceci wheel his way. The shot to the forehead was never felt as Stony crashed to the floor motionless. Spurned once again by the only woman he truly loved.

Nobody said a word as Santora retrieved the pistol from her hands and fully loaded it. Ceci looked downward at the corpse while Santora smiled knowing she would shoot Rivers. The two Cubans stood behind Rivers looking relieved that they didn't take a stray bullet.

"I knew you could do it Ceci. Not a doubt in my mind. I do think you made a bad decision though."

Santora took a step towards Derek, raised his pistol and fired a shot. Derek Sullivan was now the equal of Stony Rivers.

Chapter 42
Street Fighting Man

JONES WAS CALLING Rivers one more time without success as he climbed back into his Jeep. Then he called Graydon Bullock with the bad news which he left on his voicemail. He thought about calling Rachelle but thought better of it. One, he didn't know exactly what was going on. Secondly, he didn't want to be remembered as the bearer of bad news regarding her brothers.

The most important task right now was to find Rivers. Jones pulled out his IPAD and used his GPS tracking device to locate his vehicle. It looked like Rivers was about twenty minutes away. Rivers could be okay and working something with no viable cellphone signal. It's always a possibility on a coastline.

It only took a couple of minutes before he noticed the black Mustang in his rearview mirror. It looked like a couple of Cubans and they weren't trying to be coy. Jones decided to play it safe and stay on the main drag until they made a move. With all the police action at the crash site it wouldn't be long.

A minute later a white Mustang passed him from the opposite direction. The passenger was on his cellphone, but the driver made no effort to divert his eyes from the Jeep. The pearl white beauty made a sharp U-turn and tucked in behind its black counterpart. If there was any doubt before, Jones knew he was the next target.

The options were few. Jones knew he couldn't outrun the Mustangs in his Jeep. He didn't want a gunfight on the streets, neither. Calling the cops crossed his mind but these Cubans would have them outgunned. Besides, he was too tired and pissed off to hand his problems to someone else.

Jones decided the best defense would be to go on offense. He punched the gas hard as he pulled out his Glock and made a sharp right turn. A quick glance in the mirror showed both Mustangs easily made the turn. Any minute they would split up and try to trap him on a side street.

Jones decided to control their maneuvers by making a hard-left turn and crashing through the white flimsy gate of a parking garage. The black Mustang flew by the broken gate and gunned around the garage to cut Jones off on the other side. The white counterpart followed him into the parking garage trying to trap their prey in a crossfire.

The cover in the parking garage was better than the open streets. Jones stopped the Jeep right before the gated exit and jumped out to take a position behind a silver Ford pickup truck. The white Mustang jammed on their brakes realizing they were in a bad spot. It was too late as Jones opened fire. The passenger tried to return fire but swiftly reached for the steering wheel as Jones placed a shot right between the driver's eyes. It rolled backwards onto the street where it was struck by a passing UPS truck.

Jones spun around and faced a five-foot high brick retaining wall between him and the street. As the black Mustang came around the corner he lifted the Glock above his head, over the wall and opened fire spraying the passenger side with bullets. Broken glass flew as the black Mustang raced away choosing to fight another time. He was unsure if any of the occupants were hit but Jones knew they would be meeting up again very soon.

Chapter 43
Follow the Trail

IT WAS DARKER THAN USUAL in the late afternoon with rolling thunder clouds lighting up the sky. The periodic rain lightened up as Jones parked the Jeep along a tree line. Per the GPS, River's vehicle was up the marina road near some dry storage warehouses. The rest of the way would be on foot.

Jones made it to the warehouse despite intermittent lighting that lit up the skies. Luckily, nobody in the marina was expecting him or he could have been an easy target. The marina seemed deserted with the inclement weather, but it was River's vehicle parked there. He wondered what Rivers was investigating and why he didn't tell him. After last night, he felt better about their working relationship. It was his own fault he missed his calls, or he would have known by now. No time for regrets though as regret is a good way to get killed.

The door knob turned effortlessly as he listened for noise coming from inside. It seemed too easy for his liking, so he declined the easy way and made his way to the back of the warehouse along the inlet. The backdoor was also unlocked as he turned the knob thinking this had to be a trap. He had a bad feeling as he peered through a two-inch crack waiting for his eyes to adjust to the dim security lights.

He ran through his options as he opened the door a few more inches. Bullock could be sending out the cavalry, but they had no idea where he was. He could reach out to Dade County for backup, but he was undercover and needed Bullock for assistance there. His safest bet was backing off and watching the warehouse from a distance. But, if Rivers was injured or needed assistance that decision could be fatal.

No, he needed to go in now and take care of business. Besides, it could be empty and Rivers elsewhere. As he felt around the inside of the door he detected the light switches and an open key box full of boat keys. Security wasn't a high priority unless it involved luxury yachts it seemed.

Leaving the main lights off, he walked a slow and silent perimeter along the inside of the warehouse. Numerous boats halfway through repairs scattered the main area with various toolboxes on wheels along the walls. The air smelled of stale motor oil as he kept his Glock pointed straight ahead. After a couple minutes of the silent walk, he was feeling satisfied that he was alone until he spotted two shadows lying on the ground ahead.

Neither shadow was moving. Jones could feel his heartbeat pounding in his chest. He slowed it down as he was trained and moved straight towards them prepared to fire if they moved aggressively. They were about ten feet apart as he approached, and he realized they were dead bodies. Two empty chairs were tipped over next to them.

He glanced around the entire building one last time as he was now in the middle looking down at the late Agent Rivers. There was a single gunshot to his head and he was lying in a small puddle of blood. He could tell by the blood pool that this didn't happen more than an hour ago. Body decomposition was a skill he unwittingly picked up over the years of his army tenure.

Deep down he had a certain level of fondness for Rivers. He wasn't overly aggressive towards this specific case for some unknown reason, but he was an old-school guy. Most people viewed him as a charmer with a bit of dry wittiness. Not a genius but smart enough which he proved last night. Now he was gone as Jones put a finger on his neck checking for a pulse that he knew was non-existent. His FBI badge had fallen out of his pocket, so Jones picked it up and placed it in his own back pocket.

As he walked up to the second body he recognized that it was Derek Sullivan. Stunned and surprised, Jones had no clue as to what went down in the warehouse. Sullivan also suffered from a single gunshot to the head. Judging by the two chairs it looked like an arranged sit down.

Possible scenarios were running through his mind when he heard cars coming down the marina's gravel road. He ran towards a window and looked out to see the black Mustang being accompanied by a green Ford Explorer. It looked like five or six men total. They were looking to finish what they started earlier. They guessed right figuring he would find Rivers.

The front entrance was cutoff and there was no way he could make it back to his Jeep without being detected. They probably left a man with it in case he returned anyway. He thought about locking the front door but that would be pointless and a valuable waste of time as he only had a couple minutes to make a getaway.

He threw a call into Bullock and left an updated message on his voicemail. At the backdoor, he turned off the security lights and grabbed a numbered boat key from the lockbox and headed outside to the docks. He laughed out loud when he stepped onto slip eleven. It was a worthless marina maintenance boat about thirty years old. No wonder they didn't bother to lock the keys up.

Jones dialed 9-1-1 as he untied the boat and saw the entire warehouse light up. He reported shots being fired at the marina. There hadn't been any shots fired yet but there would be shortly. The maintenance boat fired right up, and he thrust it into full throttle which wasn't much.

It only took a short thirty seconds before bullets started flying over his head and into the hull. Jones was thankful for the dark storm cloud cover as he hit the deck steering the boat from his knees. He hoped to be out of range and hear police sirens within a couple minutes. It would be relatively easy for the police to block the marina drive and corner his adversaries.

This day was spiraling out of control as Jones heard a boat engine behind him. Judging by its speed the bad guys grabbed a better boat key which is why he should have grabbed all the keys. No time for critical analysis as it was time to make a new plan on the fly.

Jones rummaged through a storage department and found some hefty bags and a flare gun. He emptied his pocket contents including his gun into a bag. Then he double bagged it with a tight knot and pointed the boat full speed towards the rock jetty. More shots came over his head as he emptied a five-gallon gas tank on the front deck.

He didn't need to look back to see that they had cut his lead in half. The engine noise told him all he needed to know. He counted to ten while lowering himself over the boat with his new hefty suitcase tied to his belt. He fired the flare gun as he let go of the side. By the time his head bobbed up over the water line the maintenance boat was burning brightly. He was swimming hard for shore when it crashed into the jetty full speed causing a small explosion.

Jones ducked under the surface as the other boat approached the jetty. Nothing could be heard under the water but a glare from the fire could be seen. They only stayed at the wreckage site for a few seconds then turned south and gunned it out of the bay.

He stayed under the water until his lungs were about to burst then swiftly rose to the surface. At that moment, he could hear and see the sirens at the marina. No doubt they would send the Coast Guard out to investigate this explosion. Jones swam to shore knowing a stupid mistake almost cost him his life.

Chapter 44
The Wet Walk

IT TOOK A GOOD HOUR for Jones to walk back to the marina. Every time a car approached he ducked behind a palm tree to avoid making any new Cuban friends. He approached the squad cars very wet and tired with his Hefty bag over his shoulder. Both shoes were lost to sea creatures and his feet were a bit cut up.

"Identify yourself?" detective Marshfield's voice rang out in the dark storm clouded air.

"Relax officer, I'm just a poor Hefty bag salesman named Sinjin Jones."

"Bullock was right. You are a smart ass."

"You know Graydon Bullock?"

"We go way back. He received your message and called me direct. I'm in homicide. High profile. You finding Derek Sullivan dead ruined my dinner plans," Marshfield replied with a firm handshake.

"Sorry about that. But I lost two members of my task force. In fact, I'm the last one left. I need some answers."

"I was hoping to pick your brain a bit. This looks a bit bizarre even by Miami standards. Let's go inside."

Both men entered through the front door with bright lights on and CSI performing their investigation. Jones closed his eyes for a long second hoping for a different scenario but both bodies remained where he had seen them before.

"We're going to run gunshot residue on their hands, but CSI told me it doesn't look like either man fired a shot," Marshfield stated.

"Yet, both men are dead."

"I can't figure out the chairs. What do you make of that?" Marshfield asked.

"I have no idea. Rivers played it close to the vest. I'm sure Agent Oliver knew more about what he was doing than me."

"Let's call him in then," Marshfield replied.

"Didn't you hear? Oliver was in that chopper explosion today. This is all connected. Somehow the task force lost its cover. They came after me to."

"How the hell does Sullivan fit into this?"

"Not very neatly I'm afraid. Anything else regarding Sullivan, you better ask Mr. Bullock," Jones answered.

"I will. He'll be in Miami soon. You're free to go here but you need to meet him at the Sullivan residence at 7pm. He'll be there with one of his units. I'll have a squad run you back to your hotel."

"Thanks. But my Jeep is parked up the drive. If you had to make a guess, what the hell happened here?" Jones asked.

"Well, I'd think it was someone who despised both men for some reason. I know most of Sullivan's local associates. I always thought he was kind of dirty, but Senator Warren cleaned him up good. Without knowing Rivers it's hard to add it up. Judging by the guys chasing you, probably Santora's posse. He must have charged a small mint for this job. The helicopter explosion, strange coincidence if it was an accident which I doubt it was. I'm not going to lie to you. This one might go unsolved and get swept under the rug. Too messy. The Senator wields that kind of power around here."

"Thanks for the info and the heads up. I'll guarantee you one thing though. I won't let this go."

Chapter 45
Looted and Broken

JONES PULLED HIS JEEP into the Sullivan's driveway with his hair still damp from his five-minute shower. The compound was alive unlike his previous visit the night before. It was almost a relief to walk through the front door without having to be a burglar. The site that greeted him was totally unexpected.

Crime scene investigators were spread throughout every room. Uniformed officers were on the outside grounds searching the area by flashlight. A half-dozen men in casual clothes walked around talking on phones and Jones guessed they were Bullock's crew. Empty wall spots were redundant throughout every room as someone had stripped the house of every single painting. Nothing was left hanging. It was like the Ambassador heist but more thorough. Somebody evened up the score with Derek Sullivan in more ways than one.

"Are you Jones?" a middle-aged man with a bushy mustache clad in jeans asked.

"Yes," Jones replied in almost a hush.

"Upstairs in an office. Bullock is expecting you."

"Is he in a bad mood?"

"He's always in a bad mood," the man replied with a laugh.

The winding staircase looked vastly larger with bare walls if that was even possible. Elegance gone, replaced with an insurance nightmare. Technicians were lifting fingerprints, but everybody knew they were wasting their time. This was a professional job and sloppiness wouldn't be tolerated. Detectives at the top of the stairs were talking about the missing security detail. No bodies were found, possibly they were the culprits. Jones knew that was wishful thinking.

Jones walked into the Sullivan office which he knew too well. Graydon Bullock was sitting behind the desk peering into a computer screen while an agency computer geek smacked away on the keyboard.

"Good evening Mr. Jones," Bullock offered while not taking an eye off the computer screen.

"Good evening sir. What happened here?"

"Well, somebody looted this place of every piece of artwork. Mrs. Sullivan is upstairs with a nervous breakdown and her attorney says somebody hacked into all the Sullivan accounts and took every last cent."

"She lawyered up already?"

Bullock finally looked up at Jones and paused for a second.

"The rich are lawyered up twenty-four seven. Funny how that works isn't it. A normal response from a victim would be complete cooperation. Instead, I'm greeted from behind a wall of silence by an over-priced mouthpiece that doesn't appear too smart. You would think he would be helping us if he ever wanted to get paid. His client doesn't have a cent to her name now."

"It's been a low information case from the start," Jones countered. "Even Rivers and Oliver kept me in the dark for the most part."

"Sorry to hear about their demise. I am glad you're alive though."

"Thank you."

"It's tons of paperwork every time I lose someone."

Bullock didn't break a smile and Jones couldn't tell if this was a half-hearted attempt at humor. His first platoon leader in Afghanistan was a lot like Bullock. His name was Finnegan who was hard as hell to read. Then one-day Jones was pinned down in a hostile village holed up in a ten-cent hut running out of ammo.

Just when things looked bleak, Finnegan rode to the rescue with a half dozen Humvees and saved his ass without saying a word.

"The FBI will handle the investigation regarding Rivers and Oliver," Bullock stated shaking Jones from his trip down memory lane.

"I'll be glad to help them with the investigation."

"I appreciate that. I really do. Unfortunately, the Bureau is pissed at me. Losing two agents will do that. The chopper crash was due to a small bomb like we thought. Any idea what Oliver was doing with the Sullivan boys?"

"No sir and judging by his phone messages Rivers was in the dark also. Are you sure I can't lend a hand? On the unofficial down low of course," Jones asked with a slight degree of childish pleading.

"We'll stay out of it for now. But take a walk into that little room for a minute."

Jones looked towards his right where Bullock motioned and could barely believe his eyes as he walked toward a small doorway in the wall. It was a secret door, three feet wide leading to a very elaborate small room. The dim room lighting concealed it quite well.

Bullock escorted Jones to the room and flipped on the light. It was more of a viewing room than a safe room. A brown English oversized leather chair sat in the middle of the room with a small wine table next to it. On the table sat a single bottle of wine next to a short-wave radio and an empty Bordeaux glass. The ensemble faced the south wall with a dust free rectangular spot in the middle of the wall where a painting recently hung.

Inside the spot hung a single Polaroid photograph. Jones walked up for a closer look with Bullock beside him sporting a slight smile. Jones started smiling himself while looking at it.

"That's right Mr. Jones. It's a photograph of the other Dutch Sister which was hanging in this very spot."

"An art thief with a sense of humor I see," Jones stated.

"Indeed," Bullock replied. "Very interesting that Dunbar gets caught red-handed with one of the Dutch Sisters and Sullivan has the other one stolen from his house. The dirty bastard must have spent hours in this room gazing at his prized catch. All these years and it was in Miami nearly the whole time."

"A lot of people died for that painting and I was just feet away from it last night," Jones offered about his impromptu mission."

"Yes, I know. We found a couple of your bugs. Nice placement although a bit risky and against my advice. I'm sure you would have heard this happening if not for the afternoon distractions."

Nothing but distractions Jones thought to himself as he was reminded about his pleasant afternoon with Rachelle. Although he was certain Bullock was referring to his late FBI colleagues.

"Where is their daughter Rachelle?" Jones asked cautiously.

"Nothing on her location. With a dead husband and two burned up sons that would bring some sense of relief to her mother. We've tried her phones, went to her residence and even called Senator Warren. Nobody has seen her since yesterday it seems."

Jones stared off in the distance. She must have known something was wrong, but everything seemed perfect in the afternoon. Maybe she was in danger and that was her way of saying goodbye. An empty feeling was settling in.

"Would you mind if I had a word with Mrs. Sullivan? I know she has a lawyer, but I believe I could find something useful," Jones asked.

Bullock thought for a moment while breaking into a small grin.

"I should warn you, she seems a little loopy. I think she doctored up also."

"That might work to our advantage. I can handle the attorney."

"Let me lead the way then," Bullock replied.

Both men walked down the barren hallway and Bullock knocked on the door. A few seconds later a gray haired corporate mouthpiece in a navy-blue pinstripe Hugo Boss suit, opened the door with his yellow power tie trying to make a statement.

"Do you have some news?" the lawyer asked in an even monotone.

"No sir," Bullock replied maintaining his civility even though he was tired from a lifetime of speaking with attorneys. "But I have a friend of the family here to offer condolences."

"Let them in Frank!" Ceci shouted reluctantly in a beaten down tone from a hell soaked afternoon of terror.

Lawyer Frank opened the door and gestured them in with his right hand to oblige Ceci.

"Mrs. Sullivan, my name is Sinjin. I'm a friend of your daughters."

"You look vaguely familiar. Do you know where she is?"

"No. But I will look for her. I was hoping you could run down the last twenty-four hours?"

"I've made it very clear gentleman. Mrs. Sullivan is making no statements today," The exasperated attorney interrupted.

"I'm just talking about Rachelle. I'm trying to help Mrs. Sullivan."

"That's fine Frank. I need to help anyway I can."

Ceci sighed deeply and looked left trying to recall events in a semi-drugged out state.

"She was here last night for a little while. She dropped by unexpected. I only talked to her for a minute before going to bed with a migraine that's been lingering for a while. She talked to her father last night for a while. That was nice. They drifted apart once she started working for the Senator. That was more her father's fault than hers. He always guarded his privacy"

"Do you know what they talked about?" Jones asked.

"Let's keep the conversation on a straight road please," Frank interjected.

"I'm sorry," Jones replied with a peace offering gesture of the hands. "How long did she stay?"

"I'm not sure. She was gone before the first theft last night. Do you think it's related to that? A kidnapping maybe?"

Bullock and Jones stole a glance towards each other. She was the first person to mention last night's theft. It was minor league compared to what happened here today. Jones wasn't even sure the Sullivan's noticed it let alone reported it to the authorities. Maybe his mission last night with Rivers set off a chain of unseen events costing people their lives. He was feeling a bit guilty now and was silently stuttering at a loss for words until Bullock came to his rescue.

"We are investigating everything Mrs. Sullivan. When we find something out, rest assured, Frank here will be my first phone call," Bullock replied with a line similar that he had used hundreds of times before.

"Did you talk to her today?" Jones asked.

"No, I didn't. I meant to give her a call around lunchtime. Unfortunately," Ceci paused to measure her words carefully, "events happened and when I called her to break the bad news, her phone was no longer in service."

The conversation was basically worthless, and Ceci Sullivan was fading with every passing minute. In another ten minutes, she would be sleeping off the pain of a broken heart only to have it return with the sunrise.

Bullock gave a weak wave towards the sad woman. "We'll let you get some sleep. If you remember anything else have Frank give me a call, please."

Ceci stood up and walked towards Jones grabbing his hands. "If you find her, please tell her that I love her like my handpicked angel."

Jones nodded while staring Ceci straight in the eyes. "I'll find her Mrs. Sullivan."

Chapter 46
Nice Work

THE SLIGHT BREEZE FELT perfect with nothing but sunshine as Graydon Bullock sat down at the table for a poolside breakfast. Jones would be down any minute and he wouldn't be very happy with the news. At least this atmosphere would lighten the disappointment he hoped. It was such a gorgeous day, quite the opposite of the storms of yesterday.

Bullock saw Jones across the pool as he took the liberty to order the eggs benedict and mojitos for them both. He was due back at headquarters for afternoon meetings, so breakfast and de-briefing would be rushed. Jones made it to the table as the waitress delivered the mojitos.

"A little early for mojitos, isn't it?" Jones asked with a smile.

"I have an early plane to catch. I'm trying to seize the day as they say. They found a burned-out van this morning in the Everglades. Two scorched bodies inside. It looks to be our missing security detail."

Jones grimaced. "I wasn't holding out much hope for those poor bastards. All the witnesses eliminated along with a van full of possible evidence. Very efficient."

"You did a really good job Jones. We appreciate it."

"I didn't do that much. Too many people died in Miami yesterday."

"You stayed alive despite a bunch of bad guys trying to kill you. In this game, staying alive is half the battle. Listen, I know you were trying to make a mother feel better, but in the future, don't make promises like that," Bullock stated.

"It wasn't exactly a promise. But I do think I can help find her," Jones replied taking a sip of his mojito.

"That's the other reason I'm here. And this is straight from the top. We're shutting it down on our end."

"Are you serious? We don't have all the answers yet. Two FBI agents are dead. The Sullivan's have three dead with one still missing. The Ambassador heist is still an open book." Jones rattled off with his voice rising.

Bullock shook his head. "Sometimes we don't get all the answers. That's life. We were purely assisting on this one. Dunbar and Sullivan were obviously connected to the heist. We even recovered one of the masterpieces and know that the other one is on the move. The FBI will keep looking for it and they will investigate the death of their own just like we would. The case is officially closed on our end. I guarantee you this though. I will use you again. You impressed the hell out of me kid."

"I appreciate that. I know it's not your fault, but this doesn't sit well with me and I'll leave it at that."

"Understood. Stay here another night on Uncle Sam and enjoy the sunshine. The FBI will sort this out. They already cleared out their rooms. I have no idea what if anything they found. Trust me though. They will make someone pay for Rivers and Oliver. It might take a while, but someone will pay."

After Bullock left for his plane, Jones ordered another mojito and went for a walk on the beach. He realized his spirits were at rock bottom when the bikini clad South Beach crew barely gained his attention. Letting things go never came easy to him. Somebody needed to be held accountable for Rivers and Oliver.

Even more bothersome was the disappearance of Rachelle Sullivan. He refused to believe that she might be dead floating somewhere in the Everglades. Most people didn't hold similar beliefs with three members of the Sullivan clan confirmed dead. She was tough and resilient with incredible street smarts. Personal interest aside, he wasn't going to stop looking for her although he tried his best to keep that from Bullock.

Nobody alive seemed to have any answers. The only person who might know everything was Santora. Finding this man was damn near impossible. Miami was his town. Bought and paid for with everybody watching his back. Every time he seemed close to finding him, someone tried to take him out. That made it personal and nobody was stopping him from doing his own personal investigation on his own dime even though those dimes weren't in great abundance.

Jones stopped and grabbed a Red Stripe at the Sand Bar. It was time to formulate a game plan and do this his way. Rivers wasn't here to ride herd over him anymore. He needed to track down Santora by any means necessary.

It took ten minutes to track down Detective Marshfield. Under the guise of working the copter crash he asked for an address for a license plate number. It happened to be the plate number that Ruben's mother gave him or sold him depending on your point of view.

A dispatcher reached out within a minute to give Jones the information. Sitting in front of him written on a white wrinkled bar napkin was the likely identify of a man only known as Simon. He was the man in the Miami Underworld who seemed to know all the players and all the angles. Jones decided to order another Red Stripe and enjoy a South Beach afternoon. He would visit Simon tonight and the information was going to be free.

Chapter 47
Low Profile

JONES WAS GETTING ANTSY as he was nearing the three-hour mark parked and waiting about a block from the North Miami address that dispatch had given him earlier in the day. He knew it was the right place as the car in question had returned to the white stucco two-story house about an hour before. It was a nice house but nothing extravagant like the palatial Sullivan estate.

Both the house and the car belonged to one Peter Cromwell. It sounded British, but Jones didn't know for sure. A thorough background search didn't turn up one single fact about this man. That's how Jones knew it was his man for sure. These days someone must try very hard to stay off the radar. It's nearly impossible but this guy appeared to be a professional's professional. He was a low profile mastermind to the maximum.

On the way to his new private mission Jones stopped at a hardware store and bought some rope and bungee cords. Along with his Glock he was prepared for anticipated trouble. Making someone give up information was never easy if it was their livelihood. The act of persuasion wasn't in his comfort zone, but he wasn't about to walk away empty handed. He only had one chance with Cromwell and he was going to get his information with whatever means necessary.

It was almost ten pm and Jones was getting antsy to make his move. There was an old-fashioned service door on the side of the house. He could softly break out a window pane and let himself in the house. A brick wall encompassed the entire yard, but it was more a pleasing visual effect rather than hardcore security. No security cameras were visible. The man's product was in his head. It couldn't be stolen. He was exceedingly smart and didn't draw any attention to himself.

Jones passed a small Cuban coffee shop about a mile away. He decided a pit stop and a Cuban coffee would be a good idea. When he returned, everything would be a go and most of the neighbors in bed or watching the late show with loud air conditioning units smothering outside noises.

On his way back from the coffee shop, he changed the plan. There was too much risk of getting shot like a common burglar. He needed to get up close and personal to decrease those chances. He parked about two blocks away and walked the rest of the way.

The fence was easy to vault even with a half full cup of coffee in one hand. He leaned against the fence finishing his coffee then tossed the paper cup down a drain. It was a quiet evening and all the immediate neighbors seemed to be minding their own business. If things went south, he had Detective Marshfield's number on speed dial.

Jones knocked on the front door and could hear footsteps almost immediately. They paused for a second to look out the peephole before flinging open the door in an angry haste. A muscular man with dark eyes looked at Jones with a mixture of impatience and audacity. Jones assumed the man was armed so he would need a moment of distraction to fell his prey.

"Is this the Shula residence?" Jones asked.

"You have the wrong house mister. How did you bypass the gate?" the dark eyed man asked.

"I jumped the wall. Sorry, you're the only house that looked occupied. I'm looking for my friend Glen. I don't have my glasses." Jones pulled a piece of paper from his pocket. "Can you look at this address and point the way please?"

The man started to close the door, but Jones shoved the paper towards the man.

"Please sir. You're my only hope."

Reluctantly, the man grabbed the paper and looked down at it. Before he realized it was blank, his jaw was the recipient of a right cross that sounded like a baseball hitting the sweet spot of a bat. He fell backwards hitting his head on the Mexican tile floor. Dark eyes laid out cold as Jones closed the door and dragged him by the collar back into the house.

Jones could hear a television on in the back of a house. He creeped along the edge of the wall and opened the door a crack. A shaven headed man about sixty years old was sitting at a counter eating a ham sandwich. The room was solely illuminated by the television light. Here sits another wealthy man trying to keep his power bill to a minimum.

"Don't move," Jones said in a calm steady voice while pointing the Glock at the man's bald head.

The man looked up from his sandwich with obvious surprise. Yet, he had calm eyes and Jones could tell that it wasn't the first time he looked down the barrel of a gun.

"Is there something I can do for you, young man?" the older gentleman asked still holding his sandwich.

Jones didn't offer a reply as he walked up to the man. His message was obvious as he brought the Glock full force down on the man's shiny skull.

About ten minutes later Cromwell woke up tied to his kitchen chair. He was pissed off and his head was throbbing with blood starting to dry on his scalp. His driver was tied up in the next room. Jones made a cursory search of the house, but all the occupants were accounted for.

"Go ahead. Loot the place and get the hell out." Cromwell stated barely raising his tone.

"I'm not here to rob you. I want information. Where is Santora?"

"I don't know who that is?" Cromwell replied without hesitation.

"Yes, you do. You're the information man. You know everything in South Florida. People, places, you can even arrange a jailhouse murder. Or do you call it assassination?"

"Listen kid, you have me confused with someone else. Untie me now and leave. I suggest you do it right now."

Jones anticipated this reaction and wasn't going to play games. There was too much on the line, so he produced an eight-inch stiletto switchblade knife with a white pearl handle from his back pocket. Without saying another word, he thrust the stiletto blade right in the mid-point of Cromwell's left thigh. Judging by Cromwell's excruciated look the tip of the razor- sharp blade must have hit the femur. Jones leaned down and smiled while starring into Cromwell's eyes. Remarkably the eyes returned to a state of calm almost immediately.

The wound was hardly bleeding. The knife was sharp like a surgical instrument. It wouldn't cause a lot of damage or more pain unless someone chose to twist it around in the flesh. It was a favorite interrogation technique employed by the Japanese during World War II. The idea came to Jones during the afternoon on the beach while he was thinking about his earlier encounter with the prison guard. If it worked so well unintentionally, he figured he might as well give it a whirl on purpose.

"I suggest you tell me where Santora is and avoid causing yourself any more pain."

Cromwell laughed while muffling in the stinging pain with a knife sticking out of his leg. Most men would be blabbering out information by now but clearly Cromwell wasn't an ordinary bloke.

"Obviously, I misjudged you. You wear the hippy beach look well. It doesn't change the fact that I have no information for you nor do I have the slightest bloody idea what you are talking about." Cromwell responded through clenched teeth to control the pain but more so his anger. He learned a long time ago that calmness served him better when the opponent expects anger.

Jones looked down at the protruding knife and reluctantly moved his right hand towards it to accomplish his mission. A man doesn't always need to enjoy his job to do it well.

"Before you do that son, you might want to give Senator Warren a call. My guess is you're some sort of government agent. A rogue FBI agent maybe? Make a phone call before you get yourself into a mess that will swallow you up. He will set you straight about me."

Cromwell's response caught Jones totally off guard. The man with calm eyes was good, very good. He was even more connected than Jones thought if he was telling the truth. It was never good to make a poker bluff when your opponent has a knife sticking out of his leg. Options were becoming very limited.

Jones paused for a few seconds choosing his words carefully. "Two of my friends are dead. Three members of the Sullivan family are also dead, and one is missing. Santora knows something and you know Santora. I simply wish to speak with him which is no skin off your back. Better to lose some professional standing than your life mister."

"No offense but I don't think this Santora fella would like the way you speak to people. And I've seen the news. I have nothing to do with your late friends. Do both of us a favor and call the Senator?"

Jones thought hard for a moment about his dwindling options. He couldn't kill this guy and walk away without repercussions if he was connected to the Senator. Chances are that someone would eventually figure it was him and then he would be looking over his shoulder for eternity. Calling the Senator for a quick chat would lead to a phone call from Bullock. He was in a box. Going rogue was more complicated than he bargained for.

Jones tied a tourniquet around Cromwell's leg and gagged both men. This guy wasn't talking that much he knew. He made a reservation on the next flight for the Capitol. If the Senator knew Cromwell, he would be back the next day to release him. If the Senator denied Cromwell's existence the neighbors should smell the flesh rot in a week as he turned off the air conditioning.

Chapter 48

The Red Eye

JONES PACKED ALL HIS GEAR and loaded it in his Jeep. At Miami International Airport, he parked in a highly visible secured spot and tucked away his gear as best he could. It was too damn easy to steal things out of a Jeep Wrangler, but he hoped for the best since he planned on returning later that day. TSA gave him a good once over since flying these days without luggage was suspicious. Once they verified he had a round trip ticket he was cleared to board the 727.

Despite being void of solid sleep the last two nights he managed to keep his composure with a crying baby two rows in front of him. An old man in an aisle seat was snoring before the plane taxied to the runway and Jones tried unsuccessfully to follow suit.

Jones was a man without a detailed plan. He was about to barge into the office of a United States Senator and ask about a mutual acquaintance in North Miami. He decided to leave the part about a knife sticking out of Crowell's thigh out of the equation. Obtaining a meeting with the Senator might be the hardest part. Knowing if he was lying would only take a minute. No matter how good of a spin master old man Warren was, he wouldn't be able to create a believable story in a situation like this. It was vital to catch him off guard and put him on the spot for some real answers.

Everybody could feel the humidity the moment the plane doors opened at Dulles Airport. It was the usual circus trying to get off the plane. At least the cab stand was efficient, and Jones arrived at the Dirksen Building in about forty minutes.

The Senator's office was even bigger than he anticipated. Secretaries and staffers were sitting everywhere in their own side offices. Trying to get a drop-in appointment with the Senator would be tough. He certainly couldn't drop Bullock's name anymore since the Agency shutdown their end. It would be huge trouble if Bullock caught wind that he was in D.C.

He approached an elderly secretary with gray hair thinking he could work her with some charm. She appeared close to seventy years old and it always bothered him to see older people working that late in life. Maybe she was a true believer in the Senator but he highly doubted that to be the case.

In a roundabout way, he tried to get an appointment without explaining why it was needed. The lady politely listened to his story since he was a constituent. Deep down she was wishing he would get to the point. Once he dropped Rachelle Sullivan's name her demeanor changed, and he was given an immediate appointment with a female staffer down the hall. It wasn't the golden goose, but it was a start. Hopefully he wasn't short in the charm department today.

Samantha Jensen was a tall dark former beauty queen who was hanging up her telephone as Jones walked through her doorway.

"You must be Mr. Jones," Samantha stated with smiling approval. "Please sit."

"I am. Thank you for seeing me on such short notice."

"I understand you're looking for Rachelle Sullivan. She spends most of her time in the Senator's Miami office. She hasn't been in D.C. for well over a week."

"Yes, I'm aware of that. I'm a friend of the family's. Her mother is concerned so I told her I would come up here, look around and speak with the Senator personally."

"A telephone call would have been easier. Unfortunately, he isn't in this office today."

"What do you do for the Senator?" Jones asked trying to take the conversation to a more personal level.

"I'm a senior level assistant. I keep track of the Senator's D.C. schedule much like Rachelle does for the Senator down in Miami."

"Did you know Rachelle very well?"

"I've known her about three years. We've had some good times. I'm sure this is a scheduling mix up. She will show up soon."

"Spoken like a good lawyer." Jones replied with a smile.

"D.C. is very competitive Mr. Jones. All in all, we hit it off fine under the circumstances. Our world is a bit different than yours I imagine."

"Actually, our worlds seem to be colliding. I don't like it, but it was inevitable I guess. Any chance I could get a moment with the Senator?"

"He's not in the office now. He has a lunch appointment followed by a meeting. Then happy hour with the Chief Justice."

"Yes, doing the work of the people." Jones replied with a sarcastic smile.

"I'll personally get a message to him. Could I get your number?"

"Allow me."

Jones leaned over her desk, grabbed a pen and leisurely wrote his number on a piece of paper. A clipboard on the desk revealed a daily schedule. Even upside down, Jones could make out Occidental Grill at 12:30pm.

He gazed into her eyes as he pulled back from her desk with a whiff of sweet perfume permeating the air.

"Please give me a call if you can think of anything helpful?"

"You have my word on that," she replied with a silent dismissal.

Jones retraced his steps confident that his phone wouldn't be ringing anytime soon. Even if she knew some real information she wouldn't be revealing it to him. The Senator would make sure everyone was silent on this front. Jensen wouldn't risk her job to help a rival nor him. Rachelle Sullivan would stay lost unless he pushed some buttons.

As he was almost back to the receptionist area he caught a glimpse on his left of Rachelle Sullivan's name plate next to a closed door. Without hesitation, he opened the door and took a couple steps inside. It was a tiny office bearing a desk and a single chair next to it. It was obvious this office was seldom used. Besides a Miami skyline print there wasn't anything else of substance besides a dusty desktop computer.

"You were close friends I presume?" a voice from behind him inquired.

Jones turned around to see the elderly receptionist who intuitively found her grandmotherly inner self within the last ten minutes.

"Just a friend of the family," Jones replied with a small guilty smile.

The receptionist smiled knowing that was a company line.

"She has been seeing someone the last three or four years. I never met him though. Not even a photo. She was biding her time trying to figure things out I imagine. A career girl you know, wanting to make her own bones in this world rather than being a trust fund kid."

"When was the last time you spoke with her?" Jones asked inquisitively as this woman seemed to have some sort of personal connection with Rachelle.

"A few mornings ago. She was in a car accident where the whole vehicle exploded. She was taking the day off and I figured she turned that into a few more days."

Jones stared straight ahead not offering a comment. He'd been trying hard to forget that incident and recent events made that impossible.

"She said she met someone new." The receptionist continued. "She seemed rather enchanted by him. Sadly, she said the timing wasn't right. I think that was bothering her quite a bit."

Jones gazed at the lovely lady and wanted to give her a hug. Besides the bad timing part, the enchantment was mutual which greatly pleased him.

"I wouldn't worry yourself to death. She'll show up soon."

"No offense, but how do you know that?" Jones asked knowing that the real world isn't always a happy ending.

"Because she's a tough broad just like me," she replied with a wry grin.

Chapter 49
Capitol Lunch

JONES CABBED IT TO the Occidental Grill rather than take a leisurely stroll in the late morning humidity. He had ninety minutes to kill and hunger pains were reminding his body that he needed to eat. After he arrived, he went straight for the bar and ordered a Corona without lime and a lunch menu.

The brunette bartender with a sexy smile tried to make small talk but Jones was more interested in the Chief Burger medium rare with a side of fries. He had enough time to eat and clear his head. The Senator could fill in the missing pieces and Jones wasn't leaving D.C. without some answers.

The lunch seemed to energize Jones or perhaps it was the three Coronas. Whichever it was, Jones ordered one more Corona and settled his tab. Senator Warren was due any moment, so he turned his seat to keep an eye on the front door. It was a popular place for all the movers and shakers. Congressman, lobbyists, mistresses and high-priced hookers all filled the joint. They all had the same underlying purpose. They were looking for a little action in one way or another.

Senator Warren arrived five minutes ahead of his reservation by himself and was escorted to his table. Jones watched the arrogant bastard decline a cocktail and grab the menu without a measure of kindness. Jones didn't have time to lecture him about basic human manners as he seized the moment and walked up to the table and took a seat opposite the Senator.

"Good afternoon Senator. I'm a friend of Mrs. Sullivan and I'm helping her find her daughter

Rachelle. You remember her, don't you? Since you aren't lifting a finger to help find her, I thought I would give it a shot."

Senator Warren starred at Jones in disgust but not dismay. There wasn't a hint of surprise in his eyes which alarmed Jones.

"I know who you are asshole. Don't think you're smarter than me. Simon had that knife pulled out of his leg this morning. You're messing with the wrong guy."

Jones was taken aback that Simon found help and the Senator admitted to knowing him. He underestimated Simon who must have had a safe system in place for events like last night. The Senator wasn't the least bit intimidated, but Jones put on his best poker face and pressed on.

"Let's talk about your friend Simon for a minute."

"Let's not," The Senator replied. "I'm leaving now but you can talk to the gentleman two tables behind you."

As the Senator left Graydon Bullock took his seat across from Jones. He sighed heavily and looked down at the white linen tablecloth. So much for Jones keeping a low profile in D.C. Bullock nodded to two men behind Jones and they took a seat at the table directly behind them.

"It's my own fault," Bullock stated matter of fact after taking a sip of water. "I debated telling you more in Miami, but I thought perhaps you would go back to Key West and do whatever it is that one does in Key West. Obviously, I was mistaken Mr. Jones."

"Obviously," Jones replied finally looking up to meet the icy gaze of his boss.

"You can't bust the chops of a United States Senator and not expect repercussions. Luckily, I'm here to repair the situation."

"What is the situation sir? Perhaps if you could enlighten me, I could lend you a hand."

"Lend me a hand? Or, lend Rachelle Sullivan a hand?" Bullock asked in a hushed voice.

"I'm here to help. There's still more to learn about this heist and there's four kids missing. Plus, Dunbar and Sullivan have a criminal empire to expose and the Senator knows something about it. This whole damn mess blew up right in his face. In Miami!"

"That's right, it blew up. It's a mess. In Miami! But not all messes need to be solved. Sometimes they just get swept under the rug."

"Well that's obviously happening here," Jones replied in disgust.

Bullock slapped the table hard in anger and looked around before lowering his voice to a harsh hush. "Don't think I like it any more than you do. You want some answers? I'll give you some answers."

"I would appreciate it," Jones replied.

"It's quite simple really. Warren is the Senior Senator in Florida. The crusty old fart is extremely popular and connected as you already know. He helps us with our Cuban problem. Anti-Castro, Pro-Castro, he knows them all and he's quite versed in playing both sides and keeping us apprised of every situation, so we can get ahead of it. In return, we turn our heads for some of his friends."

"Like Dunbar and Sullivan?"

"Like Dunbar and Sullivan," Bullock replied pausing to take another sip of water. "To be fair, they weren't even on our radar. He kept them under wraps pretty damn good."

"It doesn't hurt that the crusty old fart is a ranking member of the committee that keeps you well financed?" Jones asked already knowing the answer to this question.

"That's correct," Bullock replied as he was quite impressed that Jones was quickly learning the way that Capitol Hill truly worked.

"How does Simon fit into this?"

"Easy, he's the Senator's bastard brother. His father had a thing for Havana whores. They are half-brothers, although he portrays a British persona, he's a Yankee through and through. He does the heavy lifting. Specializes in political assassinations and that is classified information Mr. Jones."

"Thank you for sharing. Rest assured, I know how to keep my mouth shut."

"I don't doubt that. Now that you have some answers, I need you to go back to Key West. We'll handle it from here and I'll let you know what develops. These two men will give you a lift to the airport and see that you make your flight."

The two men stood up and took positions on each side of Jones. He looked to both sides and grinned sarcastically at Bullock. If he wanted to make a point bad enough he figured he stood a decent chance of knocking their teeth in despite a combined weight of nearly five-hundred pounds. But, it wouldn't do any good to make a scene. Bullock had clearly made up his mind to ice him out. Instead, he simply gave up the moment with a parting shot.

"I thought you were my friend Graydon."

Chapter 50
Never Give Up

CECI SULLIVAN BARELY TOUCHED her fruit plate as she listened to her attorney spell out more dire straits. On an ordinary day, the view from the Sullivan veranda would make even the most intense person relax. But today, Ceci decided she wanted vengeance at any cost and she knew it would cost her plenty. Finding her daughter was the only way to pick up the pieces and move on. She could make the family funeral arrangements herself, but she needed her attorney Frank to help on the vengeance front.

Frank had been a law school friend of Senator Warren and knew where most of the skeletons were buried in Miami. The Senator was circling the wagons and keeping a low profile while Ceci Sullivan lost most of her fortune in less than twenty-four hours. There was only one thing the Miami Elite didn't tolerate in their ranks and that was poor people. Ceci would soon fade into oblivion and Frank knew that. He was only keeping her counsel now because this information could be valuable later.

"I understand how bad you want to find Rachelle. I don't think there's anyone better to find her than the authorities. They have a lot of resources for that kind of thing Ceci," Frank stated in a lawyerly type manner.

"I need to know if she's safe. Right now, I don't know if she's dead, kidnapped or in hiding. I'm hoping for the later, but I need her found."

Frank was known throughout the Florida legal community as a straight shooter. If he believed a client guilty he would let them know that and double his fee. Out of respect for Derek's recent demise he was softening his edges a bit and it was getting him nowhere with his delusional client.

"Ceci, let's face the cold hard facts together. You are broke. Your money isn't coming back unless there's a major miracle. While I have the connections for this type of operation the funds to bankroll it aren't there dear."

"I have the resources Frank. Resources that Derek didn't even know existed. I always have a backup plan. Always," Ceci replied completely fed up and aggravated with Frank's assessment and overall defeatist tone.

At this point in her life she found it astonishing that Derek fooled so many intelligent people. It was his gift as a grifter she surmised. She made most of the important decisions and let Derek believe they were his decisions. That was her gift, fooling men her entire life.

Frank thought heavily on what Ceci just said. Maybe she was making it up as a last resort for help. After all, desperate people say desperate things. Derek Sullivan seemed so sharp and astute. Could he have been fooled? Maybe, but he needed to know for sure.

"What kind of resources?" Frank asked.

"I have safety deposit boxes full of cash in rural community banks throughout the state. I have jewelry that can be unloaded fast. At least a dozen cars with no notes and plenty of life insurance coming my way that nobody knows about. Plus, this damn house. Those thieves couldn't get to it all. I'll let you know when I'm flat busted Frank but if you underestimate me one more time you'll become my ex-attorney."

Ceci had been preparing for this day the moment the Ambassador heist was over, and nobody did it better. Sure, she wasn't close to a billionaire anymore, but she knew the odds of keeping it all weren't great. Everybody has a hand in your pocket and somebody is bound to find it sooner or later.

"Calm down Ceci. I will help you," he said apologetically. "Understand though that the Senator can't. He needs to insulate himself from this situation. Can't you use your usual muscle? It will be cheaper that way."

"It's complicated." Ceci hesitated thinking of how much she should reveal. After all, some of her muscle was responsible for recent events.

"If you find someone, someone damn good, I'll give you a million in cash to make it work."

Frank didn't hesitate to stand up and dial a number that he had memorized. It was for extreme circumstances and the source was only to be used sparingly as he was expensive.

"What can I do for you?" a monotone voice answered that seemed more preoccupied by something other than a possible business arrangement.

"Hello Simon. This is Frank. I have a job for you."

Simon's leg was stitched up and the pain medication put him in a groggy state. The leg was protracted in a straight position and physical therapy would be required to rehabilitate his quadriceps muscle after the stitches were removed. His professional shield had been penetrated by some government clown named Sinjin Jones and he wasn't happy about it. He was surprised to be getting a job offer but apparently word of this fiasco hadn't hit the streets yet. Under the circumstance, he thought he better take this job in case work dried up for a while.

"I need someone to find Rachelle Simon," Frank stated.

"That's a pretty tall order. Everybody is looking for this broad. The authorities are all over it. I would hate to commit resources and expenditures to find her only to have them run upon her first," Simon replied not liking his chances of finding her first.

"I understand that. I'll make it worth your while. Half million if you find her and a hundred grand if you don't to cover your expenses."

Simon thought about the proposition for a few silent seconds. "Well, I do know someone who's in need of a decent payday."

"Is he any good? Ceci Sullivan has an acquaintance looking for Rachelle, but I don't harbor much hope in that guy."

"Of course he is, but what's her guy's name? I don't need my professionals running into amateurs."

"Sinjin Jones. He was at the Sullivan's house. I'm not sure how he fits into this to be honest."

"Under the circumstances my good friend, I accept this deal. I'll keep you updated."

Simon hung up the phone with a gleeful smile despite the dull ache in his leg. To make a profit while getting revenge was but a dream about to come true.

Chapter 51
The Banishment

JONES WAS SEETHING from his official escort out of the Occidental Grill. His escorts weren't merely satisfied with dropping him off at the airport. They put him on the plane flashing identification at various security points. He felt like a terrorist with his fellow passengers shooting him a nervous glance wondering about their personal safety. At least the flight was short but now he was even more determined to find Rachelle Sullivan.

Bullock sat in his government office and leaned back in his plush chair massaging his temples as he felt a headache coming on. He was already up to his ass in conflicts and problems. He had one of his operative running guns in Afghanistan to friendlies with a blown cover. Except the operative didn't know that and getting word to him was proving difficult. Another operative was in deep Mexico with a rogue cartel member and he was a week late contacting Bullock.

Jones was testing his patience, but the kid was growing on him. He reminded Bullock of himself when it came to initiative and wanting to bring down the bad guys. That's exactly the way Bullock played the game when he was a field operative. Now, he sat mostly behind a desk calling the shots and making nice with various members of Congress to keep his department funded and protect them from themselves half the time. How he yearned for the old days.

There was no doubt that Jones would look even harder for the girl now. Bullock would be disappointed if he didn't. Shrinks would call it suppressed motivation. Part of him wanted Jones to find Rachelle

Sullivan and bring this whole shit show to a conclusion no matter who ended up being exposed. If Jones went international, he had better resources to keep an eye on him.

Bullock threw in a call to his FBI friends at the Miami office. They could operate under the pretense of Jones interfering with their agency investigation which wasn't far from the truth. They could only detain him for twenty-four hours. They didn't have the available manpower to deal with him longer anyway.

As Jones disembarked the plane and entered the terminal he was greeted by FBI agents LaRue and Hanson. They were casually dressed men with even more bulk than the set of guys that put him on the plane. Instantly, they put an official document in front of his face for a quick read.

They needed information for their end of the investigation and Bullock granted his permission with the utmost cooperation. Jones knew this was more of a roadblock than cooperation, but he would play their silly little government game, at least for now. Bullock was a smooth operator to drop a dime on him like this.

Chapter 52
New Kid in Town

THE VENEZUELAN USED many aliases over the course of his career. He had not uttered his birth name in at least two decades to the point where it was almost forgotten. At six-foot two and a two- hundred and fifty-pound muscular frame he rather liked his moniker, 'The Venezuelan.' His piercing brown eyes, goatee and short graying hair gave off a menacing look without even trying. His real name wasn't important anyway. Simon would provide him with expert workable documents and a passport that would never be questioned. Whatever name Simon gave him, The Venezuelan would become. He was a professional down to the bone.

The Venezuelan was coming out of retirement. At forty-five years of age he had been out of the game for six years. His career started out as a general thug hijacking trucks and robbing drug dealers throughout his homeland. One day he was arrested while sleeping off a twelve-hour whoring and drinking binge. He was offered eight years of hard time or four years of military service due to his exemplary build.

The choice was easy, and he worked his way through the ranks into a special unit where he received a small taste of political warfare as he helped plot two political assassinations. When his enlistment was up he was offered a favorable track to military enrichment but decided to try his luck as a private contractor. He was never suited for strict discipline and the private sector pay grade was more to his liking.

Throughout the next decade, he was the major suspect for three political slayings in Central America and being the chief enforcer for a South American oil conglomerate. A

drug cartel was hired to take him out once. It was a bloody
situation with The Venezuelan killing for free. He became
to infamous and well-paying contracts dried up overnight.
With twenty million in Swiss bank accounts he decided to
retire to the good life.

The last six years had been a quiet and peaceful
retirement. His penchant for gambling and expensive
hookers eventually erased his bankroll along with a margin
account full of tech stocks. Nearly broke he started making
calls looking for work. Most of the calls went unanswered
with other connections either dead or languishing in prison.
The few contacts he spoke with offered him nothing
figuring he was a government snitch or too old being out of
commission for so long. Yet, his old pal Simon still believed
in him.

Simon politely took his call a few weeks ago but didn't
have anything suitable at the time. When his phone rang
with an offer he figured Simon performed his due diligence
and a bit of recent background investigation to make sure
he was on the up and up. From Simon's perspective, The
Venezuelan was his best bet from a low cost, high reward
standpoint. It was a straight forward offer. He would
receive one-hundred thousand dollars for finding Rachelle
Sullivan. Plus, there was another one-hundred thousand
dollars for taking out Sinjin Jones. The kicker was a bonus
of the same amount if he could accomplish both. A passport
and expense money was awaiting him at a Cuban coffee
shop in Little Havana. The only caveat was that he must
give Jones ten days to find the girl.

The Venezuelan was on a freight plane to Miami
courtesy of an old military friend who owed him a favor
because he didn't have any valid credentials for travel. He
was picked up by a delivery truck and shuttled over to Little
Havana where the courtesy of his favor ended.

As he meandered his way through the streets of Little
Havana he could see the fear and respect in the eyes of all

who passed him. It wasn't fake or put on. If one lived long enough in this profession the swagger developed and took a life of its own. Without confidence, a long life wasn't likely.

The Venezuelan found the address and took a seat at the coffee shop counter. He ordered the most expensive coffee and took a hard look around the shop and the streets. Everybody looked to be local. The ten-minute walk took thirty minutes as he doubled around the block several times looking for a tail. He carried a simple beige backpack with a couple changes of clothes. He was weaponless for now but would visit that avenue when he determined he needed one. If he found trouble today he was okay using his fists.

The teenaged Cuban counter girl brought him his coffee and set a small package down next to him. She walked away without saying a word. The Venezuelan sipped his coffee while reaching for a newspaper. He ignored the package trying to figure out if he was being setup for some past sin. Caution was the only way to go even though she was probably an ordinary service worker. He motioned for another coffee while the package containing his documents and expense cash sat on the counter.

The counter girl brought him a second coffee while The Venezuelan finally spoke without removing his eyes from the Miami Herald front page.

"How do you know I'm the man that package belongs to?"

The waitress gave up a small forced smile. "This package belongs to a lost soul who precisely matches your physical description."

"How would you know I'm a lost soul?" he asked softly.

"Because, I looked deep into your eyes."

Chapter 53
Delayed Journey

JONES EXITED THE MIAMI FBI building into a cool breeze which felt good on his tired face. The debriefing as it was officially called had heated moments but was cordial for the most part. Several agents that knew Oliver well felt that Jones was withholding information which he wasn't. Towards the end, they seemed to accept the truth and probably thought of Jones as lackadaisical or incompetent which bothered him deeply.

He hailed a cab as he wasn't offered a ride back to his Jeep. It was just as well because it was still at the airport and he was advised to stay in South Florida in case further questions were needed. It was the standard line. They didn't really expect Jones to adhere to those instructions and he was going to do what he needed to do.

The two underlying themes that appeared to bother both agencies were that Terrence Oliver was neatly packed and ready to go somewhere. It struck Jones as odd. The one time he was in the room it looked like Oliver had moved in permanently with clothes and equipment all over the place.

Even more irksome was Oliver in a helicopter with the Sullivan boys. There was no plausible reason that he should be acting alone. Then again, Jones went out alone on his staged burglary plan until Rivers caught him in the act. Maybe Oliver was also tired of Rivers dragging his feet and rolled the dice on a plan of his own. He didn't strike Jones as the gung-ho type to put his neck on the line for anyone but himself. His laptop didn't reveal anything useful, but Oliver was too savvy to use it for shenanigans. Funeral arrangements were being made by his relatives and Oliver would be buried with full honors.

Stony Rivers was another story altogether. It wasn't stated for the record, but everybody seemed to believe that Rivers was on another playing field with his own agenda. Because he was involved in the investigation from years back his involvement timeline would take a bit more time. Whatever game Rivers was playing it became too personal.

Rivers struck Jones as a bit of a mental hypochondriac. Whenever fellow agents looked at him he believed they saw a failed agent. Most likely it was his messy hair or wrinkled shirt. Sure, everyone knew his backstory, but everybody gets the rug pulled out from under them occasionally. The full truth might never be known. Despite a rocky start, Jones was fond of Rivers. They would have had fun together on Duval Street.

As Jones rode in the back of his hired cab he made a mental list. Grab his passport then purchase a ticket for the next flight to Paris. The luggage in his Jeep would have to suffice. He could catch up on his sleep during the flight. If he was going to find Rachelle Sullivan, he was going to start from scratch. Everything started in France and there were questions to be asked and answered.

With Rivers and Oliver gone the investigation was going backwards. Ceci Sullivan wouldn't be talking anytime soon and there was a worldwide search for Santora. Money trails would be tracked but finding anything useful would be slim. The money hiding elite were very good at covering their trails.

Chapter 54
Back to Basics

THE VENEZUELAN WAS finishing his greasy American burger lunch when Simon's man called him on his new cellphone. Jones was on the move and flying to Charles DeGualle Airport. Simon booked him a seat on the same exact flight. Ordinarily, he wouldn't get too close to a target so soon but under the circumstances he had no choice. The flight departed in two and a half hours.

That was plenty of time, but The Venezuelan found himself a bit anxious. Obviously, Jones had business in France. Paris was an elegant historic city which he visited often. He still had an associate in Paris, a gunrunner. It was a family business since World War II and a profitable one at that. A plan was starting to formulate, and The Venezuelan threw out a call for some assistance.

Passing through Customs and Homeland Security was a breeze. Simon was the best in the business when it came to documents. Being retired didn't hurt his cause when it came to Homeland Security. He had fallen well off their radar and he was certain that no authorities had a recent photograph of him for at least fifteen years. He didn't have gray hair back then.

As he boarded the Paris bound flight The Venezuelan passed a man in aisle L who was already counting sheep. The pony-tailed man wearing khaki pants and a blue long-sleeved hoodie matched the description of Sinjin Jones. He didn't look overwhelming or tough. The Venezuelan was suddenly feeling confident and didn't see what the fuss was about. He could take Jones out anytime he wanted to.

The Venezuelan took his seat in the last aisle and followed his marks lead by grabbing some shut eye. Everything was set in motion and he was feeling much more at ease. His only worry was the plane staying in the air and that was out of his control.

At the end of the flight Jones exited the plane and went through Customs. The Venezuelan was slow to wake up as his body was still on South America time. He was stuck behind two-hundred passengers but made himself be patient. Jumping over seats would make a scene and he couldn't afford to be noticed. By the time he was off the plane and through Customs, Jones was nowhere in sight. Despite the urge to run through the terminal he kept it to a brisk walk.

It had been fifteen minutes since he last saw Jones and his heart was racing feeling his prey had totally disappeared. Finally, he spotted Jones in the middle of a long cab stand line. With a slight bead of sweat on his brow he turned and walked the other direction when his text alarm went off.

With Jones inching closer to an available cab, The Venezuelan jumped into the backseat of a silver Mercedes and handed the front seat passenger a manila envelope with five-thousand American dollars in it. In return, the man named Pavlor gave The Venezuelan a shiny Glock with some extra ammunition.

"Inflation must be hitting you hard amigo with these prices," the Venezuelan stated.

Pavlor laughed. "The Euro sucks these days. It's been a decade since I've seen you my friend. A lot of things have changed. Besides, I said I would throw in some surveillance. Where's your mark?"

"In the cab line. Ponytail, in a blue shirt."

"He doesn't look very tough," Pavlor remarked.

"I know. Taking him down will be easy. I just need to keep him in sight. I'm grateful for your help."

"We go back a long way. It's good to have you back in play. There are so few true professionals anymore. Most of the punks today will blow up an entire building to get one person. Integrity seems to be a thing of the past," Pavlor lamented.

After fifteen minutes, Jones was awarded for his patience with a beat-up taxi and a driver who had a liquid lunch. Traffic was backed up in rush-hour, so Jones wasn't too worried about getting into a high-speed collision.

The Venezuelan was ducked down in the back seat as his escort followed the taxi three car lengths back. In this traffic, it shouldn't raise any suspicions. The Venezuelan figured Jones would be checking into a hotel, but he figured wrong. The cab dropped Jones off at the entrance of the Sainte-Barb Library.

After watching Jones disappear into the library, they parked next to a curb and sat in silence pondering their next move. Finally, Pavlor broke the silence.

"If he's going to a library first, he must be doing some research or meeting a friend."

"He's doing research," replied The Venezuelan. He intentionally left out the details about Rachelle Sullivan. He didn't need additional competition looking for this woman.

"Probably so. Park in that lot there and go inside the library," Pavlor instructed his driver. "Keep a tab on Jones and we'll take a position from the front of that bistro across the street."

Jones walked around the inside of the massive historical library gazing at the high ceilings and taking in the permanent sound of an echo. He was oblivious to his welcome party outside planning their strategy. Since his only year of French was a disaster his sophomore year of high school he would need some translation help. It didn't take long to find an American hippie girl from UC-Berkeley doing some graduate work in Paris eager to offer a helping hand. The pretty girl offered Jones a dinner companion as well, but she settled for a phone number and a promise. Jones was too tired for fun and too desperate for some useful information.

It was a two-hour research project with his new assistant who kept hitting him in the face with her dreadlocks whenever she turned to tell him something. Jones peered over her shoulder at the old newspaper articles on the screen even though he couldn't read French. The photographs were of excellent quality including photos of the crime scene and a young Stony Rivers. Rivers was a good-looking man in those days and took a lot of heat over the theft in both countries. He had a better understanding of the man unfortunately it came after his death.

The crime itself was horrific with dead children and servants. The nature of the art itself caused international tensions. So much art went missing in World War II and much of it was never recovered. The Ambassador resigned rather than talk any further about his ownership of the Dutch Sisters. His wife died broken hearted from cancer about eleven years later and he died a recluse at his vineyard six years ago.

Their holiday friends Mr. and Mrs. Brown who accompanied them to Monaco also suffered the loss of children. Mr. Brown died in an automobile accident along with his mistress over twenty years ago. Mrs. Brown was alive at the time of the latest article and never left France. She couldn't bear leaving the country if there was a chance her missing children were still in France. She lived in a small town only a few hours outside of Paris.

Most of the politicians and assorted legal authorities had long passed away since the incident. Rivers was the one of the exceptions until recently. Two French authorities appeared to still be living. General Intelligence Directorate Chief Henri Albert retired to a peaceful life in South Africa. Inspector Andre Baudin was retired and still living in Paris.

A conversation with Inspector Baudin seemed to be in order and no better time than the present. Jones gave his dread headed friend a c-note, a phone number and a kiss on the cheek as he left the library in a sober cab this time.

The Venezuelan emerged from the bistro and followed in another cab. He was hoping that Jones would head straight for a hotel but didn't feel confident that he would do that. There's something about a man's step as he leaves for someplace and The Venezuelan recognized the step instantly. Jones was a man on a mission.

Chapter 55
Inspector Baudin

JONES WAS DROPPED OFF at the Inspector's townhouse address. He knew the Inspector spoke English as one of his four languages. Whether he would be answering any of his questions or give some backstory speculation was purely another matter. As Jones rang the doorbell the Venezuelan's cab passed the townhouse and stopped a couple blocks away where he paid the driver and exited the cab.

After a full minute, a middle aged brunette housekeeper answered the door. She had Jones wait outside and went to find the Inspector. He lived a decorated career with the Ambassador Heist being one of the few crimes that went unsolved. As a child, he fled his native France with his parents only to return after the liberation. In recent years, he had become a rather sad and lonely man but not from any unsolved crimes or childhood trauma.

No, last year he lost his beloved wife Doreen. It was two months before their 45th anniversary and she couldn't fight the cancer any longer. They never had children and now he felt empty inside without the only woman that he ever loved. The Inspector had slowed down physically in recent months but mentally was sharp as a tack. Upon hearing of an American visitor at the door wishing to discuss the Ambassador Heist his energy perked up as he walked to the door to greet his unexpected guest.

The Inspector opened the door with a polite smile and graciously invited Jones inside to his plush library with over-sized English brown leather chairs. The Inspector poured each of them a small Scotch without asking and cheered his new American friend. To have an afternoon cocktail with anyone these days was a joy.

"So, tell me Mr. Jones a little bit about yourself and your keen interest in the Ambassador Heist?" the Frenchman asked in a very polite manner. "Are you a reporter?"

"No Inspector. I was part of a joint taskforce concerning the Dutch Sisters. In fact, I saw one of them that they recovered at an FBI office. I can't expound more on that aspect of the operation. Unfortunately, I was only about fifteen feet away from the other painting without knowing it. It was hidden in a secret room in a Miami mansion."

"I know how it feels to get so close to something only for it to slip away. It happened to me a couple times over my career. So, now you're back in France looking for the missing one?" the Inspector asked in a puzzled tone.

"Not exactly," Jones replied. "The rest of my taskforce was killed. I'm starting my own investigation from the very beginning to see if I can get some answers. There's a missing girl. I would very much like to find her."

"That's what intrigued me on this case. It wasn't the stolen art. I could give a rat's ass about the art." The Inspector paused for a moment in thought. "No, it was the children. Some murdered in cold blood and the others went missing. We never developed a solid theory on that. The valuables were obvious. No witnesses left alive, again obvious. But, why only take some of the kids?"

The conversation paused as both gentleman took a healthy sip of Scotch. Finally, Jones spoke. "It would seem like too much of a time burden to take some children for ransom demands later. You're killing people, you have a heavy truckload of hot merchandise and the children would slow you down."

"I always thought it was an inside job for two reasons," the Inspector offered. "One, the panic room was the best I've ever seen. No one could stumble on it by accident. Someone told someone about it. Two, everything you say is true. The only way a heist of this magnitude works is if someone knows the Ambassador's itinerary. It's the only way you get a head start like that. They weren't ghosts Mr. Jones. The perpetrators were already out of the country by the time we arrived at the crime scene. I truly believe that."

After another long pause, Jones being careful to let the Inspector recall events in his own time finally asked the magic question. "Did you have any suspects?"

"Well, originally I thought it might be an American after we ruled out some art thieves and no ransom demands ever arrived. Art thieves by nature are not violent."

The Frenchman didn't offer a name and Jones didn't know whether to press him on the issue or not. Time was short, so he sucked it up and asked the magic question bluntly. "Who was the American suspect, Inspector?"

The Inspector smiled. "Well, it wasn't your Ambassador. He took a beating in the press. Buying stolen Nazi paintings has never been in vogue. Besides, the fat cat didn't need the insurance money."

Jones stared at the Inspector with steady eyes and a slight smile but remained silent. The Frenchman nodded and smiled back with respect.

"You're very good Mr. Jones. You've learned well. Sometimes not prodding and observing makes a person divulge more than they are initially willing to say. Something tells me you grew up around a poker table?"

Jones let out a wide grin. "Very astute Inspector. Now who was your suspect please?"

"Well, I don't suppose I have anything to lose by telling you. It was an Embassy man, head of security for the Ambassador. A man named Stuart Rivers."

Jones stared down at his empty Scotch glass and made a simple request. "Would you mind if I had another?" the Inspector poured them both another generous round. They both sat back in their seats sipping Scotch in silence. Finally, the Inspector spoke.

"Judging by your reaction, you knew Stuart Rivers?"

"Yes, I did."

"Well, I changed my mind over the years. My gut feelings are usually correct, but I believe they failed me this time."

"Why is that?" Jones asked.

"Well, for one, I periodically checked his finances and never found one bit of evidence that he profited from the heist. Secondly, he never struck me as a cold-blooded killer. That man also took a complete beating in the press and it bothered him immensely. No, I was wrong about him. He called me at least once a year to see if I had any new developments. Those ceased though once I retired. I was surprised to receive a call from him last week."

"You're kidding me?" Jones asked.

"No. He asked a few questions about the four surviving children."

"Three," Jones replied politely correcting the Inspector.

The Inspector sat slowly finishing his Scotch while in deep contemplation about his next sentence.

"No, I meant four. Even my dear Doreen didn't know that. Just Mr. Rivers, myself and a couple others sworn to secrecy. I insisted on that for the child's own safety. The youngster survived a shot to his head. Either the muzzle was too close or perhaps he turned his head at just the right moment. He was in a coma for two months. The Brown's flew him to a hospital in Germany. It was the best kept secret in France."

"It certainly was." Jones said in agreement. "I read all the agency files about this case twice. Never a mention of a fourth survivor."

"It's what government agencies do best when things get too messy. Sweep it under the rug," the Inspector stated matter of fact.

"I'm afraid I have some bad news. Rivers was part of my taskforce. He's gone Inspector."

"I'm so very sorry to hear that," replied the Inspector as he poured them another finger of Scotch. Jones was never a Scotch enthusiast, but it was starting to suit his needs as he raised his glass towards the Inspector who did likewise in a silent cheer in memory of the late Stuart Rivers.

"I feel like I let him down a bit. The man took a beating professionally. Nobody could look the poor bastard in the eyes, they were so sad like he lost his entire world. I was going to call him tomorrow. The only thing I could dig up was an address for Mrs. Brown. She's still alive and never left France in case her children returned," the Inspector offered.

"Does the survivor live with her by chance?"

"I was unable to ascertain that. I was willing to make the journey and see for myself this week if Rivers thought it was important."

"I'm sure Rivers would have appreciated that. Did the child ever speak about the ordeal?" Jones asked.

"We never had a chance to approach him. The Ambassador pulled some strings and put the kibosh on that the moment the child came out of the coma. He felt it would be too traumatic. Who knows, he may have been right?"

"Maybe, maybe not," Jones responded. "I would like to take a shot at speaking with Mrs. Brown. May I have the address Inspector?"

The Inspector smiled in admiration and looked off into the distance. "Maybe a fresh face would be ideal for this situation. I like your aggressive approach. Let me write it down for you. It's about a three-hour train ride from here. Lovely country it is."

"Thank you for your confidence Inspector. I really appreciate it."

"You're quite welcome. Your best bet is to catch the morning train. It would be too late to go now. You're welcome to spend the night here before your journey."

"Oh, thank you but I have a few other things to check up on. Plus, I'm in the mood for a walk. I'll find a hotel close to the train station."

Jones stood up and walked to the door followed closely by the Inspector who offered one last bit of parting wisdom.

"You might want to keep this real quiet until you find something solid. One, it's obviously dangerous if somebody took your taskforce down. Secondly, the political hacks buried this once and they'll likely try again."

"Yes, I agree on both points. Good night Inspector and thank you again for the hospitality." Jones opened the door and turned around. "Especially the Scotch."

"You're old school just like me Mr. Jones. May you succeed where the rest of us failed. Godspeed and goodnight."

It was rather dark now as the Inspector made his way upstairs. He looked out the window to make sure Jones was heading in the proper direction which he was. He also noticed another man who inadvertently looked up and made eye contact with the Inspector. He seemed interested in the path Jones was taking with his almost two block lead.

The man looked back towards the sidewalk and followed Jones, but it was too late. He already aroused the suspicions and instincts of a career law enforcement officer. The Inspector donned a hat and coat while retrieving his RMR revolver from a desk drawer. His colleagues gave him a good-natured ribbing because he never upgraded his arsenal after the RMR. It never bothered him the least as the RMR felt second nature in his hand with a perfect balance. Besides, the RMR helped him put five terrible human beings in the graveyard during his career so he looked at the weapon as a source of pride.

Chapter 56

Doreen My Love

THE WARM PARIS AIR didn't require a coat, but the Inspector used it to conceal his RMR. It's possible he was mistaken about the sinister nature of the stranger, but he decided to error on the side of caution. Jones made a left turn onto a side street and his stalker picked up the pace, so he wouldn't fall behind too far. The Inspector burst into a slow jog which considering his age and the Scotch intake was merely a fast walk.

Jones was tired from his day of traveling and oblivious to the cat and mouse game behind him. He was lost in thought with his new information and the Scotch lowered his awareness level. His top three priorities now were finding a train schedule, a quick meal and a hotel in that order. The three-hour train ride would give him plenty of time for some question preparation.

The Venezuelan was walking pissed off at himself for making such a rookie mistake. The old man was now following him. Maybe he had been out of the game too long he thought to himself. He was just trying to read an address on the townhouse and now he was hoping the old man wasn't alerting Jones via phone or text. As he turned the corner he braced himself in case Jones was waiting for him, which he wasn't.

There was a garbage alley approximately twenty meters up on the left. The Venezuelan needed to make a decision. Avoid loose ends and confront the old man. Or, continue following Jones and hope the old man ran out of gas. It was getting darker on the dimly lit streets making the decision even harder.

The Inspector finally made it to the corner and turned left. Jones was nowhere in sight, but it was possible he was safe. The stranger was no longer visible. Maybe he lived in the neighborhood after all. That was unlikely though as the Inspector knew almost everyone in a six- block area. He walked these streets twice a day and even more since Doreen passed away. It's something a lonely man tends to do. The stranger could have been a musician. The music saloon a few blocks away had plenty of characters like the stranger around. He decided to walk a few more blocks since it was a beautiful night and see if he could locate Jones.

The Venezuelan heard the old man breathing hard before he heard his footsteps. He was crouched down low by the alley entrance concealed by a garbage can. His black leather belt gripped firmly in his hands. With a quick glance around, he determined nobody else was close. He didn't need another witness to deal with tonight.

As the old man passed the entrance way, the Venezuelan pounced and slung his belt around the neck of his prey. The Inspector's hat fell to the dirty ground and his hands instinctively reached for the belt around his neck instead of his RMR revolver. It didn't really matter as the Venezuelan was much stronger and pulled him further into the depths of the alley. The Inspector put up a gallant fight for a man of his age. In his youth, he would have had a fair chance against his adversary. With his last gasp of air, he died with a faint smile on his face. He would be with his darling Doreen once again tonight

Chapter 57
All Aboard

THE FRENCH BREAKFAST WAS exquisite Jones thought as he boarded the train to Angers. An omelet, fresh fruit, croissants and steaming French roast coffee hit the spot. He slept a bit better than the previous four nights thanks to the medicinal Scotch. He found a rundown hotel only a block away from the train station, so he didn't have to rush. The train departed on time and Jones found the tranquil countryside rather comforting much like the Nevada desert. He found himself wishing he was on vacation rather than on a mission to interview a long grieving mother.

The Venezuelan was wishing he was on vacation himself. He bushwhacked an old man in an alley like a common street thug and lost his position on Jones in the process. He stayed up all night peering into hotel lobbies and pubs without success. He asked a couple working girls if they had seen Jones, but no information was offered. Getting tired with few options he decided to re-visit the library and hope that Jones eventually returned. He made a call to Pavlov to be on the lookout for Jones. His sidekick told him to look for an American girl with dreadlocks. She had helped Jones with translation the previous day.

Angers was a peaceful mid-size town with a history that dated before the French Revolution and was well preserved. It was the perfect place where someone trying to live a drama free life would adhere to. The mid-morning air was perfect as Jones slung his bag over his shoulder and walked the downtown area. The market was full of green grocers and wine depots. After ten minutes of walking and taking in the sites Jones spotted a motorcycle shop which he entered. After a bit of cash exchanged and some written directions, Jones was on the road with a faded orange 1978 Harley-Davidson MX250 dirt bike.

Jones drove approximately five miles along a narrow roadway without passing a single vehicle. His destination address was clearly marked, and he guided the Harley onto the driveway and parked. It was situated on a hill with a lot of vegetation and three other homes within a hundred yards. The Brown residence had an empty look and the yard needed a good mowing. A quick glance through a window showed an empty interior except for a few empty cardboard boxes scattered about. There wasn't a for sale sign anywhere on the property.

He noticed some children playing across the street, so he walked over to say hello. A little girl ran into the house and a pleasantly plump grandfatherly man came out. When he realized that Jones only spoke English, he went back into the house and emerged with an equally pleasant blonde man about twenty years old.

"May I help you sir?" the blonde man asked.

"Yes, thank you. I'm looking for your neighbors across the street, the Browns.

"They left two, maybe three weeks ago. Very suddenly. We were gone but our neighbors said a moving truck pulled up and left within three hours. We haven't seen them since."

"What moving company was it?"

"I didn't see it myself."

"Of course. Any idea if it's temporary and they'll be coming back?" Jones asked satisfied that the man was telling the truth now.

"Hard to say. She lived there with her son and they kept to themselves. They were here before we moved in about twelve years ago," he answered.

"How old was her son?"

"Around thirty. Are they in trouble Mister?"

"No, no, not at all. I'm just trying to help them out with something. Did they ever get any visitors?"

"Occasionally, a lady would pull up in a fancy rental car. She was here a month or so ago."

"Do you know her name?" Jones asked with a piqued interest.

"No sir. We never really talked to them. Father tried talking to the son once. He was standoffish for the most part. He did mention that his mother had some memory problems though."

"I see. How would you describe the woman that stopped by every so often? Was she older or younger?"

"She was hot," the blonde man grinned. "Late twenties and she was hot."

Jones grinned back. Universally, men were pretty much all the same when it came to describing the fairer sex. He was starting to get a hunch and it was leaving a bad feeling in the bottom of his stomach again. Rachelle Sullivan gave him that feeling more than any other person that he had ever met. "One last question please," Jones prefaced while pulling out his phone and hitting the photo app. "Do you recognize this person?"

The blonde man looked at the photo for two seconds before smiling. "Yes sir. That is the hot woman. A friend of yours? Very beautiful sir."

"Thank you," Jones replied almost blushing. "She is a friend. Thank you for your time and help. I appreciate it."

Jones turned back and retraced his steps to his dirt bike where he took a seat. He was puzzled about his next move. The Browns took off without much notice that seemed clear. He could try and track down the moving truck. There wasn't much to go on and he would need to hire a local investigator for help if he wished to pursue that angle.

There must be some record of them moving into a new home somewhere in the world. This home was abandoned, and its modest value wouldn't be missed by a party with deep pockets. A theory was starting to develop in his head and he didn't like it one bit. The number of conspirators involved was starting to become the bigger question.

Jones needed some expert research and he assumed his options were limited for an American in this region. The Inspector might be of additional help, but his resources would have suspicions aroused. No, save the Inspector as the last-ditch effort to save the investigation. Andrea his hippie friend helped him once and she did say to call if he needed anything else. Besides, she billed herself as a research extraordinaire. He could mail his new friend a check for services rendered so he dialed her number.

Andrea answered the call in a low whisper while she was in sitting in the library. She was supposed to be working on her thesis paper, but the daily local was in front of her. The front-page story was about the retired Inspector's murder. The Inspector's enemy list was naturally a mile long, but a poorly constructed sketch accompanied the story. Wanted for questioning was an American male with a short ponytail. The Inspector's housekeeper gave a description of the suspect to the Paris police.

"Please tell me you didn't kill anyone Sinjin?"

"Well okay, I didn't kill anyone. What's going on?"

Jones listened silently and sad as Andrea read him the newspaper account of the Inspector's untimely demise. It was sketchy on facts as first accounts usually are. His body was found in a nearby alley within an hour of his departure last night. He knew the odds of this event being unrelated and random wouldn't play in a Vegas sportsbook. No, somebody knew he was in town scuttling up the unsolved heist. Jones stood up and glanced down the road he travelled to see if he was under surveillance. After satisfying the belief that he was alone, he continued the conversation.

"I didn't kill the Inspector. I rather liked him a lot. As soon as I finish my current business, I will come back and bring the Inspector's killer to justice. I promise you that."

Jones knew that solving one case would solve the other case, but he didn't feel the need to explain that to Andrea.

"I believe you Sinjin. Keep a low profile though. The sketch isn't great but change your shirt and wear your hair down or even grab a hat."

Jones smiled at her concern. "Will do. I need a favor though from my researcher extraordinaire. There's five hundred bucks in it for you. I'll have to mail it to you though for obvious reasons."

"No problem. What do you need?"

"I need you to check real estate records for me. Time is of the essence so try the last few months."

"Sure, no problem. What country?"

"Umm," Jones hesitated, "all of them."

"That's going to take some time. What's the last name?"

Jones chuckled. "Brown."

"You're freaking killing me Jones. Can you narrow it down a bit?" Andrea asked.

"Try Rachelle or Marie." Marie was the missing daughter according to the newspaper accounts of the heist. Rachelle could be Marie. Or, she could be a good Samaritan just looking to help an old lady out. That's when it came together for Jones. It suddenly made more sense.

"Actually, try Marie Browning." She would only have to add three letters to her birth name. She was Bogart's modern-day muse as a new Slim Browning whose first name was Marie. He wasn't sure what the end game was, but she was reinventing a new life within the shadows of her early years.

"Hey Andrea, try Martinique first."

"Okay Sinjin. Hold tight and I'll get back to you in about an hour."

Chapter 58
Bored in Paris

THE VENEZUELAN SAT in the library pretending to read a book. This experience only reinforced his decision to never attend college or high school for that matter. He was far from ignorant though. After losing contact with Jones he called Pavlov who provided the intel. His only option was to scout the library for a good looking American girl in dreadlocks. She helped Jones the day before and hopefully he would contact her again. The Venezuelan had no problem finding her and kept an eye on her closely.

Andrea was a true non-conformist. Wearing tattered jeans, beat up boots with a black Bob Marley t-shirt and an arm sleeve of tattoos she was comfortable in her own skin. No feet were allowed on the library furniture, but her feet were almost glued in a propped position on a table. Naturally, she was an art history major who was halfway through her thesis paper.

The Venezuelan was getting more bored by the minute, but he had no other options. Jones probably skipped town the moment he saw his sketch in the newspaper. It was a nice surprise seeing someone else blamed for his dirty work. He still wasn't happy about killing the Inspector. Killing without payment was morally wrong in his book and just plain stupid. Patience was the key. He once sat twelve straight days in a hot Central American hotel room waiting for a target to enter a house across the street. Once the Venezuelan finally spotted him the target was dead in less than twelve seconds.

The girl took a phone call about twenty minutes earlier, but it only lasted a handful of minutes. Since then, she was working at a much faster pace on her laptop. Maybe it was Jones, maybe it wasn't but he needed to get closer the next time she used her phone.

After another half hour Andrea smiled and quit typing on her laptop. She certainly appeared proud of a job well done. As soon as she reached for her phone the Venezuelan casually grabbed his book and made his way about ten feet behind Andrea's back in the guise of looking for another book. Not too close to avoid suspicion but he had to strain to hear her speaking. The high ceilings in the library tended to amplify the smallest noise into a large echo.

"Hey Sinjin, you must be a psychic," she stated excitingly.

"What did you find?" he asked as he prepared paper and pen.

The Venezuelan heard her say his name which vindicated his bored and patient wait. Yet he didn't want to dawdle more than a few seconds, so he was hoping she would get straight to the point.

Jones wrote down the address. It had to be the place. It could be a coincidence, but he couldn't pick up a phone and call them. It fit the criteria. The house was purchased almost three months before by a Marie Browning. Andrea was trying to put together a dossier on this woman, but Jones didn't expect Andrea to find anything on her. She wouldn't have left a trail as she learned from the best.

Andrea quickly rose from her sitting position. The Venezuelan nonchalantly continued down a book aisle on a fantasy book expedition. At first, he was worried that he aroused suspicions then noticed the hippie chick doing some yoga stretches while talking. He heard something about a house but not its location. He surmised that the hippie chick knew where Jones was or more importantly, where he was going. Hopefully all roads would lead to Rachelle Sullivan as he was desperate for a double payday.

All the guessing and surmising wasn't doing the Venezuelan any good. He took a seat far away and kept an eye on his dread headed intermediary for another ninety minutes. Finally, she packed up her brown leather backpack and headed to the exit. He gave her a measured ten second head start but couldn't afford anything longer in case she timed a bus or taxi perfectly.

On his exit, he noticed security cameras on both sides of the doors. He spotted a few inside the library also. Those damn international terrorists with no sense of profit made life tough for professional assassins. International criminals didn't use internet service at libraries anymore as they were simple to trace. Yet, the surveillance videos were checked frequently in case someone was sloppy.

Jones sat in the patio area starring down at the piece of paper with the Martinique address. He diligently memorized it in case it became lost or damaged. Or, worst case scenario he was apprehended by the authorities. Now, this was his biggest problem. To get arrested in France without Bullock's backup would be a nightmare.

Coming up with this address seemed like the easy part now. Getting to Martinique would be the tough part. He couldn't go back to Paris or use a French airport. It would be too risky. Even with a poor newspaper sketch the authorities would be looking particularly hard for a cop killer. Though the Inspector was retired it wouldn't matter as he was a beloved and respected patriot.

Perhaps he should bring in Bullock at this point. Then again, he could be sitting in an American jail instead of a French jail. Bullock was clear with making his intentions understood at the Occidental Restaurant. No, the choice was rather obvious. He would become a motorcycle thief. Jones started up the Harley and headed towards Spain where he would fly from there to Martinique.

The Venezuelan couldn't pick out Andrea on the crowded sidewalk when he first exited the library. She wasn't to his left or to his right and a sweat started forming on his brow. A quick glance across the street was a no go as traffic was too heavy for anyone to make it across without getting creamed by a double-decker bus. Finally, he spotted the dreadlocks as Andrea made the turn south down a walkway.

He caught up with her keeping a steady thirty-meter distance between them. There was still plenty of daylight, so he had to be extra cautious. It was a picture-perfect day as they trekked about a mile through the Paris streets to an artsy neighborhood where the rents were cheap and the apartments decent but simple.

She was slowing a bit, so he stopped next to a garbage bin to wipe his brow and let the girl get a little bit more distance between them. She was wearing ear beats with music blaring and never looked back once. In the garbage lay an empty wine bottle which the Venezuelan grabbed nonchalantly and continued his pursuit.

She made a right turn into a four flat and the Venezuelan broke into a light jog while looking up and down the street. In this neighborhood, most people were catching a light nap after a wine laden lunch. She placed a key in her mailbox lock as her assailant approached quietly catching the vestibule door before it fully closed.

Andrea never looked back as the bottle came crashing down on her dread headed skull. She fell to the ground but not totally unconscious due to the full head of hair. The powerful man threw a right downward fist which connected to her jaw like a batted ball. He removed her backpack satisfied that she was merely lights out and not dead. He wasn't some street punk thug stealing cash but a professional needing to inspect her laptop and cellphone.

Chapter 59
Journey to Spain

IT WAS A SPLENDID FRENCH AFTERNOON with a duplicated forecast for the next week. Jones didn't need any rain to contend with on his motorcycle journey through Southern France. The plan was to take back roads to Spain, then fly from Pamplona to Martinique. Because of the Schengen Agreement there would be no routine immigration checks on the border. Precisely what an innocent American wanted for questioning in a murder investigation needed.

The trip from Angers to Limoges took till nightfall. He stopped at a small bistro at the halfway point for lunch and bought some fruit and water to go. He was avoiding hotels, so he slept the night away in the meadow of a small forest outside Limoges.

The morning dew made his clothes damp and he had a stiff neck from using his backpack as a pillow. It still beat sleeping in a drafty Afghanistan cave. The early start was needed anyway as he filled up with gas and grabbed breakfast in some unknown small village without a town sign. The locals looked him over suspiciously as they did with all outsiders. He departed and kept glancing over his shoulder every few minutes expecting to see a police car. After an hour, he stopped worrying and pushed on towards Pau which he hoped to reach by nightfall.

The acres and acres of magnificent vineyards were certainly a sight to see and provided a sense of relaxation. Except for his buttocks aching from various road bumps and ducking pieces of churned up gravel bits he was enjoying this period of solitude. He still didn't know what to make of the Rachelle Sullivan development, but he was getting used to her mysterious aura. Maybe she had good intentions or was just plain frightened and decided to disappear with her birth mother. Disappearing wasn't against the law he reasoned. He fully intended to hear her out.

Jones made it to Pau in Southern France by nightfall. With another tank of gas, he figured the old dirt bike would guide him to Pamplona by mid-afternoon if the border crossing was clear. He was tired and hungry, so he headed for a small rundown looking store and parked the dirt bike on the side of the building. There was nobody at the counter, so he reached for the bell when he stopped mid-motion. His attention grabbed by the newspaper sitting on the counter and softly retraced his steps with newspaper in hand.

Outside he remained casual leaning against a light pole reading the paper. Every muscle in his body ached as he tried to read a few French words that he picked up the last two days. He couldn't read the article but knew what was going on. A sketch that resembled him took up a quarter of the front page. The Inspector was more revered than just well-liked, and the Paris authorities were looking hard for his killer. Unfortunately, their only lead was for an innocent man. Too bad the Inspector himself couldn't be on the case to catch his own killer Jones thought.

The newspaper was flung into a nearby garbage can with disgust. Jones pulled out a cap from his bag and pulled it low over his face. He spotted a gas station two blocks away and headed towards it. If he was going to pull an all-nighter he'd need some food and gas before leaving Pau. His ass was starting to feel like part of the seat, so he'd pick up some Advil also.

The rickety bridge leaving Pau looked at least two hundred years old. Once he left the city he was overcome by the darkness. Street lights were non-existent unless an intersection appeared. The tiny dirt bike headlight was dim and made it nearly impossible to avoid numerous deep ruts. The Advil was helping but nothing was going to save this ancient Harley by the time they reached Pamplona.

The tiny headlight was turned off as Jones approached the border crossing. A dozen or so cars passed him since he left Pau but none in the last hour. The small inspection hut was dark and looked empty. But, if anyone came out he would stop and show his papers. If there was a problem, he'd take his chances on overpowering the guard and hoping he was alone. This place was in the middle of nowhere and he slowed to a crawl as he approached it. No lights, no movements, nothing, so he kept going gradually picking up speed. After a half-mile, he stole a glance over his shoulder and the coast was clear.

Downtown Pamplona was bristling at the noon hour and Jones could see why Hemingway loved this place. The friendly people and narrow streets fed into the energy providing a brief respite to a body tired and sore from an all-night ride. He smelled a strong odor the last two hours and finally realized that it was his own sweaty self. A real bed in a comfortable hotel with a hot shower was desperately needed. His journey to Martinique would have to wait until the next morning thereby extending his rendezvous a few more hours with Miss Rachelle Sullivan.

Eleven hours later Jones woke up feeling like a new man. He took another shower more out of morning habit followed by a huge breakfast. He was treating it like his last meal in case he became caught up in another cluster like in Paris. He already ditched the dirt bike a mile away in a store parking lot and removed the French plates. The cab ride to the airport only took ten minutes and he took a deep breath knowing his transportation request would be a translator's comedy skit. Except he didn't have a translator and his Spanish was no better than his French.

After ten minutes the airline clerk became frustrated and wrote down the itinerary in his best English which wasn't much better than his counterparts Spanish. Small airports didn't cater to Americans on holiday like most of the world. His journey included two connecting flights with layovers that quadrupled his expected travel time. Out of nowhere Jones felt a tap on his shoulder. He turned around to face a Spanish man of similar build with a five o'clock shadow despite probably shaving an hour ago.

"May I speak to you over here sir? I believe I can help you." The Spanish man walked over to a support beam by a coffee shop with a backpack over his shoulder. Jones diligently followed the man for no other reasons than basic curiosity.

"Can I help you sir?" Jones asked with a glance around the area as his defense mechanisms kicked in.

"No sir. It's more like perhaps I can help you," he stated in broken English. "My name is Ramone and I fly for a freight company. We fly cargo directly to Martinique five times a week. Occasionally, we can fly a passenger or two providing one meets three requirements."

"What are those requirements?" Jones asked, starring hard into Ramone's eyes to get a read on him.

"One, you can't be wanted by any foreign authorities and you must have a valid passport."

"I check off on both of those," Jones replied even though recent events in Paris clouded requirement number one into a gray area.

"If you can keep it quiet and pay in cash, I can provide you with comfortable transportation. No peanuts or bar service, but the seat does recline."

"That's actually four requirements but I have no problem with that." Jones peeled off five hundred dollars from his pocket. "Will this get us going in an hour?"

Ramone smiled. "For five hundred cash, I'll make it thirty minutes."

Chapter 60
Welcome to Martinique

IT WAS A TYPICAL CARIBBEAN DAY as the freight plane approached Martinique Aime Cesare International Airport. Ramone kept his word as they departed on time and the seat was very comfortable as Jones looked out over the single runway field on the landing approach. Martinique compared favorably to Key West except it was bigger with two major problems. It was home to thousands of snakes and a volcano that wiped out a town killing thirty thousand people in 1902. Locals brought in mongoose for the snake problem but could only offer prayer as far as the volcano Mont Pelee was concerned.

Martinique was one of the twenty-seven regions of France and French was the official language. Jones expected a tough time negotiating the language barrier since his French wasn't showing much improvement. His destination was in the South Region outside Les Salines with its beautiful white sand beaches. Marie Browning might have changed her name, but her modus operandi still screamed South Beach.

The airport would be the busiest place on the island as the population was around four-hundred thousand people. He disembarked the cargo plane the old-fashioned way as field handlers pushed up some rusted metal stairs to the plane door. Customs passage was brief only taking ten minutes as nobody seemed too concerned who came to the island if they would spend some money.

The Venezuelan arrived in Martinique within twelve hours after stealing the laptop computer in Paris. A call to Simon speeded up his transportation to

Martinique courtesy of a private jet. He had been watching the airport with a stealth position outside the concourse in a coffee shop. Being a one runway airport, he couldn't miss Jones providing he didn't fall asleep. The coffee shop owner loved the Venezuelan as he took in three meals a day, tipped well and left after the flights stopped for the day.

On his first day, he checked out the Les Salines beach address that he found via a google search history on the hippy chick's computer. The so called smart girl left all her passwords taped to the computer case so the Venezuelan didn't even bother taking it to an expert hacker. The house was owned by a Marie Browning and she employed a guard on the beach entrance to keep out the local drifters and beggars. Since then he waited by the airport watching flight after flight land. Jones was on the way, that much he knew for sure.

Throughout his forty-eight hour watch he noticed a Cuban looking man watching the same exit door. One day arouses suspicions but a second day made the Venezuelan feel like another hired gun was in the picture. The man wearing sunglasses and a Panama hat wouldn't remain a mystery man too much longer he told himself.

Whether he was blinded by vengeance or being a brilliant businessman, Simon was playing the game and playing it well. He kept in touch with Santora and both men played a chess match in which neither man knew the other player's next move. With Simon aware of the impending arrival of Jones, he sold the information to Santora for two hundred thousand dollars. Burned bridges be damned as Simon figured Santora was finished in Miami and therefore his usefulness as a client and informant. Santora was paranoid about Jones and Simon took advantage of that weakness. He coughed up the cash, but Simon left out the part about the Venezuelan. Simon figured he would win either way. If the Venezuelan killed Jones, he would pay him with Santora's money. If Santora eliminated Jones, then he owed the Venezuelan nothing which guaranteed him a profit and revenge. Rachelle Sullivan was inconsequential from his personal perspective.

Jones exited the concourse needing food and a weapon. The islands small Creole population was famous for their food carts in the port area which was only a ten-minute walk. There's never a shortage of shady characters in the world's ports and Martinique was no exception and full of miscreants with warrants from far away destinations. Both needs could be fulfilled easily.

Santora spotted his target in the distance. He left his car and started following Jones keeping a safe distance between them. He never noticed the Venezuelan. This wasn't a drug lord's skill set and he was too concerned with keeping a low profile himself. The Miami warrants went international by now and he wasn't about to get locked up over a revenge job. He pushed his hat down low and kept his aviators on while stashing his pistol down low in his waistband. The Venezuelan gave both men a head start unsure what to think about the developing situation.

Jones strolled through the vendor area right before the port entrance and stopped to look at some sandals. A man in a Panama hat seemed to be following him. He felt confirmation of this fact when the man never walked by him. Nobody could possibly know he was on Martinique, so it could be a variety of characters. Probably someone checking him out to sell some ganja, but he put up his hair in case he needed to fight and kept walking.

Five minutes later he stopped at a Creole food cart and ordered a spicy shrimp bowl with rice. He pointed behind the vendor towards a cooler with Red Stripe beer. As the man turned around to open the cooler Jones swiped a sharp six-inch bladed knife from the counter like a seasoned professional pick pocket. He handed the smiling vendor a twenty-dollar bill, told him to keep the change and continued his journey.

A loud whistle went off and a small stampede of dock workers poured out of the entrance. Santora kept a constant fifty meters behind Jones while the Venezuelan kept a steady gaze on both men from another fifty meter distance. The port area was emptying out fast as the Caribbean didn't have unions or overtime. Day wages were the only wages and these men were looking for a happy hour now. Then, they would wake up in the morning and return to their back breaking jobs like past generation of hard drinking dock workers.

Jones tried talking to a couple workers, but no one gave the American the time of day. He wanted some information on renting a vehicle off the grid. But their quest for a happy hour didn't lend time for some foreigner's questions. He realized this was a pointless endeavor and decided that a trip to a rowdy sailor bar might suit his purpose better.

As he turned around to retrace his steps there was no sight of his tail. Maybe he found a real customer or split for a saloon himself. As he threw away his shrimp bowl a gunshot rang out and the man who was following him fell off a loading ladder on his far right. Jones dropped his beer and started running back to the port entrance and took cover behind some cargo containers. There's nothing worse than having a knife in a gunfight he thought to himself. Footsteps could be heard coming down the dock, so he took off again weaving in and out between cargo containers.

He realized that even if he outran the shooter to the entrance there would be nothing left to hide behind. Whoever made that shot wasn't an amateur and he would be an easy target in the wide-open no matter how fast he ran. Jones tore a path on the pier next to the water and hid behind a pallet of wire cable and dropped his backpack. With no security in sight he could only rely on himself and there was no margin for error.

Jones timed the footsteps perfectly and barreled into the Venezuelan at full speed. Both men tumbled into the water as the gun bounced onto the wooden pier. The Venezuelan shot a man for free who was targeting his meal ticket. Now, he had no choice but to drown his target. He never promised Simon how he would kill Jones but drowning the smaller man should please Simon he surmised.

Jones was sinking slowly with the heavier man forcing him down and a half nelson around his neck. Natural instincts instructed his body to flail but he forced himself to relax giving this bull of a man a false sense of victory. Suddenly, he threw an elbow into the man's side and did a half turn as hard as he could to be face to face with his attacker. He could see the agony in the man's eyes before blood drifted up around the Venezuelan's open mouth which was taking in water. Jones wondered if the man drowned first or if the blood leaving his body so fast made the heart stop. Right this moment, he needed air more than answers. The man was dead, so Jones released his grip on the knife and swam for the surface. The Venezuelan continued to sink like a dead shark with his soulless eyes wide open and a knife handle sticking out from beneath his scrotum.

Chapter 61
Hello Slim

JONES COULD FEEL HIS LUNGS burning as he burst upon the surface. He didn't mind the pain though as for a minute he wasn't so sure he would be the one surfacing. He climbed back onto the pier and lay motionless catching his breath. There were no sirens in the air, so the single shot appeared to fall silent on the far side of the pier.

He finally gathered himself up with water dripping onto the wood from his soaked body and clothes. Retrieving his backpack and the Venezuelan's gun he decided to grab a quick peek at the man who was shot. He had no idea why someone in Martinique would take a shot at him as he only landed an hour ago. Even he didn't make enemies that fast and why would the man who saved his life try to kill him. The whole situation left him baffled.

As he rounded the corner to check out the gunshot victim he saw a security guard kneeling over the body. It was too late to go back as the guard turned his head for a look upon hearing moving wet clothes. Jones charged the guard and overpowered him with a blow to the head from his new gun. The unconscious guard was stripped of his uniform and tied up with some nearby boat rope.

Jones put on the guard uniform in case he had any problems going back through the front port entrance. Then, he flipped over the dead man for a Kodak moment and snapped a few photos. After the third shot it dawned on him that this was the Cuban man known as Santora. They never actually met but Rivers had a photograph of him in his dossier. What was he doing in

Martinique following him? Jones relieved him of his automobile keys and his Panama hat.

It only took two minutes of walking the parking lot and pressing the Ford key fob to find Santora's car. He was on the main road to Le Marin and should make it around nightfall. The guard would be found soon, and he would officially be a wanted man in two countries.

Jones wasn't sure how tonight would play out. The lines were so blurred that one couldn't be sure what constituted a victory or a defeat. Getting off this island would also have to be figured out. The more he thought the more questions popped into his head. Relax he told himself. Let the night play itself out and all the answers will come.

Island Security was one of the two main security firms on Martinique. They advertised themselves as highly professional guards complete with firearms, handcuffs and arresting authority for trespassers. Everybody with a beach house hired one of the two firms to guard their personal possessions from the transient drifters and impoverished locals of which every Caribbean nation was saturated with.

The memorized address would be imbedded in his head for eternity. Jones slipped on the Panama hat as he pulled into the dimly lit driveway and stopped ten feet in front of the guard house motioning for the guard to approach. It was Mr. Browning's car as Santora billed himself in Le Marin, so the guard obediently walked over. Through the tinted window, it looked like Mr. Browning but as the window rolled down the guard was starring directly down the barrel of the late Venezuelan's gun.

Within five minutes the guard was gagged and handcuffed to a tall banana palm tree in some mangroves a hundred yards away. Mrs. Browning and her brother were out to dinner, but their mother remained at the palatial estate house. The only snag would be the beachfront guard on the backside of the estate.

Jones snuck around the side path on the southern portion of the grounds. The beach guard was fast asleep in a green Adirondack chair under the half-moon sky. The term professional was certainly used loosely in the Caribbean. He disarmed the man before he even woke up and put him handcuffed and gagged into a different group of mangroves.

The French style doors off the beachfront paved patio were unlocked. The Brownings had a lot of unwarranted faith in their security team. The great room was barely lit but he recognized some of the artwork from the Sullivan mansion in Miami. The location had changed but here he was sneaking around the dark amongst the same rich person's folly.

As he entered the kitchen equipped with matching stainless-steel appliances an elderly woman's voice rang out.

"You're not Marie."

"No mam." He grabbed the lapel of his security shirt even though the company name was different. "I'm with security, I'm new and checking the grounds. You would be the mother I assume?"

"Yes I am." She smiled. "You caught me having a little snack before I go to bed. Marie and Michael should be home shortly. I didn't have the energy to go. Still a little tired from the move and all."

Jones starred at the woman for a few awkward seconds. There was no doubt she was Marie's mother. She had the same stunning eyes with the high cheekbones. No doubt she was a looker in her time, but it was evident she was battling a more serious illness than she was letting on.

"It must be nice to be able to spend time with your daughter?"

"Oh yes. You could say my motherly years were wasted but I'm enjoying what the good Lord is giving me." She smiled happily then turned sad. "Of course, I lost my husband early but this new place with my children is wonderful."

Jones forced a smile although he was becoming deeply saddened. All this time thinking about Rachelle Sullivan becoming Slim Browning and he never once thought about this poor woman and her tragic life.

Maybe he should turn around and leave Martinique. The thought of shattering this woman's life more than it was shattered from the Ambassador's Heist was an unbearable thought. Her only crime was going to the Monaco Grand Prix with friends. It wasn't fair that she returned to a lifetime of heartache. She was entitled to live out her precious remaining time in peace and harmony.

"Could I help you upstairs to your room?"

"That's very kind of you. My room is on the first floor. The old hips don't take kindly to steps anymore," she wisecracked.

Jones escorted the spirited woman to her bedroom and bid her a goodnight before walking upstairs to ponder his next move. Maybe he could get some answers and leave. Rachelle didn't kill anyone as far as he knew. It wasn't a crime to move to the Caribbean and start a new life. Sure, she robbed the Sullivans blind, but she was robbing the original thieves. He didn't care about the artwork and he realized he was starting to think like his late buddy Rivers.

He walked to the library and threw open the massive twelve-foot solid mahogany doors and was stunned at how easily they opened. They must be on some type of balanced pivot system because they weighed five-hundred pounds apiece. He fumbled around for the light switch and behind a matching mahogany desk was the other Dutch Sister. It was a beautiful painting and he thought about all the people who died trying to possess it. That wasn't even considering what the German Army did to obtain it during the war. The Monument Men tried in vain to locate the Sisters but were unsuccessful. It was a shame they were separated by Derek Sullivan and Bradley Dunbar. At least the Ambassador kept them together.

There was a fully stocked wet bar near a bronze bust of some Greek character on a pedestal. He wasn't up to a major confrontation being cold stone somber. He made himself a martini with a cinnamon twist like Rachelle ordered at the casino. Then he dimmed the lights and took a seat in the corner near the doorway while placing the pistol on the table next to it.

Starring at one of the Dutch Sisters sipping a cocktail did give one a sense of bliss. He pictured Derek Sullivan sitting in his private viewing room doing exactly what he was doing. It must have been tough owning such a famous painting and not being able to tell a soul. He wondered where Bradley Dunbar kept his painting and why Santora was buying it. If that transaction had been kept private a lot of people would still be alive.

After thirty minutes, he fixed himself another cocktail. He wondered about Michael Brown and what kind of life he lived. Very few people ever fully recover from a gunshot wound to the head. His old neighbors insinuated that he was a little slow and socially awkward. Perhaps he was old enough at the time of the heist to remember bit and pieces of his sibling's terrible demise.

Jones was making his third martini when he heard a car coming into the driveway through the open window. They would be wondering where the guard was. He hastily fixed a second drink and placed it on the desk. After turning off the library lights he retook his seat in the corner starring at the painting which looked even more magnificent under the museum light. It shined like a true gem of a masterpiece that it was.

In a few minutes the library door opened casting the most beautiful silhouette in the world. She turned on the lights and walked toward the desk starring at the martini glass which she picked up with a slight smile.

"A vodka martini with a cinnamon twist, I salute you Sinjin Jones."

She turned around and starred straight into his eyes. He didn't break the gaze, but he wasn't going to speak first. She lifted the glass to her lips and slowly drank the martini without taking her eyes off his. This woman could melt an ice cube in two seconds.

"Nice threads," she said as she placed her glass on the desk.

"Thank you. They had a big splash of a sale down at the port."

There was an awkward silence with both parties starring at each other. It became clear that she wasn't going to offer anything first, so he decided to wade in.

"I have to hand it to you. Slim Browning was a nice touch. If I remember right she was a petty crook. You sure took that one step further."

"Well, Marie is my real first name. Adding three extra letters to our last name was an easy fix."

"If we hadn't talked about Bogart and Bacall, I might never have found you."

"Probably not but I prefer to think it was our destiny to meet again."

"Maybe, maybe not." Jones paused. "I spoke with your mother. She's a very lovely lady."

"Yes, she is. My brother Michael is wonderful also even though he was maimed from what those bastards did to him."

"Is that why you did it, revenge?"

"Is that why you're here Sinjin?" You need answers to complete yourself. Derek Sullivan and Bradley Dunbar killed those kids and the caretakers. In what world is that right?"

"It isn't right in anybody's world, especially mine. You could have called the authorities?"

"It's complicated Sinjin."

"I have nothing but time," he replied.

"Okay fine. But let me fix us a couple more cocktails. Don't worry. I see the gun."

She made two more cocktails, took a deep breath and walked one over to Sinjin before retaking her seat on the desk.

"The Sullivans raised me and gave me a good life. Top notch schools, great cars, clothes and as much money as I could spend. Fabulous vacations around the world but never Europe. They would get short and uptight with us whenever we mentioned Europe."

"Is that how you figured it out?" he asked.

"No. Did you see the secret room?"

"Yes. You left it open after you looted the joint." Jones answered.

Marie smiled. "I actually thought about closing it on the way out. But the Sullivans have had too many secrets in one lifetime. Anyway, I was playing in my dad's office one day by myself. I was maybe nine or ten. I accidentally hit the mechanism and the door opened. I went in there and saw this painting," she said gazing at the Dutch Sister. "She's absolutely beautiful, isn't she?"

"Yes, she certainly is," Jones replied taking a sip of his martini.

"Rumor has it that both the paintings hung in Hitler's bedroom for a year before Allied bombers started getting too close. After that he had them moved. Whereabouts unknown until Derek Sullivan stole them and the crap hit the fan."

"So, you knew about this painting as a child and never said anything to anyone?"

"That's right. I never saw it again until I took it. There was always something different with that man. He had a terrible temper. I just figured he wanted a private place to chill out from time to time and this painting provided him comfort. It probably did with all those terrible things haunting him."

Marie stopped lost in thought, so Jones let her have a minute. Then, she started talking again.

"No. It was about three years ago, in a D.C. hotel that I learned of its significance. I stayed in my room with a bottle of wine and ending up channel surfing. I watched a documentary on famous art crimes. The Dutch Sisters were one of the features. It didn't take a genius to figure out my fake parents were international art thieves and cold-blooded killers."

"Yes, Derek Sullivan was a mastermind of a horrific crime. You should have called the authorities," Jones said.

Marie laughed as she finished her martini.

"Don't be silly. He wasn't nearly smart enough. Derek Sullivan was just a figurehead. A figurehead put out there and controlled by an evil woman who couldn't have kids, so she decided to handpick the perfect rich family."

"Come on. Cecilia Sullivan was the mastermind?" Jones asked in astonishment.

"Don't underestimate her Sinjin. That miserable wretch is a great actress but she's evil as sin. The whole thing was plotted with her old boyfriend who just happened to be the security man for the Ambassador. It was an inside job."

Sinjin cringed in disbelief over Stony. His gut feeling was correct after all. It made sense especially after speaking with the Inspector who knew it was swept under the rug. It also explained why Stony delayed the investigation so much. He was looking for a payday and a way out.

"I didn't put that last part together until I saw him speaking with that evil woman at the tennis club. She could never be rattled but she was nervous and irritated that day. I figured he was there to shake her down. There's nothing worse than a scorned man." She slightly smiled at her last witty sentence.

"So, that's why you had Rivers and Oliver killed?"

"I didn't kill anyone Sinjin. Oliver tried to blackmail Derek Sullivan and he became collateral damage. There's no blood on my hands. Greed killed them, not me."

"So, your brothers were collateral damage also?"

She fixed herself another cocktail while she continued talking.

"I'm cutting you off Jones," she laughed. "Your questions are good though. They weren't really my brother's DNA wise. We weren't blood related, I assure of you that. I think Derek took me by accident and I was certainly loved like an accident."

"You mean conditionally?"

"Exactly, you understand me. I had their last name, but I wasn't the one they really wanted. I was a Brown, not a Patterson. I'm supposed to be dead."

"So, you grab your real mother and brother and move here to live happily ever after. If anybody gets in your way you eliminate them like you did in Miami. That's a swell plan, I guess."

"Nobody died that didn't deserve to die in Miami. That's why you lived Sinjin even though you're a rotten liar. I knew you were some kind of cop yet a beautiful human being."

"Well, thank you for big favors. I'm guessing that car bomb was all you?"

"That's right. It's hard to suspect me of anything if I almost die with you."

"Pure genius, it worked. Did Ceci Sullivan get what she deserved?"

"Oh yes. That's why she's alive. She gets to live with having everything taken away. Her money, art, husband and kids, all gone, just like that." Marie said as she snapped her fingers. "I wouldn't doubt that after the press vilifies her for months that she jumps on the sword. Vanity will be her final downfall."

"So, how did a rich girl in Miami get hooked up with a thug like Santora?"

"He's far from a thug. The other Dutch Sister was supposed to be a surprise present to me until Dunbar screwed it up."

"I wouldn't blame that on Dunbar. Santora was a drug lord. No more, no less."

"He had a hard life and I fell in love with his softer side. My brother Michael loves him like a brother. It's not easy growing up on the wrong side of the Cuban government."

"Oh, save me the freedom fighter crap. He was a common street thug who saw a nice piece of ass on South Beach one day."

"No, you're wrong about him. Sure, he did some bad things, but I imagine you have also," Marie said defensively.

"Mine was a job. Strictly a job. Sorry if I wasn't edgy enough for you."

"It wasn't about that. Sure, I was attracted to you. I thought you were special but in hindsight I was hedging my bets in case something went wrong."

"So, I was your backup?"

"Don't get all puppy dog sad on me. I've been with him for over three years. When I decided to re-invent myself, I knew it would take a few years of planning. He was with me every single step of the way."

"Like mother, like daughter I see."

"That's low. We're getting married next week as soon as his documents arrive. It's taking a bit longer than expected. It seems someone stabbed our forger in the leg," she said with her voice rising in anger.

It was crystal clear now. Slim Browning knew Simon and therefore knew Sinjin was looking for her. The world's a big place she must have figured the odds were in her favor. Luckily, he remembered their conversation, or he would be looking for eternity.

"How does the muscle man who tried to drown me at the port fit into this?"

"I don't know anything about him."

"Really?" he asked with a hard stare.

"I just told you the Sullivan secret. I'm going to start lying now?" she replied returning the stare.

"Touché," Sinjin said finishing his drink and grabbing his phone.

"Where is this man who tried to drown you now?" Marie asked.

"Lying in the bottom of the bay," Jones replied standing up and walking towards her on the desk.

"You killed him?" she asked.

"For some unknown reason, he shot someone trying to shoot me. Sorry Slim." he said showing her a photo of Santora lying dead on the pier. "Your fiancé is dead."

"No!" a man's voice shouted out behind them.

Jones turned around to see a man pointing a shaking gun at him with raging eyes. He made a split decision to dive towards his gun on the table and the man fired a shot that missed. Immediately a second shot rang out and Michael Brown lay on the floor with his white Polo shirt turning crimson red.

Marie Browning ran to Michael and held his head while sobbing and choking back tears. Whether it was good or bad, she proved she wasn't Ceci Sullivan's equal as a mastermind. Ceci managed to cover her tracks for a quarter century despite replacing Stuart Rivers with Derek Sullivan. Slim Browning only managed a few days before her new world collided tragically with Sinjin Jones.

The door pushed open wider and Sinjin grabbed his revolver and pointed it straight at the figure walking through with his sidearm pointed loosely at the floor. The figure looked over towards Sinjin after surveying his damage which ended Michael Brown's life.

"Looks like I am your friend Mr. Jones," Graydon Bullock stated remembering the hurtful comment from their last conversation.

"Apparently so," Jones replied. "How did you know I was here?"

"We've been following your trail since you left Miami. When the Inspector died, I knew you didn't do it. But the sketch required me to put more assets into play. I figured you would head to Pamplona. It was the smart move. Who do you think gave you a ride to Martinique?"

Sinjin vaguely smiled at Bullock then looked over at Marie Browning and Michael. Things could have been so different he thought. Then, he looked up at the Dutch Sister for one last glimpse and hoped they would be united in a museum someday.

"There's your painting sir. Take good care of it. A lot of people think it's worth dying for. I'm going home now." With that comment, Jones started walking towards the steps.

"Really good work Mr. Jones. Really good work. We could use you again?" Bullock said while turning to watch him walk down the steps.

"You know where to find me Mr. Bullock," Jones said continuing his descent.

"Duval Street Mr. Jones?"

"Duval Street Mr. Bullock. I'll be on Duval Street."

● ● ●

Acknowledgments

I would like to give a very special thank you to Kristin Elizabeth Swangstu for being my Girl Tuesday and every other day of the week. I never could have finished this book without you. To you I am eternally grateful. Thanks to my Dad, Wayne Jacobson for all his support and making sure I made it through college. A special shout out to my pal, John Wilson for keeping me focused on this project. Last but not least, thanks to number one son Cole for all his help with the first draft.

About the Author

Todd "Jake" Jacobson is a Midwestern native who graduated from North Central College. A fairly good distance runner, he was a proud member of two NCAA cross country championship teams. After college he started a career in insurance and banking, eventually becoming a corporate malcontent.

An aspiring screenwriting career came to a crashing halt in the 90's, but a 2012 visit to Key West put the writing bug back in his blood. A successful blog led him to dust off an old screenplay and turn the story into a book and he hasn't stopped writing since.

Currently he lives in Milwaukee, WI, with his fiancée Kristin, number one son Cole, and a sassy coonhound named Mango.

ABSOLUTELY AMA*ING* eBOOKS

AbsolutelyAmazingEbooks.com

www.ingramcontent.com/pod-product-compliance
Lightning Source LLC
Chambersburg PA
CBHW070545260626
47161CB00002B/514